The Chosen of the Light: Book One
Spirit Summoner

By

Jon Carlin Shea

Jon Carlin Shea © 2013

Spirit Summoner
The Chosen of the Light
Book One
Copyright © 2013 Jon Carlin Shea

Editor: S.R. Howen

ISBN-10: 0-9985714-1-5
ISBN-13: 978-0-9985714-1-6

If you are interested in purchasing more works of this
nature, please stop by www.joncarlinshea.com

DEDICATION

To Jenniffer and Jacobi, my family and my home, you have made this book possible through your love and understanding during long nights of editing and writing, but mostly through your laughter and your smiles.

You are the reason I continue to write.

To Patrick, my best friend, you have made this book possible by reminding me how important "the story" is. Your professional expertise on writing and analysis continues to be a constant source of inspiration. Also, you're a giant geek, just like me.

You are the reason I want to write.

To Mom and Dad, my biggest supporters, you have made this book possible because you both challenged me to be whatever I wanted to be. You might've tried to direct me where you wanted me to go, but you allowed me to be myself. I became a dreamer and a writer.

You are the reason I love to write.

ICTAR

Stern

Mt. Keridos

Dis

Lowlands of Derro

Darlholme

Tyfor Valimere Mts.

The Barricades

Karahesian Wastelands

Oasis

Dwarf Borderlands

Navila

Tower Castle

Arcnor

Nicwazian Line

Fora Lake

Crossroads

Jacova

Triker Forest

Cruv

Ormirion Sound

Sanctum Lake

Vanla

Magna Vaults

Mord

Firearm Mts.

Dragon Territory

Murmackling Passage

Forgotten Mountains

Spirit's Reach

The Norstag Plume

Plaid

Exed

The Ladornaleah

Kee

Greenflyre

Qued

Copyright 2014 Matt Campbell

Chapter One

"Before this land of Ictar came into being, before even the Ancients, chaos engulfed this world. The Four Elements and life itself had no meaning.

Then the Sephirs of Earth, Air, Fire, and Water appeared, and the Archons within them spread their Light to every corner of this land. The laws of nature passed down from the Sephirs and enforced by their Archons, organized the chaos and balanced the Four Elements. Mountains rose, waters settled, and air became clean. The spirits flooded the hidden realm of the Currents and life flourished in this new land. The Light, the power of life and death, ruled them both."

~From A Current History of Ictar, as told by Nidic Waq

A fall breeze cut through the afternoon air, rustling tree branches and sending brightly colored leaves cartwheeling across the path along which Darr Reintol walked. The sun wouldn't set for another hour or so, but already the day had grown cool enough to wrap his travel cloak tight against his body. Overhead, the tree limbs interlocked and screened away what little heat and light remained in the day, but Darr found he didn't mind.

He liked to get away from the confines of the village and his life there. Tyfor might be a prosperous farming community, nestled within the forests of the Valimere Peninsula, a virtual paradise to most of its visitors, but Darr saw a solitary island lost in a sprawling ocean. These journeys into the surrounding countryside, to deliver packages to the farmers along the coast, were a chance for him to pretend Tyfor existed in a completely different world. It allowed him to believe his old life had ended, ushering in a new era of travel and adventure.

Darr sighed wearily to himself and let such thoughts drift away with the leaves at his feet. He couldn't indulge in fantasies. Their lack of fulfillment simply hurt too much. The luxury of leaving Tyfor wouldn't come any time soon. His obligations to his family would always come first.

He found a loose stone along the path and kicked at it absentmindedly. He was stuck in place. The middle child, he did what he was told. His older brother, Erec, was a soldier in training, a warrior who would make the family proud. Jinn, his younger sister, looked to be the ghost of his mother, a woman loved and respected by many. Darr was just a young boy grown only halfway to adulthood, yet still falling short with his scrawny limbs and awkward movements. He had a lot of trouble making his body do what he wanted it to, and being a Spirit Summoner added to those difficulties.

Before he could catch himself, the voices of the spirits intruded on his thoughts. Their voices began as a faint whisper in the back of his mind, turning rapidly to a scattering of words carried over the rustling of the leaves until they were all around him. They came to him like this, every time he thought about Summoning or about them, their messages always unclear and indecipherable.

The spirits were hundreds of thousands of souls, flowing freely within the Currents, a place distinct from the physical world. As a Spirit Summoner, Darr had been born with an invisible connection to the Currents, allowing him to hear the voices of the spirits, and in turn, communicate with them. Strange, that he should know so little about something he was so deeply connected to, but life hadn't filled in the gaps in his education. He had adapted to his ignorance.

At times, the voices of the spirits were his inner voice, their visits soft and unobtrusive. He never really questioned what they were trying to say to him. The Currents were a spiritual plane, yet somehow, the voices of the spirits connected him to their world, if only by the smallest pinch. So far, he'd chosen to remain silent to them. He often wished they would extend him the same courtesy.

The methodical rhythm of his breathing took over his body and mind like he had been taught. The young Summoner breathed deeply into his diaphragm and concentrated on the rock he kicked along the path. He focused on the sound of his breath entering and leaving his body. Within a few moments, the voices of the spirits disappeared completely.

Darr sighed gently, brushed his lanky, brown hair out of his face, and continued towards Tyfor, fighting the urge to dwell more on the spirits.

Dusk had fallen when the trees finally bunched together into a giant wall that gave way to the road marking the borders of Tyfor. The village sat on the western most region of Cortaz, homeland to the Cortazian race of Man. At the edge of the foothills, on top of the mountain rich soil, and bordered by the protective confines of the forest, Tyfor's buildings sprawled out from the center of a vast clearing, lost to the rest of Ictar except for the random hunter and trapper.

Ahead, the mountain peaks of the Valimere climbed up from behind the trees. He'd been beyond them only once, and only to Stern. His mind wandered again to thoughts of travel and exploration, of mountains rising up from the trees in other places, other lands.

Farmhouses and barns appeared in the distance, nestled among the protective conifers, the buildings lone sentries guarding over patches of black earth. The village took shape, and Darr quickened his pace. Yes, he loved the world outside Tyfor and dreamed of escaping the ordinary life he lived there, but Tyfor was his home. He doubted he'd get that feeling anywhere else.

The forest and farms gave way to homes and cottages, all tended and maintained with daily care. The citizens of Tyfor took great pride in their community. If one person grew unable to tend their land or buildings, others would come to help them. Darr knew he might not find such a powerful sense of fellowship anywhere else in Ictar.

As Darr approached the town center, he slowed his walk, more intent on taking his time. He would enjoy the few last moments he had to himself as he walked the main road running through Tyfor's center. One side of the road held the Tyfran General Store—the other side held Arn's Inn, the blacksmith's shop, and a cluster of smaller houses. A few people were still out, finishing their daily business in the light left to them. With their customers gone home for the day, the general store and the blacksmith's shop were closed, but Darr heard voices and laughter from the brightly lit interior of Arn's Inn.

He and his siblings spent many nights at the inn, listening to the tales concocted by the hunters and trappers who visited. Lately, they had only been hearing ghost stories.

Satisfied with what he saw, Darr turned towards the Tyfran General Store and started along its wood-planked side. His house sat some twenty-odd yards behind the store, nestled amid a gathering of aged cedar trees. Darr's father had built it ten years ago, after the death of his mother. Amid the towering cedars, the brown and white trimmed house appeared small and insignificant, but its insides were open and welcome. He'd only been gone for the day, but a pang of joy welled up inside Darr.

The Summoner bounded up the stairs of the porch and threw open the front door, momentarily forgetting his father hated surprises. He stood in the doorway and breathed a sigh of relief, examining the stuffed couch and chairs. His father was nowhere in sight. Darr took off his travel cloak and shut the door in the same motion. He hung his cloak on a hook by the door and walked leisurely towards the kitchen. A fire burned in the hearth on his left, and down the hallway on his right, darkness came from the bedrooms. Except for the smell of something cooking, it appeared no one was home.

He slid past the dining table on his way to examine the contents of the stew cooking on the wood stove. A voice called out from behind him, causing him to startle.

"I thought you'd be back earlier," his father said with a hint of disappointment in his voice. "I was getting ready to send out a search party."

Darr shook the hair out of his face. The shoulder length strands tried to fall back. He looked his father in the eye, trying to convey the shock the old man had given him.

His father smiled and walked stiffly to one of the kitchen cabinets, his thickening body moving slower than it used to. His father brought down two bowls and spoons from the cupboard along with some day-old bread wrapped in a baking cloth. With precision that belied his old age, he set the table before taking a seat facing Darr, who still stood over the pot of stew.

His father stared at him. "Well, what're you waiting for, boy? I'm sure you're starving."

"Aren't we going to wait for Jinn and Erec?" Darr asked. He used woven pads to lift the small pot to the table.

His father chuckled and snorted at the same time, a strange sound he often made. "We'll be waiting for a couple of weeks, or better, if we do, and I'm pretty hungry right now." The old man's mouth twitched. He was teasing him. "They left right after you did this morning. I sent them to Stern to see what's holding up our ale shipment. You know how people get around here when there's no drinking all winter." The old man's eyes took on a distant look. "One of these days I'll convince old Tyer to brew those apples he grows into cider, then we won't need Stern's wares at all."

Darr used a spoon to scoop the stew into a heap in his father's bowl before filling his own. The daylong excursion had left him more famished than he'd thought, and he ate in silence, concentrating on his meal.

When they were finished and had set their bowls aside, his father asked, "So how was the trip?"

The Summoner described in detail which paths he'd used and any problems he'd encountered, how his customers were doing and which packages he'd delivered. His father was only testing him. With Erec going off to Mertz to join the army in the spring, his father wanted to make sure Darr could make the supply run to Stern when necessary.

When Darr finished his summary, his father nodded in approval and smiled, his gray hair bobbing around his head. "You'll be ready for Stern in no time, my boy."

"You know I really want to go, Father."

"I know. You will," his father said with profound understanding. "You know I'd never keep you here, Darr. Not you or Erec. As much as I'd miss having you around, you both have to go out there and take a look around."

Darr nodded, almost embarrassed by the strength of his father's words. "You know I couldn't go, Father. Not anytime soon, anyway. Not with Erec going away to Mertz."

The old man grunted and straightened in his seat. "Not Mertz anymore. It's been a busy day for travelers," he said with a half-grin.

Darr scrunched up his face in confusion.

The old man left him perplexed for a moment longer before continuing, a game he often played. "A soldier came here today, well several of them if you want to get exact about it, and they didn't come from Mertz. They came from Darlholme."

"That old outpost. Why?"

His father's smile held no warmth. "Apparently, our King, Lord Ariel Forn, wants to try to unify the northern and southern provinces," he said, a heavy rebuke. "He's strengthening the fortifications at Darlholme so he can be closer to the south-make them feel more included. He's also uniting the militias in the south and integrating them into the main army, naming the combined force the Cortazian Army."

Darr shook his head. "This doesn't make any sense. Lord Forn must know the southern men won't allow that. They may owe allegiance to the crown, but they have never been respectful to it. What about Mertz? What is he going to do to the capital city?"

"He'll change it, I suppose," his father said, leaning back in his chair. "From the sounds of it though, Darlholme is going to be the new capital, once the north and south are fully integrated."

Darr continued to shake his head. "That will never happen though—not without a major war. The whole thing is ridiculous."

"Well, you haven't even heard the most ridiculous part yet." His father's tone was incredulous. He folded his big hands before him. "This whole business with the Cortazian Army and Darlholme came about three months ago over the summer. It's in response to the threat of the Soul Seekers."

If Darr had been confused before, he was dumbstruck now. "The Soul Seekers? But they're only a myth. The hunters and trappers that come here think so, well, most of them anyway. They're nothing more than a fairy tale cooked up by the Divine to scare people into not going near magic anymore."

The old man nodded. "I know, boy. Me and half a dozen townspeople, Arn included, tried to tell these soldiers the same thing. They wouldn't listen. Just following orders, they said. Said we would do well to heed the warnings. They requested volunteers to go to Darlholme, and then they left. It's a good thing Erec wasn't here or he'd be off fighting Ariel Forn's demons for him."

Darr smiled at his father's attempt at a joke, but quickly let it fade. Something about this business didn't make much sense. Ariel Forn was a young, untested king, but the organization of such a massive force suggested the "myth" of the Soul Seekers might have more truth behind it than what he'd heard. Men of power, especially kings, couldn't allow themselves to be taken in by rumors and superstitions. Not after what had happened during the Aeon Wars.

His father pushed back from the table, stretching out his

arms and yawning. "Well, it's best not to think too hard on these things, boy. Let those in power do what they think is best. When they decide to wage war west of the Valimere, then we'll worry."

The old man rose from the table and started towards the hallway, the shadows beginning to fold around him. "Goodnight, Darr. I'll see you early at the store." He disappeared into the gloom of the hallway on his way to bed.

Darr sat at the table, listening to the fire crackle in the hearth. After a while, he got up and cleared the table. He worked for a few minutes, wiping down the counter, cleaning the bowls, and storing the leftover stew. When he finished, he walked into the sitting room and collapsed on the feather couch next to the hearth.

He thought about the soldiers' cryptic message about the Soul Seekers. The rumors about the Seekers were fragmented and vague, and Darr had heard them only from the hunters traveling through the village. No one knew who they were, but everyone agreed the Seekers used magic lost since the Aeon Wars, and they ripped the souls from the bodies of those they killed.

The mere thought of the stories chilled Darr, yet logic reminded him the stories were just that. Magic no longer existed in Ictar, save for the magic contained in the Sephirs, the ancient relics that bound the Four Elements of Earth, Air, Fire, and Water. Nobody could tap into the Sephirs, not now when the Divine were entrusted with their protection, decreed by the Kings of Ictar. No one could harness such power. It was forbidden to do so.

Of course, laws had always been broken throughout the course of Ictar's history.

The warmth from the fire seeped into him. For a second, Darr thought he heard the spirits whispering unbidden in the back of his mind. Mistaken, he reached up and pulled down a blanket, letting sleep claim him.

Chapter Two

"When the Ancients rose to power, they made use of their science to erect giant cities. Over time, their science unbalanced the Sephirs, and so they explored new avenues in which to grow. They discovered the ability to pass into the Currents from within their own minds. The Ancients used this newfound ability to walk the Currents and communicate with both the spirits and the Archons. Together, they balanced the Sephirs and restored order. Despite their vast knowledge of both science and magic, the Ancients maintained strict discipline in using their power."

~From A Current History of Ictar, as told by Nidic Waq

A glimmer of gray daylight splintered through the sitting room window, bringing Darr awake with a headache centered in his temples radiating down his face. He'd never experienced anything like it. He lifted his frame halfway up on the sofa, holding his hand to his forehead.

The spirits came to him, their presence sudden and intrusive.

Erec and Jinn must've returned during the night, he thought. He'd simply overheard a conversation with their father. Darr clamped his eyes shut. The voices came from within him, from the part of his mind connected to the Currents. The voices of the spirits flooded through him, their messages jumbled, but insistent. They wanted to be heard, whatever they were saying. Darr struggled to an upright position, fighting past the pain in his head. Perhaps this invasion by the spirits caused his headache, though he couldn't be certain since nothing like it had happened before. The spirits only came when he thought about them, and they were never this persistent.

He took in deep breaths, sending air into his midsection

in steady motions. He closed his eyes and concentrated on the silence in the house. The confusion of sound in the Currents and the throbbing of his head made them difficult to ignore, but not impossible. The air he breathed, and the comfort of his home, became his sanctuary. After a few minutes, Darr's body and mind begin to relax, and with it, the voices disappeared. His headache became a dull tingle behind his skull, but with the spirits no longer present, he could function.

Cautiously, Darr rose from the couch, testing to see if either his headache or the spirits would return in force. His father was gone, departed before dawn as he always did. Darr hurried through the house to the sparse bedroom he shared with Erec. The Summoner washed up in the water basin between the two small beds and threw on brown pants and tunic. He ran his fingers through the brown tangle of his hair to straighten it out halfway to presentable. Dressed and refreshed, he bounded down the hallway to leave the house.

He stepped out onto the porch and examined the overcast skies. A sharp coldness bit into his cheeks and nose. He promptly reached back into the house to grab his heavy cloak. As he started out across the field towards the Tyfran General Store, Darr puzzled over the mysterious onset of his headache. The feeling persisted, nothing more than a minor inconvenience now, but it bothered him that such unexpected things still happened.

Twelve years ago, when his summoning abilities first surfaced, Darr would wake in the middle of the night, screaming out unintelligible words, mimicking the jumbled messages of the spirits. There were some more serious moments, when the spirits would come unannounced during the day, flooding his mind and leaving him crumpled on the ground, screaming until they stopped. His father grew worried and went to the village elder, explaining the attacks. The elder couldn't help directly, but he knew of a man living in the foothills of the Valimere who could assist. The man,

Aeranth, came at once.

Aeranth was a Summoner himself, a kind but shy man, he spent almost two months teaching Darr how to shut out the spirits when they came spontaneously. Deep breathing techniques and focused meditation were the primary forms of control. Rather quickly, Darr noticed a change in both his body and mind. He learned how to shut the spirits out of his head when they came to him, and how to summon them if he chose to listen. Darr chose to do the former because even Aeranth couldn't see any real reason to listen to the spirits. The spirits spoke in jumbled words and fragmented images, and they did so in unison. Deciphering those messages became something short of hopeless.

Aeranth taught him of a city called Navda, far south and east of the Dwarf Borderlands. Spirit Summoners gathered from all over Ictar to study and learn about themselves, the Currents, and the spirits. Some of the Summoners there were rumored to listen to the spirits and communicate with them.

Darr thought if he ever left Tyfor to travel the world, Navda would be the first place he would want to see. He'd always questioned the purpose and function of Spirit Summoners in general, and in particular, because his own experiences seemed pointless. He thought maybe he could find his answers among others who shared his ability, and by learning to understand the messages of the spirits, he might understand the purpose of being one. He might have learned more from Aeranth, but his reclusive nature made him uncomfortable around others. After he'd left, Darr never saw him again.

He came up along the front of the Tyfran General Store. The old building's weathered but sturdy plank siding and roofing stood strong. Large wooden barrels sat out front below the windows to encourage a quick sell, some contained grains, others had seasonal fruits and vegetables. Signs meticulously designated the contents of the barrels, an indication of the intense amount of professionalism his father put into his work.

Darr walked past the barrels and opened the wood plank door. The smell of lemon oil struck him first, his father's cleaner of choice for use throughout the store. After all these years, that smell hadn't grown old. Inside, at the counter near the far wall, his father talked to a couple of farmers from the coast and two trappers he'd never seen before.

His father looked up momentarily from his customers and smiled at him. Darr walked to the counter and stood alongside one of the trappers and listened.

"Well, I don't know anything about an army, but I do know you'd all do well to mind that warning about the Seekers," one of the trappers said, a dark skinned man, a Dwarf from the looks of him.

"Bah! Nothing but a bunch of ghost stories," Tyer said, an apple farmer from Tyfor's south end. "Everyone knows magic doesn't exist anymore. It can't, not with the Divine monitoring the Sephirs."

His father nodded in agreement. "If the Seekers were going around hurting people, well that'd be one thing. But, rumor has it they're using magic, and no one's seen magic used in over two hundred years. It's been banished by the kings for spirit's sake."

The farmers grumbled their approval. Confined to silence, Darr found himself unable to make an opinion. The other trapper, this one most definitely a Dwarf, marked by his stocky build and his dark brown skin, took a step towards the two Tyfran farmers.

"'Aos—you people are blind," he scolded, his voice so rough it startled Darr. "You only see what you want to see. I've seen them though. I've seen the Seekers with my own eyes when they killed one of my own. Saw 'em from a distance, you know why? Because if I didn't, I wouldn't be here telling you."

The Dwarf turned sharply and started for the door. "You people have no idea what's comin' for you," he called out over his shoulder. He opened the door and stepped out onto the street. The other trapper nodded curtly, thanked his father for his services, and followed his companion.

"Who in chaos do they think they are, Hydle?" Tyer started, but his father silenced him with a raised hand.

Still in shock, Darr stared out the door after the two trappers. Whispered secondhand accounts and word-of-mouth stories were one thing. Hearing someone had actually seen the Seekers upset Darr. Someone dying from the encounter was more disturbing.

"Darr," his father grumbled, "I want you to go down to the storeroom. It needs to be cleaned out to make room for the winter supply order."

The Summoner recovered his composure, nodded politely to Tyer and the other farmer, before he walked to the back of the building where the storeroom entrance sat underneath the foundations. He used a key to bypass the lock, and once the doors were thrown open, he went down the steps. The only light in the storeroom came from the tiny cracks in the floorboards above. Darr could still hear the muffled grunts and protests from the men gathered there. He stumbled around long enough to light an oil lamp, filling the storeroom with an orange glow.

He began work immediately, pulling unused crates free from piles on the basement floor and hauled them up to the field behind the store. A few minutes into his work, the Summoner was sweating freely despite the cold, and he stripped off his cloak. After clearing the room of pallets, he began the tedious project of reorganizing what little supplies were left.

The project didn't bother Darr much despite the tedious sorting. He liked jobs that required attention and forced his mind to focus. The memory of the two Dwarf trappers who'd been in the store earlier lingered. He'd seen a few Dwarves in his life, and never any of the other races like the Elves or the Ogres. The Dragons, he'd heard, were only a legend. Darr wanted to know more about the races who he shared the land of Ictar with. He didn't know much about the Dwarves being that Tyfor was so isolated. Besides, the Cortazian men who shared the Dwarf Borderlands didn't welcome outsiders, a prejudice left behind by the Aeon Wars.

Darr's thoughts strayed until the spirits came rushing back into his head with a numbing jolt.

He braced himself, letting his mind clear, but he'd claimed only a moment of silence before an explosion rumbled in his ears. While distant, Darr knew instinctively the sound must've come from somewhere close by. The Summoner turned for the door, but lost his footing and tripped over his feet, awkwardly crumpling to his hands and knees.

He began clawing for the steps leading out of the storeroom, when a second explosion rocked him to his belly, this one stronger and much closer. Darr struggled to his feet and fought to regain his breath, choking on dust shaken free from the building's foundations. With new intensity, the spirits began a tirade of whispering petitions, but he ignored them and raced up the steps, trying to muffle the spirits with his heavy breathing.

Outside, smoke wafted on the air. He took in deep breaths. Simultaneously, he took in the scene and tried to silence the spirits. For whatever reason, the voices wouldn't be dispelled, so Darr ignored them and ran around the building to the store's front where his shield of calm faltered before falling away completely.

Across the road, next to Arn's Inn, flames engulfed the village blacksmith's shop. Tyfran's citizens ran in every direction around the scattered remnants of the building. Some carried buckets of water, while others shoveled dirt in wide swatches where the flames weren't so high. The building itself looked hollowed out, as if the fire had consumed everything inside in a matter of seconds. Darr watched in horror, imagining what must've happened to the blacksmith and his apprentice, both of whom were close friends.

Taken aback by the spectacle, Darr turned. The front of the Tyfran General Store had caught fire. It appeared a piece of debris had flown from the blacksmith's shop and into one of the windows, leaving flames licking up the cedar paneling in its wake. The Summoner carefully looked inside through the opening.

An angry orange glare gleamed back at him.

Darr called out for help. Without waiting for a response from anyone, he threw the door open and leapt inside. Heat rushed against his face, stinging his eyes and nose, filling his nostrils with the acrid smoke. Fear rose up, but Darr forced it down, covered his mouth with his tunic, and forged ahead into the smoke. Flames licked greedily up the left wall of the store, fighting for position and racing towards the ceiling. The piece of debris from the explosion had shattered shelving and set products ablaze, sending them flying in all directions. It appeared everything inside the small building had caught fire simultaneously.

A man writhed on the floor near the counter, his body covered in flames. Darr charged towards him as the man's screams of agony reverberated through him, turning his bones to ice. An image of his father burst into his mind. Darr's hesitation gave the spirits a chance to flood in once more. Their voices buzzed urgently, a warning.

Darr reached up for his travel cloak to use it to smother the flames, but he'd left it in the storeroom. The man's screams were growing more frantic. The fire ripped through the victim's flesh and his fingers clawed at the charred floorboards. Darr searched along the counter in a frenzy to find something else to smother the flames, and instead, came face to face with a ball of flame. It floated in the air. The spirits howled.

Shock paralyzed the Spirit Summoner. The ball of fire had form. Blunted legs ran up to a thick torso, and pointed ears jutted out of its head. Two pinpricks of white-hot fire glared out at him.

Darr had heard of creatures such as these during his lessons on the workings of the Currents.

The creature before him was a conjuring from the Currents, an elemental. A firehound.

The firehound stared at him from across the span of a few feet, waiting for its prey to make a move. Indecision coiled about Darr, a prison chain of fear. The spirits' voices pounded in his head, preventing him from thinking clearly.

Darr reacted out of desperation, running for the door. He needed help. The firehound's massive body crashed through broken shelving and snapped at the back of Darr's legs and boots with the quickness of the element it embodied. The raw heat of it seethed through his pants and tunic, searing his skin. The soles of his boots were burning. He'd barely reached the door when the firehound leapt over his head, a living cloud of flame, cutting off his escape and sending up a new curtain of flames in its wake. Darr doubled back, heading for the counter and the window located in the back of the store. The firehound chased him, its fiery paws clawing up hot ash with every leap.

The Summoner crawled over the counter in time to see his last chance at escape fall away. He looked back through the curtain of flames. A tall, white-robed figure stood in the doorway. The spirits abruptly stopped their tirade, the voices shattering with the fragility of brittle glass. Perhaps he might have been frightened by its suddenness had it not been for the charging firehound.

The robed figure stretched out his arm.

Blue light gathered on the stranger's fingertips and the air about him rippled outward like the surface of a pond. No, not the air. A sheet of water had materialized before the robed figure, its surface heaving outward by some unseen force. The stranger dipped his hand into the glassy surface, stirring it, causing it to shudder before a rippling geyser of water exploded across the charred ruins of the Tyfran General Store. The geyser found its mark in the body of the firehound, as it leapt at Darr. The elemental froze, its maw split wide and its body contorted in upheaval. Then it fell to the ground and evaporated into smoke and steam.

Dumbfounded, Darr clutched the top of the counter for dear life, staring open-mouthed at the stranger. He could see him clearly now, incredibly tall, his face hard and set, dominated by piercing green eyes set above his wide nose and close-cropped beard.

The stranger raised his other arm, and the white robes around his body shimmered softly. The same blue light, this time laced with tiny sparkles of yellow, swirled around his hands and arms. The man gathered it up and sent it spinning upwards to the ceiling. Darr jerked away from the motion, but the chill of a misty dampness caressed his face. When he looked up again, the flames were beginning to die away. A downpour of rain fell all about the room. The raindrops swirled about the interior of the store, a miniature squall hanging on the ceiling, and yet visibly there wasn't anything of the sort. At the center of the maelstrom, the stranger held his arms up high with glowing fingertips.

When the rain had washed away the fire, the stranger lowered his arms and his conjuring ceased. With eyes fixed on Darr, he started forward. The Summoner found he could only stare at the stranger's face from his perch on the counter.

I know this man, but from where?

Without a sideways glance, the stranger walked to the man who had been on fire. Stunned, Darr rushed over. The Summoner lowered himself down beside the kneeling stranger. The stranger's hands moved over the withered form, touching it, checking it in places. After a few moments, the stranger looked up, and his piercing gaze found the Summoner's own. Untold knowledge glowed in those eyes. This man knew things no mortal could comprehend. A chill descended over him.

"Do not worry, Darr Reintol," the stranger said, his voice oddly reassuring. "This man isn't your father. It's unfortunate, but there are worse ways to die these days."

Questions flooded Darr's mind, but he forced them away. The man's charred remains lay before him, and a feeling of sadness and guilt washed through Darr over his relief that it wasn't his father.

The stranger rose, his white robe enfolding him, armoring him. He walked to where a shelf had been overturned near the front of the store and carefully tipped it away. His father lay underneath it, his clothes covered in ash and soot, his face bruised. Despite being unconscious, his father's chest rose and fell steadily with each breath.

Darr ran to his father's side, checking the old man's body to see if there were any broken bones or permanent damage on the surface. It appeared his father had been knocked out, but was otherwise all right.

When Darr looked up to thank the stranger, the man had vanished, gone as suddenly as he'd come.

Chapter Three

"Centuries went by, and the Ancients accomplished great things. The Sephirs' Light flowed freely through the Currents, and the land and the people prospered. The Ancients advanced themselves both mentally and physically, furthering themselves as a race until they were near perfect beings. They shared the land with the primitive species of Man, Elf, Dwarf, and Ogre, but they kept the solitary Dragon race at a distance, wary of their knowledge of the Sephirs."

~From A Current History of Ictar, as told by Nidic Waq

The hour after dusk found Darr within the shadow-dappled interior of the Tyfran General Store surrounded in the glow of oil lamps hung from the ceiling. It had taken him longer than expected to clean out the building. With the task near completion, Darr approved of the amount of work he'd done. After his father had been examined by Tyfor's healer and put to bed at the house, Darr and the innkeeper, Arn, began the difficult task of cleaning up the damage done by the firehound. Of course, Arn and everyone else in Tyfor, didn't know what had caused the destruction.

The ruin caused by the firehound started in the blacksmith's kiln, an explosion that killed the blacksmith and severely injured his apprentice. Tyfor's population believed the Dwarf fuel sources the smith used had ignited the blast. The third casualty, the man burned within the general store, had been Tyer, the apple farmer.

With all the rumors surrounding the Soul Seekers, the last thing anyone needed to hear was that an elemental had caused the devastation. So, Darr said nothing about the stranger or the firehound. Better to leave out the details rather than stir up trouble.

Darr could tell Arn suspected the morning's events

19

weren't what they seemed. The old innkeeper had known him all his life, and the tale of a piece of flaming debris being thrown from the blacksmith's shop to the general store in the explosion was partly believable. Darr suspected Arn saw through his account of fighting the fire using the water barrel on the side of the building. The innkeeper had simply known him too long and knew he wasn't a risktaker. Once his father was healed, Darr believed Arn would begin asking more questions.

The Summoner sighed inwardly, distraught at his inability to talk with anybody about the truth of what happened. Had Jinn been around, he would've confided in her. He stood in the golden halo of the oil lamps and swept up what remained of the scattered glass and ash.

The stranger who'd saved them was Nidic Waq.

Nothing else made sense. He'd never met the man, in fact, he'd only heard stories of him. From the stories Darr had heard since early childhood, Nidic Waq was the self-proclaimed prophet of Caeranol, a loner and an outcast almost everywhere he traveled. He appeared in random towns from time to time, narrating detailed accounts of the Aeon Wars and of times before, when the Ancients inhabited the land.

Despite his knowledge, he possessed far too much detailed information to be considered sane and it gained him little respect. Many people maintained Nidic Waq could read a man's thoughts by looking at him. He could even divine the future.

From the moment the white-robed stranger had disappeared from the store, and the spirits had gone silent within him, Darr suspected Nidic Waq's presense. It bothered him more that the man might be connected somehow to the firehound. After all, both the elemental and the prophet used magic. What if the stranger had created the firehound? Of course, if that were true, why did he come to destroy it?

One certainty had come from the experience, Darr would no longer be willing to dismiss talk about the Soul Seekers. The sight of the firehound alone, not to mention the display of magic let loose by the stranger, convinced Darr the Divine had less control over the magic they guarded than anyone suspected. Darr had a sinking feeling magic could be harnessed without the use of the Sephirs. The other option placed the mysterious stranger among the ranks of the Soul Seekers.

He swept a pile of glass and soot into a tray. The Tyfran General Store had been mostly cleaned out. All of the salvaged goods and shelving had been stored down in the basement or over at Arn's Inn. The fire had done surface damage, which would require some heavy scrubbing and waxing, all of which could be taken care of within a day or two. Darr was planning what supplies he'd need for the repairs, and who he could get to help, when a knock came at the door.

At first, Darr mistook the sound for the old building settling or a siding plank shaking in the wind. The knock came again, this time accompanied by a gentle urging within the Currents, a voice he felt rather than heard. The tray and its contents slipped from his fingers and fell to the floor. Darr shook his hair from his face. He turned towards the door and stared in silence, straining to hear within the Currents, but nothing reached him.

He recognized who reached out to him, though he didn't know how anyone, besides the spirits, could enter the Currents.

Darr lowered his arms and walked to the door with precise silent steps. The light from the oil lamps dimmed suddenly, as if what waited for him outside stole away their light. Or perhaps he drained their light, for he was shadowed somehow, separate from events conspiring around him. He stood in front of the door and took a deep breath before reaching down and opening it to the night air.

The tall, forbidding figure of the stranger rose up before him.

"May I come in, Darr Reintol?" the man asked, his voice smooth. Darr hesitated, uncertain, but he nodded anyway and stepped aside.

The stranger walked through the doorway, his tall form stooping slightly in order to pass through. The man intimidated Darr, and not by his physical height and appearance alone. Outwardly, he appeared calm and disciplined, but Darr sensed within the stranger's frame a greater brilliance. He radiated some inner power. The Summoner reached back and shut the door. When he turned around, he faced an elder seeking reprimand.

"Who are you?" Darr asked uncomfortably, wondering what the man wanted.

The white-robed figure stood in the center of the room, looking up and around, searching for something. Finally, his piercing green eyes fixed on Darr and his wide mouth parted into a smile. "I think you already know who I am," he said in so much of a whisper the Summoner barely heard him.

Darr's breath caught in his throat. He stared at the man, his own suspicions now confirmed. "You're Nidic Waq."

The man nodded and the yellow light from the lamps above shimmered off the long strands of red hair tied behind his neck. "I apologize for the attack by the firehound," the prophet said, his voice low and smooth again, yet his gaze never left Darr's. "I confess, the elemental broke free because of my presence. The Currents are delicate now, spread out through Ictar like a spiderweb, and Summoners are like bears traipsing through them. I truly am sorry, but in this time of war, there are risks we must take if we are to survive. Navigating the Currents is one such risk."

So, Nidic Waq was a Spirit Summoner. Darr tried to decide whether he told the truth though somehow it was obvious.

"Wait a minute," the Summoner blurted out, shaking his

head in disbelief. "What do you mean? I'm not at war with anybody, and I'm certainly nothing like you."

Nidic Waq smiled, another slight lifting of the edges of his wide mouth, and before turning away said, "Ahhh..."

Immediately frustrated with the prophet, Darr remained calm. How could he be close to the same as Nidic Waq? Darr didn't have a hint of magic, let alone the desire to learn. Magic was forbidden for a reason. Besides, why would a man who preached about the errors of the Aeon Wars choose to equip himself with the same forces that had instigated it?

Nidic Waq stepped to where a few empty crates had been left stacked near the counter. He effortlessly lifted two from the stack and brought them over to the center of the room, setting them on the floor. Nidic Waq sat down, his legs stretched before him, facing the other crate. Darr hesitated, debating whether he should stay or run out the door, but after a moment gave into his curiosity and sat down.

The prophet kept his gaze steady for an instant, but it was enough time to send chills running down Darr's spine. "Do you know the story of the fall of the Ancients?" Darr nodded his head, but the prophet smiled mockingly and remained silent, apparently testing his knowledge of Ancient Ictarian history.

"Well, I've always heard the Ancients were an advanced civilization," Darr said. He looked up at Nidic Waq for approval but found nothing. "They built great things using magic and machinery. But something happened with one of their creations. It got loose from them and destroyed their civilization."

Nidic Waq smiled sadly and leaned back. His intense eyes focused directly on Darr, and the prophet said, "I could tell you the truth of what happened all those years ago. But what difference would it make? The story of the Ancients is set in your mind like stone, as it is for the rest of Ictar. History has become a story for us, and the only way for you or anyone else to discover the truth is to discover it for yourself."

The Summoner started to protest, but the breath left his body and he couldn't. Something about what Nidic Waq said made a connection, and Darr found himself wanting very much to know more about that connection.

Nidic Waq continued, his tone softer. "What I call history, and what you call stories, are merely words we use to color the truth. The reason I'm here is because you and I are both Spirit Summoners, and as such, we have access to a very old, yet very powerful magic..."

"Wait," Darr interjected, his hands raised slightly in protest and defense. He didn't like the way the prophet changed subjects so abruptly, almost in subterfuge. "I've never heard Spirit Summoners could do magic, not even during the Aeon Wars, and I certainly know I can't, so somewhere along the line, I think one of us has been misinformed."

The terrifying smile on the prophet's face forced Darr to recoil not only physically, but also within himself.

"Yes, Boy, one of us has been grossly misinformed." Though he continued to sit, Nidic Waq bore down on him, a towering wall of rage. "Did you think I would come here if I didn't know what I spoke about? Did you think I would waste my time approaching you, if I didn't think you were capable of what I am asking? What you have heard of me, and what you will come to know, are of such vast difference one should be stone and the other one air."

Petrified by the the prophet's words and powerful gaze, Darr found himself unable to break away despite his fear. Something more than Nidic Waq's physical actions held him spellbound. The longer Darr sat there, the more he realized Nidic Waq used the Currents to accomplish this.

In response, Darr let his mind slip away from the prophet, and the air about Nidic Waq shrank. His fear deteriorated. The man's eyes were calm once more, his voice smooth and reassuring.

"Now, if you'll allow me to continue uninterrupted." Darr

nodded his head ever so slightly, and Nidic Waq smiled in response. "Good. The information you have about Spirit Summoners is not complete. Yes, we are connected to the Currents in such a way that allows us to hear the spirits, and in turn, communicate with them. This is a fraction of what a Summoner's potential amounts to. It isn't only the spirits that lend a Summoner his meaning in life, though it's certainly an important aspect. An integral piece to the puzzle of the Summoners is our connection to the Currents."

With caution, Darr watched the prophet, not willing, or wanting to believe his words quite yet, but he didn't want to discount him either.

Nidic Waq leaned forward, and his gaze held Darr's own. "In all of Ictar, only the Spirit Summoners can experience the connection shared between the Currents and the spirits. Only a few of those Summoners know that all life on Ictar is connected to the Currents as well. Now I ask you, Darr Reintol, if you know the importance of this association?"

The Summoner shook his head, his eyes wide. Nidic Waq continued.

"When I say everything on Ictar is connected to the Currents, Darr, the Sephirs are included. They are connected to the Currents in the same manner of all living creatures. What this means for a Summoner is one can acquire the skill necessary to navigate the Currents, thus enabling them to call upon the Archons within each of the Sephirs. This is the true power of a Summoner."

Darr stared in confusion, still unsure what exactly Nidic Waq wanted him to understand. The prophet raised his hand and a ball of white fire flared to life, causing Darr to flinch before it died away.

"Every Summoner is capable of finding the skill needed to summon the Archons, thereby harnessing the elements of Earth, Air, Fire, and Water. There are some Summoners that possess this skill naturally, gifted from birth with the ability to traverse the Currents with little effort."

Darr sat frozen in shock while Nidic Waq's words echoed through his mind. He no longer doubted what the prophet told him. He had the strange feeling, again, that he'd known all along, and Nidic Waq merely confirmed the information. Darr couldn't be sure of the source of this feeling, especially since he'd already experienced something of Nidic Waq's power over his mind.

Darr built up his courage and asked, "How is it I know you speak the truth? I want to believe you, but like the rumors I've heard, you've imposed your will on me."

The prophet nodded somewhat sadly. "I don't impose my will so much as I bring to surface and intensify those emotions that control you the most. The spirit realm allows me to see deep into the Light dwelling within living creatures. It allows me to either suppress or intensify those emotions and memories of their soul they would keep hidden." Nidic Waq hunched forward on his seat. "Despite the rumors, my young friend, I am not a mind reader. I am a listener of the spirits, and the knowledge of the spirits is vast. Sometimes they know of things that are to come. Being able to listen to the spirits and not be confused by their words is another skill that takes practice and time. But, I think you will master the skill quickly."

"So what do you want from me?" Darr asked, his voice wavering. The prophet wanted him to use his summoning abilities in some way, but Darr couldn't imagine how.

Nidic Waq's posture didn't change. "I want you to explore your potential. I need you to become the kind of Spirit Summoner you were born to be, not because of me or your own desires, but because Ictar's survival requires nothing less."

Darr shook his head in protest, but Nidic Waq held up his hand, halting him.

"You don't need to know everything yet, but you must know the Soul Seekers are real. They are as real as you and I, and if they're ignored, they will do to us what they did to the

Ancients."

A numbing cold washed through Darr. "You mean that story...?" he asked in a bare whisper.

"Yes, Summoner," the prophet replied. "The Seekers are spawned from the Devoid, the very same creation that rid this world of the Ancients. Neither you, nor the might of all the races combined, can bring an end to them. Though the Devoid is sealed away by the Light of the Sephirs, it has been chipping away at its prison for some time now. All we can do is buy ourselves some time, for as we speak, our guardian and protector, the great Archon, Caeranol, searches for a way in which we'll all be free."

"Caeranol?" Darr interrupted. "I thought he was only a myth."

Nidic Waq gave him a dark look. "No, young Summoner, I can assure you Caeranol is very real. He is an Archon of vast power, one who is bound to Ictar in ways you cannot imagine. Caeranol's objectives in this matter are of little concern to you now. What matters is you're in a position to aid me, and thereby aid yourself and all of Ictar."

Darr nodded hesitantly. "Even if I could learn magic, if I have it in me to do it, what chance do I stand against something that destroyed the Ancients?"

The prophet's brow furrowed and he adjusted his seat. Darr wanted nothing more than for the prophet to get to the point. Nidic Waq cleared his throat before continuing.

"All living things on Ictar, the Sephirs included, are possessed of the Light and subject to its laws. The Light contained within the Sephirs is potent and vast, but like every other living creature, it is finite. When the Light from a Sephir is extinguished, the magic controlling its element is extinguished as well, and if the Light of all the Sephirs fails..."

"Chaos." Darr breathed the word like a curse. "Before the time of the Ancients, the world was chaos. But an unknown cataclysm brought life to the world by binding together the

Four Elements through the creation of the Sephirs. How the Sephirs were brought together was a mystery even to the Ancients, but without them, the world would revert back to its true form of chaos."

"Yes, young Summoner," Nidic Waq said, nodding his head solemnly. "Chaos. That's exactly what the Devoid is after. Unleashing chaos would allow the Devoid and its Soul Seekers to reap the Light from every living creature on Ictar. More to the point, the return of chaos would break the walls of the Devoid's prison. What's more frightening is the Devoid has discovered the means to drain the Sephirs, and it's been doing so for some time now."

Darr's jaw dropped slightly. "How...?"

Nidic Waq shook his head. "I'm sorry. I wish I could tell you everything, but my time grows short. At this point, either you've made up your mind to believe me, or not. I need your help, and while I cannot tell you everything, I can tell you this—only a Spirit Summoner with potential such as yours, Darr Reintol, can restore the Sephirs to their original state."

Darr stared for a moment before his words tumbled out in a rush of disbelief. "So that's it? The Sephirs have started to fail and you want me to go with no more information than what you've told me?"

Nidic Waq nodded again, his eyes dark and solemn. "I have already explained what is necessary for you to make a decision. All you need now is the willingness to explore your potential in order to learn."

"I can't do what you've asked!"

"You've never tried."

The prophet remained motionless, a statue sitting before him. Darr watched him with the caution, but also with resignation. He sensed truth in the prophet's words. Besides, Nidic Waq was giving him the opportunity to travel Ictar. It gave him an excuse to leave.

The Summoner looked back at Nidic Waq. He remembered all the stories he'd ever heard of the prophet.

The people of Ictar shunned him largely because they didn't want to hear what he had to say about them. Darr realized the same was true for him. He wished Nidic Waq had never come to Tyfor, revealing omens of doom and shadows of Darr's own self, shadows he somehow already knew.

He wished he wasn't a Summoner, carrying with it a legacy of magic he never knew existed. More surprising though, Darr wished he'd never wanted to leave Tyfor. He wished desperately he could live out the rest of his life in the confines of his town and never know anything beyond.

He knew he couldn't do that though.

The desire to know the truth about himself and the world was too strong. Likely, Nidic Waq knew this as well.

"Fine," the Summoner said softly. "I'll go." He looked up into the prophet's eyes, seeing a tender look there. "I don't know what I can do, and I'm not sure where to begin. I'm afraid for myself, but more for those I'll let down if I fail."

Nidic Waq's smile broadened, lending Darr a small bit of courage. "It's enough for now that you simply begin. The rest, as I said before, you'll learn along the way." The white robes closed tight about Nidic Waq's frame as he rose. "As for your fear, remember this—we feel fear when we're alone, when there is no one to help us. You are a Summoner, and as such, you're never alone because you will always have a foot in the Currents. The spirits will aid you, if you listen carefully to them. The spirits will never abandon you."

The prophet brushed past Darr and patted him lightly on the shoulder. With long strides, he went to the door. He reached down for the handle but stopped as if catching himself in mid-thought. "Remember the lesson of the firehound," he said, his tone dark. "The Currents are severly disrupted as the Light of the Sephirs are draining away. Elementals like the firehound are a spontaneous effect of the failing Sephirs. They can break free anywhere, but they will be drawn to Spirit Summoners when we're in the Currents. Always be wary of the bindings of the elements around you."

The prophet nodded at Darr before he straightened his robes one final time. His wide-featured face took on a hard cast. "I know all of this is new and confusing, but you will not be alone in this even though I must leave you."

The whole world fell out from underneath Darr. "But I thought..."

"I know. You thought I would be going with you, but I've other matters I must attend to. The Devoid intends to keep me from securing the Sephirs, and so it is moving its Soul Seekers strategically. But it doesn't expect there to be someone like you." Despite Darr's shock, Nidic Waq showed no sympathy. "Don't worry, Summoner, for I would never send you away alone and unguided. Head first to Stern and the Sephir of Water. I have arranged for someone to guide you. Leave at first light—you will be found on your way."

The prophet nodded, turned immediately back towards the door, and opened it to the night.

Darr charged forward, a fury of confusion and objection running through his head. "I can't leave right now. My father isn't well, and my brother and sister..."

"Leave at first light. That's all the time you can spare," Nidic Waq said before stepping out of the light of the oil lamps and into the darkness of the road beyond.

The prophet didn't look back.

Chapter Four

"Not all of the Ancients were content with nurturing the land and her people. Some believed the only way to sustain, was to control and conquer. Such was the case of the elder named Symdus.

Symdus hoped to conquer and control death, and at first, his intentions were noble. He was a respected elder, his knowledge of science was profound, and his ability to navigate the Currents, was both accomplished and unique. A rare gift possessed by only a few of the Ancients allowed Symdus to hide himself within the Currents."

~From A Current History of Ictar, as told by Nidic Waq

In the hours before dawn, Darr sat before the hearth in his house. The fire danced as he contemplated his decision to go on Nidic Waq's quest to secure the Sephirs. Sleep was impossible in light of all he'd learned, so after a few hours of lying in bed, he went to the sitting room to think. He would leave after dawn, after he told his father.

After Nidic Waq left him staring wide-eyed into the night, he'd been frozen by indecision. Fear alone didn't paralyze him. The shear uncertainty in determining whether Nidic Waq spoke the truth froze him in place. Deep down, Darr believed the white-robed stranger about the Soul Seekers and their creator, but on the surface, the beliefs the prophet expressed concerning the Light and the Sephirs were foreign, and, truthfully, a little hard to swallow. Everything Darr had ever heard concerning the Currents said the spirits were the ones connecting all life on Ictar. Similarly, the Sephirs connected the Four Elements.

The Light, an unseen force that could be taken away by creatures like the Soul Seekers, both frightened and astonished him.

Perhaps it was so hard to believe because of his fear, but Darr wouldn't allow himself to be bound by fear and ignorance. He would forge ahead down the path Nidic Waq laid out for him, whether he knew its destination or not. The path would take him on the adventure he'd always wanted to experience, and because doing so would save Ictar.

How would his father react? The old man could barely comprehend his life as a Spirit Summoner, let alone an innate ability to do magic. If he told his father Nidic Waq had chosen him to save the Sephirs from certain destruction, his father would, without a doubt, think he'd lost his mind.

Darr sighed and looked wearily out the front window. The skies were turning a faint leaden gray with the promise of morning. His insecurities melted away, replaced instead with the excitement of what he knew he'd be able to accomplish. This is my chance to see the world, he thought with eagerness and sadness alike.

The Summoner rose from the couch, unable to contain himself, and walked down the hallway to his bedroom. He stripped off his ash-dusted clothes from the day before, washed, then dressed. He took in the familiar sounds and smells of his room, not knowing when he would be there again. It felt odd to him to be leaving, but it also felt right, despite the circumstances.

The Summoner finished off his outfit with a leather belt, and as an afterthought, took out his long hunting knife. It would be his only weapon. He secured it to his belt. Everything else he needed was kept at his father's store. Darr took one last glance around his room, sighed deeply, and moved into the hall, taking slow footsteps to the door at its end where his father slept.

Carefully, he reached down and turned the handle, opened the door, and slipped inside. He walked on cat-paws to the bedside. His father slept soundly, his bruised face showing no trace of discomfort. Darr smiled to himself. Even in sleep his father defied everything and anything he possibly could. The Summoner sat down on the bed and waited for his presence to wake the old man.

"Darr?" his father whispered, his eyes flickering open. "Is something the matter?"

Darr shook his head, letting the words funnel through his mind before he spoke. "No, father, nothing's wrong. I came to check on you before I left."

His father chuckled softly. "Out to start work on the store early, huh? You got my work ethic, boy, that's for sure."

Darr smiled and looked down, then back up into his father's eyes. "No, not to the store, father. I'm leaving Tyfor for a while."

If the old man was shocked, he didn't show it. He simply laid there, his head resting on the pillow. "What brought this on?" he asked in a weak voice.

Darr cleared his throat, preparing the lie. "Those soldiers who came here yesterday morning returned last night. They heard about what happened with the fire and thought we might need assistance. I had a chance to talk with them, and they convinced me of the importance of enlisting in the Cortazian Army. I told them I didn't want to be a soldier, and they said there were other ways I could serve. I think the fire changed me, Father. It showed me I could lose you. Maybe there is something I can do to make a difference."

The old man's eyes lost their focus for a moment, turning lost and vaguely sad. He nodded his gray head. "Maybe, Son. Maybe. But, why do you have to go now? Why now when the store's a mess, and Jinn and Erec are gone? And why go off fighting ghosts and whatnot?"

"Because I don't think they are ghosts, Father. I think they're real." Darr swallowed hard in spite of himself. He'd finally admitted it. His reasons for going weren't all selfish, but centered on a belief that the Soul Seekers were real, even if the rest of Ictar didn't believe it.

His father grunted and shifted his body. "Well," he said

with a sigh. "Well, I always did raise my children to think for themselves. Besides, I suppose I can get along without you for a while. Arn will help me out 'til I'm back on my feet, then no one will be able to stop me." The old man reached up and grabbed onto Darr's shoulder, squeezing tight. "Are you gonna be okay? How are you getting to Darlholme?"

"I'm going with the soldiers," he lied again, feeling all too uneasy with how good he was at it. "I have to be going soon."

The old man nodded and smiled fiercely. "You take care of yourself, and you better have a whole cartload of stories for me when you get back, Boy."

Darr smiled and nodded back. He imagined he would, though not the ones his father expected to hear. The Summoner rose and looked down on his father one final time. The old man smiled again, then closed his eyes and returned to sleep. Darr smiled in response, both sad and excited.

He walked swiftly from the room and down the hallway. In the sitting room, he retrieved his travel cloak from the back of one of the couches. After taking one last look around the house and whispering an oath to see it again, the Summoner opened the front door and bounded off the porch into the morning light.

A horrible weight had lifted off Darr's shoulders after he'd spoken with his father, though the tactics he'd used were questionable. Nobody in Tyfor really understood his desire to leave. Most everyone was content with their lives, and they would never know anything beyond the borders of the village. Even though his reasons were selfish, knowledge about the world was a good thing.

Once he reached the cellar of the store, Darr momentarily forgot his doubts. He found his backpack there, a relic if he'd ever seen one, but he cherished it because it had once belonged to his mother. It was also coated with a resin that would protect its contents from the elements, almost as if his mother continued to watch out for him. Darr crammed in a heavy blanket for the cold and a flint for starting fires. Of the little traveling he'd done over the years, he'd never been away this late in the fall. At the back of the room, he went into the cold locker and removed a loaf of bread, cheese, and a pouch of dried beef, foods that didn't require him to carry heavy cooking equipment. Satisfied, he blew out the lamp.

Everything he needed he had with him. With stunning disbelief, Darr faced the beginning of his journey. Tyfor had nothing more to offer him except a homecoming. He took a final look around at the dawn dusted buildings and homes, and at the carefully tended fields off in the distance that for so long had been a prison. The Summoner knew he'd be longing for the entire landscape in the days to come. With a casual wave, he turned down the road leading east out of Tyfor.

One main road led out of Tyfor and straight to Trenton Pass, and from there, to Stern. He knew about navigating the pass from Erec's stories of his travels there. Even though Nidic Waq said there would be a guide, Darr had his journey planned out. He didn't want to put his quest in the hands of someone else.

The Spirit Summoner made his way up the road at a quick, but steady pace, careful not to let his body tire too rapidly. He passed by the outlying farms and houses, keeping his head lowered for he knew the inhabitants would be awake by now. No need to draw attention to himself.

Darr hiked steadily, following the rolling hills upward. Tyfor and its encompassing forest turned into a dark smear in the background.

Morning bowed to afternoon, afternoon waned into evening, and time melted away in the cool fall air. Thick clouds had been rolling in over the past hour, studding the overcast skies with humps of black. A storm approached, and Darr intended to reach the pass before it struck.

He climbed over steep terrain that made his progress more difficult. The Summoner cinched up his pack, keeping his eyes focused on the cut between the mountains before him. Where was the guide Nidic Waq said he'd send? He'd seen no one. Perhaps his guide wouldn't show and he'd have to complete his journey alone. The clouds overhead grew darker as he climbed higher into the foothills. He pushed on against the cold rush of wind now blowing down out of the Valimere, scrambling up the high slope in a desperate effort to reach the safety of the pass.

When the first few raindrops started to fall, Darr realized he might not know the way to Trenton Pass as well as he thought. A deep ravine cut across his path, barring his passage into the mountains. The Summoner believed the ravine stretched a short distance in length, yet the further he traveled, the longer the ravine grew in width and depth. After another hour of climbing, and with darkness rapidly descending, Darr admitted failure. The ravine was an impassible stretch of overgrowth dragging on for miles up into the Valimere.

When he looked back the way he'd come, the foothills below were small folds of grass and miniature trees. Rain fell in steady sheets, and combined with the wind and darkness, the cold turned from bothersome to miserable. Darr needed shelter, and he knew he wouldn't find it on the open mountainside.

With fresh resolve, the Summoner climbed into their shadowy folds. The terrain lost its stability as the rocks of the Valimere completely overtook what remained of the foothill grasses. Trenton Pass was a natural thoroughfare of the Valimere. There should've been a road or a path, but Darr saw nothing anywhere in the distance. His confidence slipped away, and with it, his patience.

The Summoner continued to berate himself when he went down in a flurry of loose rock and mud. It took a moment to recover, but when he did, he was completely soaked and disoriented. The rain fell in sheets now, and with nightfall upon him, he couldn't tell which way to go. The slope of the hill led upwards, but he couldn't be sure any longer if he would be led back towards the edge of the ravine or further away from the pass.

Doubt evaporated from his mind with the streak of lightning that lit up the sky behind him and the clap of thunder that followed. Darr started up the slope, concerned only with seeking shelter, hiking faster now as he dashed from muddy slide to muddy slide in an attempt to prevent another fall. He made good time, congratulating himself he'd made it as far as he had. Before long, he'd be resting within the shelter of the Valimere. He managed a quick smile. Another bolt of lightning flashed, breaking the Summoner's concentration as the entire mountainside lit up.

The flash sent him off balance. Darr went down in a heap. He fell harder this time, striking his head against a clump of gravel and mud. He lay for a minute and let the rain beat on him, dazed from the blow. He reached up to his face to check for damage and after finding none, scrambled back onto all fours. The weight of the pack fought against the mud and the angle of the slope, and when he tried to stand, he slipped and fell onto his back.

For a moment, Darr lay in the mud in disbelief, letting the rain wash over him. Everything had gone wrong, leaving him lost, cold, and wet. He tried to sit up, but the weight of his pack pulled him down. In a moment of hoarded frustration, he yelled. He didn't yell at anyone in particular. The Summoner howled in pure annoyance of his situation, his voice carrying over the sound of the storm itself.

His voice cracked, and the small moment of silence allowed the spirits to come flooding into his mind. The spirits snapped Darr to attention, instantly making him aware of their presence.

Then they were gone.

Darr blinked in surprise against the downpour of rain. What had just happened? It was like a door to the Currents had been opened long enough to feel the presence of the spirits, then closed.

The Summoner lifted his head and looked down the slope. A black shape approached through the torrent of rain. Startled, Darr writhed in the mud, attempting to regain his feet. He managed to roll over and get up on one knee. The black form was right on top of him, a massive, frightening shape. Lightning flashed across the sky, and Darr saw it clearly, shaped like a man, robed and hooded. Soul Seekers!

Without a second thought, Darr leapt to his feet, clawing his way up the high slope. A massive hand clamped down on his shoulder and pulled him back.

Chapter Five

"With the blessing of High Elder Caeranol, Symdus went to work unlocking the secrets of immortality. He established a workshop to conduct his experiments and brought together a team of men and women to assist. Symdus and his assistants studied the Currents, examining its timelessness and searching for ways to apply its secrets to the physical world."

~From A Current History of Ictar, as told by Nidic Waq

In an instant, the truths Darr perceived about the world were shattered and his life changed forever. With grating clarity, Darr knew the forbidden power of magic had come back into being, and he was somehow a part of it. When the massive hand closed about his shoulder, the hand that belonged to some unimaginable evil, the Summoner automatically joined with the Currents. The spirits flooded in and all truths were laid bare.

And Darr knew no Soul Seeker pursued him, instead, an Archon, somehow brought from the Currents into physical form had ahold of him.

Archons were ghosts, he told himself—they were the spiritual presence residing within the Sephirs, guiding their magic across Ictar in harmonious balance. They weren't real people and certainly had no physical form. The iron grip spun him around.

"This way, follow me. Quickly now," the Archon's voice rumbled, as if born from the stone of the Valimere.

Darr didn't hesitate. He followed the dark-robed figure down the slope a short distance until they were met by the jagged edge of the ravine, its black maw lit by another flash of lightning.

Hesitantly, Darr looked down into its depths through tearing wind and rain.

"Careful now, young Reintol," the Archon said above the noise of the storm. "We only have a short distance left to go."

The Archon started down without slowing, and Darr charged blindly after. Slick and treacherous, the slope had become a muddy wash of rain and loose rock. The Summoner pitched headlong into the ravine with each step, but his guide stopped at every misstep Darr took, an immutable wall, always in the right position to provide support.

They reached the black base of the ravine in a matter of minutes. Scrub brush and thick-limbed pines choked any visible passage, but the Archon forged ahead, making his own path through the darkness and cold. Darr followed after in near blindness, pushing right up against the Archon to prevent separation. They were traveling along the base of the ravine, working their way steadily upwards into the Valimere from what Darr could tell. With each step, he grew weaker and colder. The storm crushed down on them with suffocating force. His legs were beginning to tire, and Darr knew it wouldn't be long before his entire body gave out.

Why here, he thought, lost in darkness at the bottom of the Valimere? My journey hasn't even begun.

He dwelt on the thought for a moment before his body crumpled, and he fell into the darkness of the storm and the ravine.

His body floated upward, lifted by unseen hands. Massive arms cradled him and kept him safe, and in their embrace, the spirits of the Currents were close by. They told Darr he hadn't failed. His journey was only beginning. A warm drowsiness slipped over him. The spirits' words slipped through his mind, and he slept.

* * * *

When Darr woke, a fire crackled before him, hot and bright. The close confines of a cave surrounded him, but his exact whereabouts were a total mystery. The Summoner raised his body to a sitting position and crossed his legs before him. Directly across from him, on the other side of the fire, not more than a few feet away, the cave entrance opened. Outside the storm swept on unabated, but now it felt miles away.

His pack lay beside him, unharmed. Oddly, his clothes were completely dry. He reached up to the tender spot on his face from when he'd fallen climbing the Valimere, touching it experimentally, only to find it no longer hurt. Was the whole thing a dream? The only solid thought standing out was of the Archon.

His breath caught in his throat at the memory, and the layers of confusion clouding his mind peeled away.

"Come awake now, have you," a voice rumbled from somewhere back in the cave.

Darr leapt to his feet. The voice, while startling, didn't frighten him. He stood with his back to the fire and peered into the darkness of the cave. A massive shape materialized–a robed figure outlined by the firelight–the Archon who'd rescued him.

The Summoner took a short breath and a step forward to get a closer look at his mysterious rescuer, but suddenly the spirit creature rose up before him. Darr fell back, in awe by the sheer size of the giant who'd have dwarfed Nidic Waq. The Archon took a meager two steps, effortlessly closing the distance between the back of the cave and the fire, and hunched down in front of its warm light.

Darr looked over at his rescuer. He smiled cheerfully, as if somehow amused. The Archon had human features, though he had the appearance of being hewn from stone, the flesh of his face all planes and angles. His hair fell short around his ears, an earthy brown color, but his eyes gave him away as a spirit creature. His eyes were a perfect shade of emerald, shining green through the orange tint of the fire.

Darr caught himself staring and quickly looked down at

the fire. "Did I summon you?" he asked.

The Archon shook with great booming laughs, the depth of his voice barreling out of his hulking body. Darr stared in mute horror, appalled at the spirit creature's outburst. Did the Archon laugh out of pity for him or amusement? Whatever the reasons, Darr shrunk before the roaring echo.

The Archon appeared to sense his discomfort and silenced himself, holding out one of his large hands in apology. "I am sorry, young Reintol. I meant you no harm," the deep voice coaxed. "I thought you were playing a joke on me."

Darr shook his head warily and reached out to the Archon's hand. As soon as they touched, the Summoner felt the same connection with the Currents he'd experienced on the slopes of the Valimere and quickly drew his hand back.

The Archon smiled and sat back from the fire. "My name is Racall, and I am the Archon of Earth. But you knew that when you touched me, is that not right?"

Darr nodded, but kept his gaze level. "How are you here?" he asked.

"As an Archon, I can pass freely between the spiritual and physical realms because I am composed of both. My *flesh* is born from the essence of my element."

"You're an elemental," Darr stated.

Racall smiled and shook his head. "No. Elementals are a result of imbalance between the Sephirs."

Darr twisted his mouth in confusion. "So what are you?"

"Balance," the deep voice soothed. "Or rather, I am the embodiment of balance. The Sephirs spread their magic across the Currents like a net, and this magic manifests itself in Ictar as the Four Elements. This is what we call nature, and it is the only thing holding back chaos—the true, uninhabitable form of this world. As long as the Light of the Sephirs flows freely and equally, the binding on chaos will hold."

"That sounds awfully complex," Darr said. "I always

thought the Archons were extensions of each element."

Racall nodded his head. "We are, Summoner. But we are also the extensions of balance, the sentient voices of the Sephirs, and the wielders of their magic. Without us, the Sephirs would quickly become unbalanced and fail. Chaos would return, as well as other evils."

"You're talking about the Devoid, aren't you?" Darr asked.

Racall's gaze lowered. "Nidic Waq had to tell you. It is not easy information to hear, but you had to know in order to make an informed decision to help."

Darr shook his head. "The story of the Ancient Ictarians is just a story though. I never imagined any of that could be real. All of this is so strange. The Light and the Currents and the Devoid...no one ever taught me any of this."

The Archon of Earth remained motionless. "New things come to us everyday," he said. "We are constantly presented with new information and facts as we live our everyday lives. You can believe something, but not learn from it, and you can learn from something, but not believe in it. What matters is that you choose one or the other."

Darr stared up at the Archon, lost in the principles of his words. "And what do you think, Racall? What do you think I should do with the information presented?"

The spirit creature's smile deepened. "Learn how to summon. Navigate the Currents so you can help bring some balance back to the Sephirs."

The Archon's surreal green eyes mystified Darr. Racall told him almost exactly what Nidic Waq had. Yet, unlike the prophet, Racall had a more trusting demeanor. The Summoner believed the bond they shared through the Currents allowed this trust. Though the workings of the Currents were new to him, he'd learned lying was difficult, if not impossible there. Emotions and memories alike were laid bare. The realization startled him.

Uncomfortable with his thoughts, the Summoner kicked

at a piece of deadwood in the fire, sending up a swirl of sparks. He forged ahead into the thick of his concerns. "Racall, why did you laugh when I asked if I summoned you?"

A broad smile crossed the Archon's face. "I already told you. I thought you were joking." Darr gave him a tired look, and Racall's smile faded. "In all honesty, I thought you were more experienced, but I see now you have much to learn. However..." The spirit creature looked upward as if searching for something. "...in a manner of speaking, you did summon me, though not in the way you are thinking. I am the guide Nidic Waq sent for you, and I've been searching for you for some time. Your cries on the mountain are what brought me."

The Summoner cocked his head and let the thought sink in. It had never occurred to him that Racall might be his guide. It should've been obvious to him by now. He supposed he expected someone more...

"Human." Racall finished his thought, ripping the word out of his mind. "Yes, the prophet likes his surprises. But, who better to train a Spirit Summoner than a spirit creature? Who better to guide you through the land ahead than one who is composed of it?"

Racall appeared delighted at the idea, but Darr was angry. Nidic Waq admittedly withheld information, but it appalled Darr that the prophet had done something as life altering as sending an Archon without saying anything beforehand. Darr had expressed his doubts about magic and spirits. It seemed to him the prophet had understood. Instead, Nidic Waq had shattered his beliefs in one swift strike. It made him wonder what else the prophet had in store for him.

Racall hunched forward, distracting him. "Don't let Nidic Waq's intentions trouble you, young Reintol. Caeranol and his emissary have served Ictar faithfully for a long time, and I assure you neither means you harm. The prophet has an agenda to meet, and you fall into that agenda. He does what is necessary to let you fall into place."

"You mean let me fall where *he* wants me," Darr retorted.

Racall shrugged his shoulders as if to say they were the same.

Darr studied the Archon's impassive, yet cheerful demeanor. Racall was a paradox of human traits and emotions, but Darr grew accustomed to him rapidly. The Archon was kindred. The weight of authority Nidic Waq had commanded didn't exist with Racall. The spirit creature treated him as an equal, despite the fact they had differences between them that Darr couldn't fathom.

He glanced up at the cave entrance and out into the darkness of the night. At last, the storm died off outside, turning away from its harsh pounding of rain to a soft pattering. How long had he been up in the Valimere? He really had no idea.

"You better get to sleep, young Reintol," Racall told him, more of a suggestion than an order. "We will start our journey through the Valimere and the exploration of your abilities tomorrow."

Darr nodded, feeling a slow exhaustion seep through him. He wrenched his blanket free from his pack and lay down beside the fire, wrapping himself up tightly.

His last thoughts were of the wonders in store for him tomorrow.

* * * *

When morning came, Darr found himself alone. The fire had burned to ash and the storm had subsided, giving way to sunlight. He woke disoriented, like the night before, but within a few moments, his memories returned to him, doubts and uncertainties accompanying them. The events of the last couple of days had left him hollowed out, from his decision to leave Tyfor, to the revelations blazing truth to his misconceptions.

Darr leaned back against the cave wall and reached into his pack for a hunk of cheese and a piece of fruit. He chewed mechanically on the food. What would his father think of him if he knew the truth of his situation? Would he approve of all the lying and trickery he'd used? His father wouldn't be proud of him for not being truthful in the first place. Like everything else that had happened so far, there wasn't much point in worrying about it. Better to forge ahead and not think of the mistakes he'd made.

Refreshed by his new state of mind and a full stomach, Darr stuffed his blanket into his pack and tied it off. He couldn't hide his eagerness to find Racall and start on the way to Stern. Most likely, they would have to retrace their steps through the ravine and down the foothills in order to get back on the trail to Trenton Pass. He hefted his pack over his shoulders, cinched it into place, and walked indifferently into the morning sunlight.

Darr expected to find himself within the ravine. Instead, he found himself within Trenton Pass, identified by the towering peaks of the Valimere on either side of him. More surprising, he emerged into a landscape with the look and feel of spring. Luscious green grasses, dotted with white and yellow wildflowers, littered the floor of the pass stretching upward into the mountains. Trees, both deciduous and conifer shone brilliantly with morning dew, exhibiting not a trace of fall's corrosion. The Summoner breathed deeply and his lungs and nose were filled with the sweet scents of soil, flowers, and pine.

He started to examine a nearby shrub when a huge, dark shadow fell over him. "I see you slept well, young Reintol," Racall said, his voice deep and sober.

Darr nodded and looked up at the Archon. "Racall, what's going on here? What're we doing here in the Trenton? I thought we were down on the slopes. And what's going on with these trees? Did I sleep through the winter?"

The spirit creature smiled quickly, and turned to face his charge. "No, no, Summoner. You are fine. The reason you are in Trenton Pass is because I brought you here."

Darr gave the Archon a blank stare.

"After you collapsed in the foothills, I carried you the rest of the way to the pass. Archons are not subject to the same physical constraints as humans. The magic of the Sephirs is what sustains us."

Darr tried to imagine Racall carrying him through the ravine and up the mountain to the pass. Such a task would have been formidable for the strongest of men, yet the Archon brushed it off as something less than an inconvenience. Racall's gaze turned back towards the lush greenery of Trenton Pass, a lost look lingering in his eyes.

"As for the upset in nature you see before you," the Archon began, "this is what happens when there is unbalance between the elements. This is chaos reclaiming Ictar."

Shaking his head in confusion, Darr stepped forward to block the Archon's view. "But, Racall, this is beautiful. It's the middle of winter and it looks like the first day of spring up here. If this is chaos, maybe chaos should come more often."

Racall didn't move. His massive form went rigid, and his emerald eyes never once left the landscape before them. "No, Darr, you are wrong. What you see before you is the beginning of nature's slide towards chaos. The Sephirs are losing their Light, and the Four Elements are losing coherency—they are losing balance. Their magic runs unchecked through the Currents and into Ictar. Everyday, it becomes harder for the Archons to stretch the thinning magic."

Understanding turned Darr's skin cold as he looked up at the sad eyes of the Earth Archon. "This is because of the Devoid, isn't it?"

Racall only nodded and walked up into the pass. It took a moment for Darr to recover from his shock. He ran to catch up with the Archon.

They traveled through the day, and the landscape remained unchanged as they went. A beautiful catastrophe, Darr thought.

"During the summer, the southern lands around Fora Lake were razed by thunderstorms," Racall said. "The Elven capital of Exed received nearly a foot of snow during what should have been the hottest day of the year. Most everyone believes these are freak occurences, but that will not last."

Darr looked up at him and asked, "Why?"

With a nod, Racall said, "Because the Lourcient River has gone dry. The races of Ictar will not be able to ignore that."

When they stopped around nightfall, underneath a deep recess in a cliff, Darr asked Racall what lay in store for him when they reached Stern. They sat before a fire, though the Archon appeared to be acting as if he required warmth, whereas Darr had to pull his cloak tight in order to shut out the cold.

"So, if the Lourcient River has dried up, it must be the Seekers draining the Water Sephir's magic," Darr reasoned. "But how could they do that when the Sephir is protected by the Divine? It's not like they could go into the Currents because isn't that what the Archons do—protect against invasions?"

Racall nodded, and Darr's eyes widened in disbelief at his next thought.

"Could someone have stolen it—the Sephir, I mean?"

"Very good, young Reintol," the Archon said, his face beaming. "In the physical world, one must be in possession of a Sephir in order to use its power. Just think of the destruction the races would have caused during the Aeon Wars had they known of a way to use the magic without the need for the Sephirs. Spirit Summoners could have changed the direction of history."

Darr shook his head, shrugging off Racall's speculation. "So one of the Seekers stole the Sephir of Water and is now draining it of its Light."

Racall shook his head. "Not the Soul Seekers, young Reintol. The Devoid created the Seekers for one purpose, to collect the Light from the living. It summoned something else to drain the Sephirs, something more efficient."

"Regardless, how am I supposed to restore the Sephir?" Darr asked with a hint of frustration building in his voice.

Racall's eyes were steady and focused on Darr. "You can learn, young Reintol. It will take time, and you will have to be patient, but you can learn how to navigate the Currents and summon the magic of the Sephirs."

The desperation faded out of Darr as he sensed Racall's sincerity. "How?" Darr asked.

The Archon of Earth smiled warmly and reached over to pat the Summoner on the shoulder. Racall shifted his body so he could sit closer to Darr. "The only way you will ever be able to walk the paths of the Currents is if you learn to *hear* the spirits, not shut them out. To the untrained ear, their voices are vague and jumbled, but the spirits are a collective voice. Do you know what that means?"

Darr nodded faintly. "I think so."

"It means the spirits are a multitude of memories and knowledge, all different and all with different things to say, but they speak and think in harmony with one another, a constant sharing of their knowledge. It is a sensation unlike any you will feel here in the physical world, but one you must grow accustomed to in the Currents. Now do you see why it is hard to listen?"

Racall's voice, so smooth and easy to listen to, lightened the stress of facing the spirits for the first time. The Archon closed his eyes and breathed deeply. "Now, I want you to concentrate in the same way you learned to shut out the spirits, but instead, I want you to listen. I'll be with you, should anything go wrong."

Darr watched Racall's still form for a moment, his body a mountain before him. He used the image of the massive

Archon to gather his courage. He took a deep breath and opened his mind to the spirits. They came to him in an instant, and despite his preparations, they flooded his ears with hundreds of buzzing voices. The Summoner continued his breathing, following Racall's instructions, trying to listen, rather than shut out the voices. The spirits grew more intense, their voices louder and more jumbled. Panic set in and Darr opened his eyes in a short yelp, interrupting his breathing. For a few short moments, the spirits were still with him as he stared dizzily at the fire blazing before him, their voices still mixed and indistinct.

"What happened?" Racall asked. No disappointment appeared on his face, only concern.

"I tried. They were too many. I couldn't listen to them all."

Racall smiled kindly and said, "This time, try listening to only one. Remember, the spirits are connected one to another."

The Summoner looked up in frustration, about to protest, but Racall repositioned himself, his eyes already closed. Darr wasn't afraid to listen to the spirits or venture into the Currents. He progressed too fast, a sensation not unlike falling from a great height. Though it was his second day out of Tyfor, he was having conversations with Archons and taking trips into spiritual planes the rest of Ictar thought were unreachable outside of death.

"Are you ready?" Racall asked, peeking out of one eye.

Darr decided right then that he was, but his life would never be the same because of it.

Chapter Six

"After nearly a decade, Symdus's studies led him to theorize one could create a pocket of space called the Endless that would simulate the Currents. Within the Endless, one could reverse the effects of aging by allowing time to flow backwards. Work began on a means to generate the Endless, and Symdus anxiously awaited the realization of his dream."

~From A Current History of Ictar, as told by Nidic Waq

Racall's features were unreadable. "Remember your goal," the Archon said. "Remember the techniques I have taught you."

Darr let go a long sigh and did as Racall asked. He took in long, slow breaths, taking more time on this attempt. Calm now, he opened his mind and let the spirits rush in, another cacophony of voices.

"Easy Summoner," Racall said in a soothing tone.

The Summoner struggled right away, wanting to dash back to the mountains and the cool night air. He remembered Racall's advice about listening to one voice, but he didn't see how he could do such a thing. There were so many different voices overlapping each other.

Racall said the spirits were a collective, different voices and different thoughts, but they all acted in harmony with one another. Could listening to one really be the same as listening to all? Newfound confidence surged through Darr. He slowed his breathing again and let his body relax. Extremity by extremity, he calmed himself. The voices of the spirits roared through his head, but this time, he chose one voice to focus on.

Darr didn't remember exactly what it said, in fact, it might have been more of a memory, a composition of images imprinted on words. He heard about, or rather, he saw a tower surrounded by gardens enclosed by thorns. There were men of power walking its grounds, elders perhaps. Darr listened more intently, trying to focus on the details of the memory, fighting past the rising voices. The elders walking the grounds stopped what they were doing when an argument erupted near them.

At the doors to the tower, a tall and regal-looking man stood before a thin black-haired man. They were the ones arguing. The other elders gathered around, though they put a fair amount of distance between the two because they were the highest among them. They were arguing about the use of their power. They were arguing about life. In the end, the black-haired man stormed off and fled through the gardens...

...*Darr listened in silence, but he could hear nothing. Silence surrounded him. The voices of the spirits were gone, replaced now with an eerie quiet which Darr accepted as another failure. His vision cleared, like he'd opened his eyes but without the physical action. He didn't see the night of the Valimere. A vast world of lavender-colored light spread out before him.*

–Summoner of the Currents–

–Summoner of Tyfor–

–You are welcome–

The spirits spoke in unison, and Darr gasped in spite of himself. The spirits were nothing more than tiny specks of white light swirling around his face and in the distance, fireflies against the pale light. There were easily thousands of them, perhaps more.

I've done it, he thought, trying to fight down the invincible feeling of glee. It wasn't about listening to all the spirits at once. One voice needed to be heard, because hearing one was the same as hearing all. An overwhelming sense of panic crept over the Summoner at the realization of how far he'd come, for he had no idea what to do or how to leave.

–Do not be afraid, Darr Reintol–

—You can leave when you want—
—The Currents are yours to travel—
—Our home is now yours—
—Our wisdom is shared now with you—
"Good job, young Reintol."

Darr watched, awestruck at the greenish light swirling in front of him, coalescing into the shape of Racall. The Summoner looked down at his own body, his own physical shape mimicked by white pinpricks of light, much like Racall's. Flesh and blood didn't exist in this world, he realized.

"You have passed the first obstacle in learning your potential as a Spirit Summoner. The spirits have welcomed you into the Currents, and you have learned what is necessary to listen to them." Darr heard a difference in Racall's voice here in the Currents. While its depth matched his physical form, it sounded harmonized with other tones.

"Why do they welcome me here?" the Summoner asked, his wonder dissipating. "I'm always connected to the Currents, aren't I?"

Something Darr likened to deliberation rushed through him. It subsided the moment Racall began to speak. "What you have experienced during the transition between the Currents and the physical world is not unlike the relationship between a mother and her unborn child, still in the womb. Before the child is born, the child and mother both are aware of each other's existence, but they reside in different worlds. When the child is born, the two worlds collide, and the mother welcomes her child into her world. The transition you have gone through is very similar."

"How do I get back?" Darr asked, suddenly uncomfortable.

A deep rumbling came from all around him. It wasn't anything he felt physically, but a sense of dissatisfaction from within the Currents. He sensed a hint of delight from Racall in the same way.

"You would not offend your hosts by leaving so soon after your arrival, would you?" Racall asked. "Let us have a look around."

The Currents were a wide open space with no earth and no sky, no trees or plants of any kind, only the strange wisteria light and the fluttery white of the spirits. In the distance, weaved through the ether, there were lines of color—red, blue, yellow, and green. On closer inspection, Darr saw the same colors weaved through the air in front of him, though harder to see.

"Is this the magic of the Sephirs, Racall?" Darr asked.

"This is the Light of the Sephirs," the Archon replied. "Their Light can be summoned or taken into the physical world where it becomes magic."

Racall gestured to the lines of color, sweeping his arm back and forth towards the various directions in which they flowed.

"These Lights are the Four Elements as they work their way through the Currents, spreading their magic out into the physical world." Racall inched closer to Darr. "Think of the balance between the Four Elements like a cord woven together by four strands. If the cord is stressed too much, one of the strands might fray and eventually break. These breaks cause elementals to appear in the physical world. When you are in the Currents as you are now, these breaks will be drawn towards you. Always be mindful when you are here."

The strange lights presented a hypnotic puzzle, but Racall started to move forward, a slight drifting motion through the Currents that broke Darr's attention. The Summoner tried taking a step but nothing happened. He tried running, the white light of his legs sending up a flurry of luminousness, but still he detected no movement. With no ground beneath him, his legs didn't work.

Racall laughed. "This is not the physical world, young Reintol. However, the same rules apply here. You think of walking, and your legs move to do the work. Use the same principle here."

The Summoner stopped running, and calmed himself. He imagined himself moving forward, and he moved, but he moved so fast and so unexpectedly, he shot off into the wisteria light. Darr tried to stop himself, but somehow ended up changing directions. The sensation overpowered him, and he quit trying to move altogether. He floated in the Currents for a few moments before Racall found him, his massive form emitting a feeling of amusement so powerful Darr couldn't help but share in it.

When they had both calmed themselves, Racall said, "You must remember one thing when in the Currents, Darr, and this lesson will apply to many different tasks, so take careful note. Your thoughts mirror what you seek here. Whatever you are thinking, whatever you ask for from the Currents, is what you will receive. That is why becoming a Summoner is so difficult and bears such a burden. It is an awesome power, capable of almost anything. If you ask for a mountain, you will receive a mountain. If you ask to travel from one end of the world to the other in the blink of an eye, you will do so. Keep your requests precise and your thoughts from straying."

Darr nodded, and this time when Racall started off through the Currents, he kept an image of the Archon close in his mind. He found by thinking of Racall, he stayed close to him and matched his pace.

They drifted through the wisteria light for a while, but Racall brought them to a stop before a sudden brightening in the Sephirs' magic.

"Here," Racall said and gestured towards the brightness.

The light marking the Four Elements crisscrossed before them like giant ribbons, and aside from being brighter, Darr saw nothing different about them.

"Look closely, young Reintol."

Darr studied the colors, following the threads from

yellow to blue to green. When he followed the thread of red, the element of Fire, something gave him pause. A small fleck of white light burst from the center of the stream and brightened the colors around it.

"It looks like it's torn," Darr said, and a feeling of approval washed over him from Racall.

"As I mentioned earlier," the Archon said, "this is a break in the Four Elements. You must look for breaks such as these when you are in the Currents. Your presence near them could allow them to break free into the physical world."

Confused, Darr asked, "How do I go about fixing it?"

"In time, you'll learn," Racall answered. "For now, you would do wise to be aware of breaks like this and stay far from them."

The Archon drifted closer to the break and stretched his arms out to it. Slowly, the white light began to dim, then vanish altogether. It appeared the break had never existed.

"Your own Light has such power, young Reintol."

They drifted onward through the wisteria light. Through the haze of the light, soft pricks of bright whiteness could be seen, identifying each of the Lights of the Sephirs themselves. They could be seen anywhere in the Currents at anytime like stars.

There were pale places, clouds that were more towards where the ground would be. Racall took him in closer and told him to focus on those pale places. In a flash of blinding color, the familiar light of the Currents disappeared and groups of bodies appeared, all composed of the same white lights as Darr.

"The pale places within the Currents are where large numbers of people are gathered. With more experience you will be able to locate a single person walking across an open field." Racall edged closer and his voice became a soft echo. "Inside the Currents, being this close to someone's Light will allow you to sense what they are feeling and sometimes, if the spirits are able, they can tell you a thing or two about them as well."

"That's why everyone thinks Nidic Waq is a prophet," Darr said in wonder. "He isn't really reading their minds–he's a Spirit Summoner. Nobody knows it though because they don't know what a Summoner can do, right?"

Racall nodded, but Darr sensed restraint of some kind from the Archon. For the first time, Darr suspected Racall might not be telling him everything. Racall pushed forward, avoiding a confrontation and changing his thoughts so Darr couldn't sense his feelings. The Summoner shoved his doubts aside and followed him to where a group of the sparkling white bodies were gathered close.

A flood of emotions coursed through him. He mingled among the forms and felt their merriment and exhilaration, hostility and rage, anxiety and apathy. The feelings were so intense, for a moment, they threatened to drown him. As the sensations grew in strength, Racall's familiar presense brushed them away, lending strength to Darr and quieting the emotions boiling in him.

"Do you know why I brought you here? Do you know what this place is?"

Images flashed in Darr's head and his mind raced for an answer. He closed out the images gently before answering. "This is a tavern or an inn. I can almost see it, but I don't understand why you brought me here."

Racall strung his glowing, green arm out before the patrons and said, "This is another important lesson for you, Summoner. I brought you here to show you what you are capable of. Spirit Summoners can see into the Currents and read the Light in another living creature. What you see before you are not the physical bodies of living beings, so never deceive yourself into thinking otherwise. These are their lifeforces, their Light, mimicking their physical forms in the Currents. The Light carries within it all of their emotions and memories, and in the Currents, you are given access to all of this. However, should you try to take in too much, you will become lost. Your own Light—your memories and emotions, the very core of your being—will become indistinguishable from their own, and you will be lost to the Currents. Do you understand?"

Distress roared through Darr at the revelation. He hadn't thought the Currents could be such a dangerous place, but he'd experienced the drowning sensation once already. The Currents had the potential to consume the careless. He nodded his head in understanding, forgetting his physical gestures meant nothing, but his emotions spoke volumes.

"Good," Racall said. "Then there is one more thing you must remember. The spirits are also composed of the Light. They are a danger to you and can consume you in the same way as these people you see before you. They would not do so intentionally, but should you let them get too involved with you, they would integrate themselves with you in the same way. All of this goes back to what I told you before. This is not a place for curiosity, but a place for precision."

Unease vibrated through Darr, its source coming from somewhere other than Racall and his cryptic warning. This feeling was familiar. When listening to the ghost stories told by travelers at Arn's inn he sometimes felt like this. It was fear rooted in the unknown and the unexpected. And why did he feel so cold all of the sudden? He had no physical body in the Currents, no flesh to numb.

Racall appeared at his side, but the Summoner could sense fear in him. Fear for his charge.

"We must go now, young Summoner," Racall said. "Focus on me. The transition from the Currents to the physical world will disorient you, but if you can hold on to my Light, you should be all right for the time being."

There was no time for questions. Urgency radiated through the Currents. He did as instructed and focused on Racall's Light.

The sensation of falling came over Darr, uncontrolled

and frightening. He gasped for breath, fighting for air even though air didn't exist in the spirit realm. Racall's aura surrounded him, comforting him and protecting him, and in moments, the feeling of suffocation was replaced...

...By hardness and dampness, light and dark, cool air and crackling fire. Darr's eyes focused, and his physical body closed around him. The Currents still buzzed in his ears, awash with the incessant ramblings of the spirits, but Darr didn't have attention to give them. A wave of sickness washed through him, disorienting him. He tried to stand and found his legs gave out.

"Do not strain yourself, young Summoner," Racall soothed from right behind him. Gently, the Archon lifted him to his feet, holding him by the back of his shirt.

"What's wrong with me?" Darr asked, his words slurring together.

"Your body and mind are adjusting to the shift between worlds. You need rest, but now is not an option. Come. I have your pack."

Racall nudged him forward, and Darr's legs worked mechanically. The air and darkness of the night closed around him as Racall prodded him out into the pass. With it, came a deadening cold, but Darr didn't feel it from the elements. This cold came from inside him, radiating outward from the marrow of his bones. The night itself appeared normal and calm, but some threat lurked close by. Perhaps a predator cindercat was on the hunt, but that didn't feel right. Whatever was out there didn't feel natural.

Nothing could be seen with the eyes or heard with the ears.

Darr's thoughts grew jumbled again and he fell to the ground. Racall had him on his feet in moments, nudging him onward, his voice a whisper of reassurance. "Not far now, young Reintol."

The Summoner let himself be propelled forward. His body moved fine on its own, as long as he didn't try to dwell on whatever went on around him. He and Racall had left the main pass now, and his legs worked harder as they started up an incline. Long grasses whipped at his arms and face, but these were minor annoyances. When at last they stopped, they were on a broad ledge above a canyon, but the shadow and starlight gave no real definition.

Exhausted at last, Darr collapsed to his knees and Racall bent down over him. "I am going to leave you now, but you must stay quiet and still. Sleep if you can, but do not exert any more energy than necessary. Do you understand?"

Darr nodded, and he sprawled out on his stomach with his chin resting on his hands. Confusion persisted as to why they were running, but he no longer cared. The prospect of sleep appealed far too much. He closed his eyes and his spinning thoughts stopped. His body relaxed and peace settled in.

Time had passed. Darr wasn't sure how much. His eyes fluttered open, and through the screen of grass, the starlit canyon spread out below him. There wasn't much to see except the opposite cliff wall and a scattering of boulders. A willow grew across the way, its gnarled trunk and drooping limbs growing out of the rocky cliff. Strange. He'd never seen a willow grow out of a cliff before, but with the Sephirs unbalanced, he supposed anything could happen.

Darr tilted his head to look up for the Archon. He hadn't heard from him in a while now. Out of the corner of his eye, something darker than the shadow around him caught his attention. His breath caught in his throat. His heart stopped, and he lay still.

The dark shapes worked their way west through the canyon, their movements fluid and black. The cold returned, stronger and more debilitating than before. He froze from the inside out, his being reduced to something so small he could barely perceive it. He knew what caused it.

The Soul Seekers.

They slid out into the starlight below him, shadows come

to life, cloaked and hooded from head to toe in tattered robes. There were four or five of them. If there were more, he couldn't see them. Silver tipped claws dangled at their sides, shining and inert and anything but useless. Like specters, they floated above the ground on invisible legs, silent and stealthy embodiments of death.

Darr took in a short breath. The Soul Seekers stopped and stood motionless in the canyon between him and the willow. Their empty hoods still faced west. The Summoner's lungs froze, and a shiver of dread spun down his spine, uncontrollable.

As if sensing the movement, the Seekers turned as one, the black hoods peering up the rock wall of the canyon. They were looking right at him. They knew where he hid. They intended to destroy him, to rip him asunder like the Dwarf hunter in Tyfor had described.

Flee! Run away!

The words screamed in his mind, but Darr's body wouldn't work. With the incarnations of death standing before him, his bones and blood had turned to ice, his muscles had atrophied, and his only thoughts were of regret. The Seekers would come for him, and he would die.

The Seekers shifted their bodies in his direction, gliding towards him to finish him off. A breeze blew through the air, and Darr dipped his head, waiting for death. No, it wasn't a breeze. The air itself was still, and he lifted his head to see the willow across from him swaying, its limbs and branches shifting.

Sound exploded across the canyon, and the willow came to life, its slender branches stretching out for the Seekers, wrapping about their robes like dozens of clinging tendrils. The tree shuddered, and the branches flung outward, tearing the Soul Seekers to pieces in the process, their robes shredded and scattered into the night. Their bodies, if they had any, were torn apart and lost to the darkness.

The entire spectacle ended in seconds. Darr blinked. The

tree shook itself once before letting its branches hang limply once more. Darr blinked a second time, thinking he'd been mistaken, and the death the Soul Seekers would bring him still approached.

The Seekers were gone. Calm had returned, and the night no longer threatened. Darr let the breath he held in his lungs go and a smattering of bright spots crossed his vision. He felt sleepy and dizzy, and he shut his eyes to regain his composure.

Chapter Seven

"Despite all his planning, the Endless was not what Symdus expected. A person within the Endless was not subject to the ravages of time, but neither were they aware of the outside world. Worse, the outside world had no way of knowing a person slept within the Endless unless it was previously established. Inside the Endless, a person might sleep forever, lost within a pocket of timelessness with no body and no Light to show that they'd ever existed."

~From A Current History of Ictar, as told by Nidic Waq

Darr jerked awake with a start. Morning had arrived.

With some effort, the Summoner sat up, pulling his blanket tight against his body in order to fight off the early morning nip in the air. At first, he remembered nothing from the previous night, only a vague perception of the Currents and his time there. He examined his body, searching for a clue to what had happened. He lay wrapped in his blanket, stretched out before the cold ashes of the previous night's fire. The edge of a bluff dropping down into a canyon lay not more than a few feet away. Darr leaned over to get a better look at the canyon below.

In an icy flood, the image of the Soul Seekers ravaged his thoughts. The feelings generated by the memory of their silver claws and faceless hoods were enough to paralyze him. Alone and afraid again, Darr had no one to save him. No one except...

"Ah ha, young Reintol. You have survived after all, I see."

Racall appeared through a screen of trees beyond the ashes of the campfire. The Seekers had been ripped apart by the branches of the willow. He searched the canyon for the strange tree, but he couldn't find it.

"It was you," Darr whispered, his gaze turning back to the

63

Archon. "You were the willow. You became that tree and saved me from them."

The smile on Racall's face broadened. "You are perceptive, as always, young Reintol."

The ice in Darr's veins thawed, but the blackness of the creatures from last night still lingered in his mind. "It was them, wasn't it, Racall? Those were the Soul Seekers I saw last night."

Racall nodded and the smile faded from his face. The Archon knelt down and sat across from Darr. "They were," Racall said. "But you have nothing to fear from them, not yet anyway. While you travel with me, young Summoner, the Soul Seekers will not harm you."

Darr shook his head. He had trouble believing that. The Seekers had come out of nowhere, and now that he knew what they were like, nothing frightened him more.

Racall's flat mouth shifted into a smile. "I assure you your safety. The Seekers pose no threat to me, and I can find them long before they can find me, or you, for that matter. I detected them while we were in the Currents last night."

Darr shook his head in confusion. "Was I really in the Currents last night?"

"Of course you were," Racall replied. He brushed the nearby branch of a blossoming cherry tree, and his cheerful demeanor returned.

Darr sat in a daze for a moment longer, his mind still reeling from thoughts of Soul Seekers and spirits. He reached into his pack for a piece of bread and chewed on it. He didn't remember leaving the Currents. The whole experience left his memory blurred. While he remembered his initial acceptance by the spirits and his explorations with Racall, he retained very little else. An entire chunk of his memories had been stolen from his mind.

With his hunger sated, a new flood of questions plagued Darr. He tried to voice them to Racall, but the Archon wouldn't hear them. They would have plenty of time to talk as they crossed the Valimere. Reluctantly, the Summoner gathered his few possessions, and together, he and Racall resumed their trek through Trenton Pass.

"If I'd spent all night in the Currents, wouldn't I have lost an entire night's sleep?" Darr asked while they hiked.

Racall slowed and looked back at him. "Time has no meaning when you are in the Currents. From the moment you entered them last night, time ceased to exist. You might have been in there for what seemed like minutes or days, but it did not matter out here in the physical world. So long as you fully submerge yourself in the spirit realm, not the blink of an eye will pass while you are away."

The Earth Archon resumed his pace, leaving Darr staring after him in mild shock. "But that's impossible," he cried. "If I wasn't in there for as long as I was, why did I wake up in the morning with nothing except a vague memory of the Seekers?"

"It happens quite often for Summoners on their first attempt into the Currents," Racall soothed, still walking briskly along the ridge, not bothering to turn back. "Your mind overcompensates for the time you think you have lost in the physical world. The truth of the matter is, your mind actually stays with your physical body. It is your Light that becomes aware of the spirit realm."

"My Light?" Darr asked before running to catch up.

Racall smiled down at him. "Your Light is always connected to the Currents, but for most people, they are never aware of this connection. As a Spirit Summoner, you have learned to listen to the spirits in such a way that allows your perception to shift from your mind to your Light. This is why some of your memories are vague. Your mind is sorting out the information your Light has collected. No worries. This will get easier in time."

Darr followed in silence afterwards. Racall should've told him what to expect. Of course, making the discovery of lost time for himself probably worked out better in the long run.

If Racall had told him beforehand, he might not have wanted to venture into the Currents. It wasn't such a bad thing not having to worry about time when in the Currents. It meant he could spend all the time he wanted there.

Over the next two days, Darr learned all he could from Racall as they traveled through the Valimere. The Archon passed on new relaxation techniques, and meditations which would allow Darr to quiet his mind and enter the Currents swiftly and more efficiently than before. He learned to train himself into using a trigger, an automatic response that would take him to the Currents.

"Emotion and memory are two things you should be mindful of while in the Currents," Racall explained one evening before they stopped for the night.

"How do you mean?" Darr asked.

"While you are in the Currents, your ability to reason logically is reduced. You do not have your mind to think with, and so you must rely on your memory and emotion, as well as the spirits, to guide you."

Darr shook his head. "But I remember trying to think in the Currents."

Racall smiled. "Thoughts are still possible in the Currents. I am talking about reason. It is important that you keep your emotions under control. In the spirit realm, your emotions and memories are what drive your thoughts, not logic. And while your memories might be mindful of some consequences, your emotions know nothing of consequence."

Racall continued by explaining emotions and memories could be transferred through the spirit realm—either suppressed or intensified within the Light of living creatures.

Later that night, Darr asked about the Soul Seekers.

"The Seekers are elementals drawn from the Light itself," the Archon told him. "The Light contains the power of life and death, and it is from death that the Devoid has shaped its minions. The Seekers hold some influence over the Currents, allowing them to instill dread in their victims.

Remember that, young Reintol. Keep your wits about you and your emotions in check when they are around or else they will easily manipulate you into becoming prey."

Racall offered little else on the Seekers, and while it wasn't as much information as Darr would have liked, it turned his obsession into a mild curiosity.

The days passed quickly. Darr's connection to everything around him grew with every lesson. At night, the Archon would encourage him to venture back into the Currents to explore his potential and grow more comfortable with its complexities. Darr dove in, and he found he could move in and out of the Currents without losing time or his memories.

When the Archon and the Summoner finally reached the far side of the Valimere Mountains, late in the afternoon of their third day of travel, fall set upon them once more. It appeared the Sephirs' binding magic still had some strength left after all. The trees coming down out of the mountains and stretching out across the plains of Cortaz were bright orange fingers, waving their leaves in every direction.

Racall led him down out of the foothills and they angled south towards the Lourcient River. As the daylight waned, the crisp fall air swooped down upon them, but the skies remained clear. Darr marveled at the rolling plains of Griton before him. He'd seen them once several years ago. They had the appearance of an ocean made of grass, rolling waves of yellow and green studded with trees. Ictar still had some hope left, he thought. Imbalance might be spreading among the elements, but there were still places where the seasons fell regularly and blight had yet to ruin the landscape.

Darr's hopes ran high until Racall brought him before the banks of the Lourcient River. Once the proudest, most powerful river in the Cortazian territories, the Lourcient had been reduced to nothing more than a creek winding feebly west towards the peaks of the Valimere. Its banks stretched outward into grotesque drifts of mud, gravel, and tree limbs for miles in either direction. The water itself looked disgusting, fouled from sediment. Darr dropped to his knees. He hadn't prepared himself for this sight, and his strength and resolve fell away. In the failing of the river, the hopelessness of the task before him stood fully revealed.

"Is this because of the Water Sephir?" he asked, barely able to get out the words.

Racall nodded. "The Lourcient River dies because the magic of the Water Sephir runs deep through this part of Ictar. With it missing from its altar, its magic cannot reach into Ictar, and its element fades."

Darr watched the thinning line of the once magnificent river, in horror of the tragedy brought about by the Devoid. Nidic Waq had been so insistent in restoring the Sephirs, and now Darr knew why. At the same time, what difference could he make? He'd made the leap into the Currents, explored the vastness of the spiritual realm and come to understand much about its workings, but he still didn't know the connection between the Currents and summoning. How could he draw physical power from a place built entirely of imagery and light?

Once the sun began to set over the eastern horizon, Racall turned away, walking along the muddy banks. Darr followed, tired of staring out at the ruined Lourcient. They found a small stand of cedar to camp beneath for the night. Racall discouraged a fire now that they weren't protected by the Valimere's cover. Darr didn't mind much, except for the cold weather. He consumed his evening meal as night set in, and afterwards he leaned back against one of the cedar trunks with his cloak pulled close. With the moon only half full, there was enough light to make out various shapes dotting the landscape.

Darr felt incredibly alone in that moment. The plains shouldn't look so foreign to him, even as dark as they were. The memory of the Lourcient River stuck fresh in his mind and added to the strangeness of his surroundings. The Ictar he'd always dreamed of seeing wasn't there, buried under all the madness of the Soul Seekers and...

"Devoid." Racall said the word smoothly, but with the right intensity so it startled Darr. "That is what this world is becoming...devoid of life."

Darr sat up straight and looked over at the giant Archon crouching down next to him. The darkness grew deep around them, and Darr whispered, "This isn't what I expected at all."

Racall laughed softly. "Journeys of self-discovery seldom are, young Reintol."

The Archon's response caused Darr to wonder. "Is that really why Nidic Waq sent me? So I could find out who I am?"

"Of course he did. You cannot restore the Sephirs unless you know who you are, and part of knowing who you are is about going on this quest. Nidic Waq knew this when he chose you."

The Summoner shook his head. "You know that's not what I mean."

"I know, but does it really matter why the prophet chose you to go on this journey? He asked you to go, and you are here."

Darr looked back out across the plains. He'd been asking himself the same questions since he'd left Tyfor, and it made him feel exposed for Racall to have read him so easily. The Archon had vast intuitive powers, and up until now, Darr hadn't been bothered by the spirit creature's ability. Regardless, the reasons that set him on this journey were no longer a subject he wanted to consider.

"Racall, you said something about an altar when we were talking about the Water Sephir. You said it wouldn't be connected to the Currents since it was stolen from its altar. I thought the Sephirs were connected to the Currents all the time?"

The Archon nodded. "The Sephirs are connected to the Currents by the Light within them, the same as you are. The only way their magic can flow throughout Ictar is if they are placed on an altar. Their Light flows into the Currents through their altar, then out into Ictar as magic we know as the Four Elements."

"But if the Sephir was stolen, how can its magic be stolen?"

"The Sephirs' magic flows freely," Racall said as if he were telling a fairy tale. "To absorb its Light is the same as absorbing its magic, but to do this, someone would have to remove the Sephir from its altar, which in turn would disrupt the balance of the elements."

Darr nodded in understanding. "So the altars act like a deterrent. If you try to steal the magic, you risk destroying everything, even yourself."

Racall smiled faintly and said, "Today, with the Divine in power, the Sephirs are safe from the hands of mortal men."

"Just not from the Devoid," Darr replied.

"The Devoid wants to be free of its prison. Once free, it will consume what Light remains in the Sephirs, as well as the Light of every living creature on Ictar. When it is done, it will be engulfed in the return of chaos, and it will be indifferent to its own destruction."

A chill vibrated through Darr coupled with a sick feeling in his stomach. Racall remained silent afterwards. A flood of questions concerning summoning, the Sephirs, and the Currents inundated his mind. He still wasn't sure how Nidic Waq managed to control the magic of the elements when he was in the Currents, or when he wasn't for that matter. The whole concept of magic remained too terrifying to consider.

Darr leaned back against one of the cedars and reached for his blanket. Racall looked over with a bright smile. "You're not going to sleep, are you, young Reintol?"

The Summoner glanced up at Racall with a questioning look.

"The Currents await you," the Archon chided. "How can you expect to learn about the spirit realm if you don't explore it?"

Weariness crept over Darr, weighing down his back and shoulders, and causing his eyelids to droop. A small voice called to him, a familiar inner voice. This is what you asked for. This is your journey of self discovery. Darr forced a smile and gave Racall a perfunctory nod. He crossed his legs before him, monitoring his breathing at the same time. With no small amount of conscious thought, Darr slipped into the Currents in pursuit of his journey.

Chapter Eight

"Symdus recognized his failure with the Endless, but he wasn't ready to give up. In his experimentations, he had found the Light within all living things to be a potential source of immortality. Wary of this new approach, a handful of Symdus's assistants reported his findings to the Elder Council."

~From A Current History of Ictar, as told by Nidic Waq

Racall and Darr traveled east, along what remained of the Lourcient River, towards Stern, over the next three days. Despite the weather turning colder and wetter, Darr grew more appreciative of his lessons from Racall. When they stopped at night, Darr always found something new to learn from the Archon.

After only a few days, moving through the Currents had become as easy as moving across an open field. He learned if he allowed himself a little patience, he could feel the emotions of people in the physical world through their Light. The sensation overwhelmed him still, but with Racall present, Darr found very little he couldn't accomplish. He'd even managed to mingle with the spirits and listen to what they had to say without being overtaken by them.

While the experiences fascinated him, Darr found they affected him little outside in the physical world. There were great things he could do in the Currents, but what good were they if he couldn't be in two places at once? He had to be in the Currents in order to summon these special skills, and in order to put his abilities to use, he had to be in Ictar.

"So what good are my abilities if I can't use them in the physical world?" Darr asked Racall.

The Archon kept his gaze straight ahead, but a smile played at the edge of his mouth. "In the Currents, you must remember the futility of time."

Though cryptic, Racall offered no further response to Darr's question. Frustrated, Darr pondered the dilemma, searching for a real answer.

At noon on their third day out of the Valimere, they came within sight of Stern. The plains rolled upwards, making their rise into the foothills on which the city rested. Stern, an impregnable fortress in every sense of the word, had been a focal point during the Aeon Wars.

The Water Sephir had found its home there, and for a time, the Cortazian Kings had lived there before establishing themselves at Mertz, and now Darlholme. During that time of kingship, Stern had been transformed from a lone standing fortress into a beautifully walled city that guarded the source of the Lourcient River. It achieved this by making use of a system of locks and dams within the mountains behind the city, that also allowed control over the flow of water.

For all the good it does now, Darr thought grimly, staring up at the city. A large iron gate closed off a section on the right side of the city walls, sealing off the opening where the river should have tumbled to the plains below by way of the Hondor Falls. The Governor of Stern must've shut it in order to conserve whatever water remained.

A road became visible as the city grew closer, and the two travelers followed it past the outlying farming communities. Darr had seen few people since leaving the Valimere, and only from a distance. Now they passed many different people on their way to Stern's gates. With the weather turning cold and wet, Darr's giant companion received barely any attention while people scurried about their business.

A light rain fell as daylight faded to dusk. The high walls rose up before them, as did the stubby peaks of the low mountains guarding the city's rear. The Summoner and the Archon approached the lines of farmers and other tradesmen migrating to and from the gates.

Darr turned to Racall, intent on asking how they were

going to explain their business at the gate. The Archon had mysteriously shrunk in size. And he no longer took the shape of a man, but a boy instead. The only thing giving him away were his peculiar green eyes.

"Racall!" Darr cried out.

The Archon walked past him, looking back long enough to flash his familiar smile before dashing towards the gates. Darr ran after, trying not to look suspicious, but he drew the attention of the men guarding the raised portcullis.

"Whoa there, little fellah," one of the guards said sternly, holding Racall back as he tried to run through the open gates. "Wait for your brother there, will ya."

Several people turned to look, but the guards kept them moving. Darr ran up to the guard holding Racall, breathing heavily after the chase the Archon had given him.

"Sorry, sir. He...got away from me." Darr gasped between breaths.

"What's yer name there, fellah?" the guard asked, still keeping a firm grip on Racall's shoulders. The Archon smiled fiercely at Darr.

The Summoner glared back, but answered. "My name's Darr Reintol."

"And the boy? He your brother?"

Darr kept his gaze on Racall, finding his lie there. "Yes, of course. His name is Erec. We're here to visit our grandfather. We came all the way from Tyfor. He's a little excited, that's all."

The guard eyed him skeptically for a moment, then released Racall. "Be sure to keep a better hold of him next time."

The Summoner nodded and reached out for Racall's shoulder. The moment they touched, Darr slipped halfway into the Currents. His eyes remained focused on the physical sights around him. In a terrifying clash of color and feeling, Darr saw both the physical world and the lights of the spiritual realm simultaneously. The raw emotions and memories of the men around him crawled over him. He could almost hear what the spirits were saying about them.

One of the guards reached out and shook Darr's arm away, breaking his concentration. "Hey, what's the matter with you?"

Darr gave the guards a sheepish look. He shook his head in dismay and rushed headlong onto the streets of Stern in complete fear for his life. He ran, not only from the wrath of the guards, from whom he sensed anger, but also from Racall, who'd shown him some new aspect of the Currents. Somehow, by touching the Archon, he'd existed both inside and outside of the spirit realm, privy to all of its secrets while still remaining grounded in the physical world.

The world of concrete images and feelings and sounds fell away, leaving Darr stripped and naked. He'd felt a similar sensation when he first met Racall, but this wasn't the same. The Currents connected all life, all memory, all emotion, and for a brief moment, Darr shared it all. It made him feel sick inside, a violation not only of himself, but of everything around him.

Without seeing, he ran through Stern's streets, quickly becoming lost in their uniformity. The entire city sprawled out in a grid, with channels cut into its streets where the Lourcient River flowed on its way to the Hondor Falls and the plains beyond. All the streets and buildings had the same look to them, and Darr no longer knew where he was.

He didn't care. His world crumbled apart. The shock he'd received from his joining with Racall gave him reason to scale the city walls and run straight back to Tyfor. The power of the Currents, and whatever magic he might find there, was too far away from his idea of normal to be useful. Worse, he knew once he took that next step into the Currents, the step which would allow him to summon, there would be no turning back.

"Stop running, young Reintol," a voice called out behind him, deep and powerful.

Darr slowed. He didn't want to talk to Racall, but he couldn't run forever. He turned and looked down the darkened street at Racall's familiar giant form. Nightfall had arrived, and most of Stern's citizens were at home or walled up in a tavern. No one would bother them.

Racall walked up before him and said, "I am sorry you had to experience what you did, but sooner or later, it would have happened."

"I don't know if I can do it, Racall." Darr lowered his head, not wanting to look him in the eye. "I don't know what I saw when I touched you back there, but...I'm not ready for this..."

He trailed off, but the Archon was a pillar before him. A hint of sympathy emanated from the spirit creature, but it vanished quickly. "Listen to me, Darr. I know all of this is strange. I know you never expected this kind of journey when you set out, but giving up only means you have failed."

"I never wanted any of this," Darr whispered.

"You wanted to know more about Spirit Summoners. You wanted to know what their function was in the world. And deep down, you want to know why you are a Summoner."

It shocked Darr that Racall knew him so well, but he said nothing.

"Yes, there are strange things to discover when you are learning to be a Summoner. These things are sometimes frightening. Sometimes you will want to run away. You must remember you have great potential, young Reintol."

A knowing whisper came from the Currents, the voices of the spirits confirming Racall's words. He spoke the truth. Never before had the spirits come to him unbidden and with a message he could understand.

"What happened?" Darr asked.

Racall shook his head. "We should not talk here. We will find someplace to sit."

The city had grown quiet and dark, but echoes of laughter and shouts sounded from every direction. Lights burned from within several of the nearby buildings. Darr's apprehension melted away, though his concerns about the magic and the Currents still flooded through him.

Racall led the Summoner inside a noisy tavern crowded with a number of drunken patrons. The Archon didn't change his appearance when they entered. Racall walked past staring faces to a table in the back and took a seat. Darr sat with him, and the crowd watched them for a moment longer before returning to their nightly activities. A serving woman came and took Darr's order, a pint of ale and some food. When the food and drink arrived, Racall explained while Darr consumed his meal.

"Everything you have learned along this part of your journey, young Reintol, has been rudimentary. When you touched me, and connected yourself to the Currents, you made a leap in progress you were not quite ready to make."

"You haven't taught me anything about connecting myself to the Currents while remaining in the physical world. How am I supposed to learn anything if you don't show me?"

A smile brightened the Archon's face and said, "It is something you must discover for yourself."

"But what happened?"

"When you touched me, you were able to see through my eyes."

On the verge of cramming half a potato into his mouth, Darr stopped and said, "You said I made a leap in progress. How is seeing through your eyes a leap?"

Racall's smile faded into seriousness. "Because seeing through the Currents as I do will eventually be one of your many gifts."

Was Racall telling him he'd be like an Archon? Was this the curse Nidic Waq bore, the reason no one in Ictar trusted him?

Panic threatened to overwhelm the Summoner, but a calming sensation flowed from Racall. "The time to worry about how the rest of Ictar will view you is not now. You are not ready to face this aspect of yourself," the Archon said. "When you are ready, you will know."

After taking a long sip of ale, Darr said, "I wish I knew I was making the right decision in all of this."

Racall sat back in his chair, bearing his familiar smile. "You worry far too much. You must learn to accept what you are, and more importantly, accept the task you have been given. Once you do, you will find the Currents and its mysteries are little more than exotic flowers along the way." The Archon leaned across the table, exuding a strong sense of confidence through the Currents. "You must be strong, Summoner."

Darr gave a slow nod in response. The Archon's emotions flowed through him, infusing him with courage he didn't know he had. Racall wasn't forcing his emotions on him so much as intensifying Darr's own inner strength—some hidden reserve he'd long forgotten about. From the moment Darr had first left Tyfor, until the events unfolding before him now, everything came together. His doubts and worries fell away with the promise he would find an answer to them. He'd do as Nidic Waq had asked of him. He would restore the Sephirs to the best of his abilities, and he'd travel Ictar to all of its borders if he had to. Calm settled deep inside him, and nothing else mattered. The journey would drive him now.

Racall rose from the table, his mass casting a shadow across the entire tavern. "I must go now. Your brother and sister are nearby. They are at an inn called the Blue Star a couple blocks north of here. Stay with them and tell them what you wish. I will come for you when I am ready."

Darr turned in his chair, desperate. "Wait, Racall. My family never stays in this part of the city."

"The next part of your journey requires you be with your brother and sister, young Reintol," the Archon soothed. "And they are at the Blue Star. Why, I cannot say, but I have other matters which I must attend to for the time being."

With a polite wave, Racall turned and made his way back through the crowded tavern. Oddly, no one noticed his passing. Outside, he disappeared into the darkened streets beyond. Darr had spent the better part of a week with the Archon. Now, he felt powerless in his absence.

After finishing his meal, Darr paid with a few of his meager coins, and made his way back to the streets. The night air was cool and heavy with the steady drizzle. Darr cared little about the weather–it made him happy to be out of the stifling confines of the tavern. Cinching up his pack, he walked north along the city streets. Buildings and homes sat ragged, in various stages of disrepair. What few people wandered the streets had dangerous casts to their faces. He couldn't imagine what would bring Erec and Jinn to this part of the city.

The Summoner located the Blue Star admist its neighbors. All its windows were intact, and the siding had been painted recently. The sign hanging from the eaves, and marked with a bright blue star, gave it away for what it was. The windows stood dark, but when Darr tested the front door, he found it unlocked. Chairs and tables lay in disarray all across the room, some covered, others coated in thick layers of dust. Darr made his way to the front desk where a tallow candle, no better than a flickering stub, shed some meager light across the room.

Darr called out into the darkness behind the counter. When no one appeared, he tried the hallways on either side of the desk, but still, no one came. Finally, he searched around the desk, hoping to find some clue about his siblings' whereabouts. A ledger lay open on one side of the counter. Erec Reintol had signed his name beside room number three. Why such a rundown inn would keep a ledger was odd, though keeping records of who came and went in the city might be required by the government.

Darr took the candle and walked down the hallway to his left. A door stood in plain view with a 'three' carved into its surface. He set the candle on the floor and raised his hand to knock when a slight whisper from the Currents gave him pause. He sensed unease among the spirits. Might they be trying to warn me about something? Darr gave a quick look behind him. The Blue Star would be the last place in the city Erec and Jinn would ever come. The place had an eerie feel to it. Where were all its residents and its innkeeper?

Darr lowered his arm, prepared to return to the street and find Racall, but he didn't have a chance. The door before him burst open, and he had no time to defend himself from the strong arms reaching out for him. He cried out for help, but his captor thrust him to the floor, smacking his head against the wooden boards.

Darr saw the faint flicker of the candle before everything went black.

Chapter Nine

"Symdus met with Caeranol and announced his intentions to begin new experiments using the Light. Caeranol argued the Light was necessary for all life to continue, and using it as a way to escape death was unnatural. The secrets of immortality had eluded Symdus for over ten years, and further tampering promised to upset both the Currents and the physical world. Forbidden to continue his experiments, Symdus left the Elder Council enraged and with no intention of stopping his work. Along with several of his loyal assistants, he fled to a secret location where he carried out his experiments. Caeranol searched for the rogue elder, but Symdus's powers of deception masked him from the Currents and the physical realm."

~From A Current History of Ictar, as told by Nidic Waq

A garden swept out before Darr, its perimeter surrounded by a wall of thorns. At the center of the mass, a great tower rose among the flowering shrubbery–a tower so large it was a castle. Elders gathered on paths broke the profusion of colors. They watched a spectacle unfolding before the doors of the keep. They watched one of their own argue in anger with the highest among them. Darr sensed the futility of the argument. Only one of them could win and the gathered elders knew who the victor would be.

The argument unfolded from a distance–from a place where Darr hid, but he could see and hear everything. The voice of a black-haired man rang with intensity. His counterpart, a tall, regal-looking man, had a voice soft with reason. Both men were unfamiliar, but like the elders around him, Darr knew who the victor would be.

Defeated, the man in black wheeled away from his superior and cut along the path like a knife cutting through air–sleek and with the possibility someone would get hurt.

The elders and their superior watched him go, disappointed at the mistake he'd made.

The spirits echoed disapproval.

"Darr."

The flame of a candle danced before his eyes, and he opened them, prompted by the voice of his sister, Jinn. He knew her voice immediately. Dark brown curls fell all about her round face as she leaned over him, her physical presence almost nonexistent so light was her build. Her large, green eyes reflected both tenderness and regret, shining through to her soul. In that moment, Darr knew he would be all right.

The Summoner sat up from the bed he was laying on. Erec stood over him, disappointment radiating from every one of his strong features. In his face, he looked almost identical to Darr, though physically heavier, taller, and tougher. He grew his dark hair long, tying it behind his neck. His eyes, which in Darr reflected calm, in Erec almost always showed anger.

"What're you doing here, little brother?" Erec asked without a shred of amusement.

The throbbing heat of a bruise along the side of his face burned, and he wanted to return the favor to his brother. Any kind of physical response on his part would never work with Erec. Sometimes, he couldn't help thinking about it though.

"I came here to find you two," Darr said.

"Leave him alone, Erec," Jinn growled, a dangerous look on her face. "I think you've done enough already."

His brother jerked his hands up in exasperation. "I'm sorry, Darr. Do you feel any better?" Erec's apology didn't look remorseful. "What would you have me do? You were sneaking around outside our room. I acted on instinct."

Darr nodded, his smile faint. "All right. I forgive you. I guess I should've written a letter first."

The anger in Erec's face drained away and a smirk formed at the corners of his mouth. Erec tended to view intelligence as a weakness, preferring physical strength to any other attribute. Over the years, Darr found most confrontations with his brother were diffused by pointing out something clever. Erec held his gaze for a moment longer, then slunk over to a dusty armchair and dropped down on its cushions. The Summoner watched him out of the corner of his eye while Jinn soothed his wound with a damp cloth.

While large and open, the room's interior had few furnishings, with a single bed, the armchair Erec sat in, and a table layered with ages of dust. A single window had been cut into one wall, but it had been boarded up. Darr still wasn't sure what to say to Jinn and Erec.

Jinn rose from the bed, satisfied with her work. She walked to her pack, her movements graceful in the faint candlelight. From what fragmented memories he had of his mother, she could have been her ghost. When Jinn looked back up, fear filled her eyes. She must suspect something had happened back in Tyfor.

Guilt-ridden, Darr took a deep breath and sat up and told them.

* * * *

"And this all led to the attack..."

"What attack?" Erec interrupted, leaning forward in his chair.

Darr didn't think he could tell them what really transpired. *They won't believe me.* His gaze drifted from Erec's fierce countenance to Jinn's understanding gaze, and he knew he had to try.

"An elemental attacked the town. A firehound."

Unlike what he told Arn, Darr told Erec and Jinn exactly what happened during the attack. Darr finished by telling them their father now recovered at the house while Arn took care of the store. He left out any mention of Nidic Waq's name and everything he'd learned concerning the Soul

Seekers and the Devoid.

Jinn stood motionless before the bed, staring wide-eyed at him. Erec stared off into space, crouching forward in the armchair like he'd collapsed in on himself.

Darr broke the silence. "I'm sorry I had to leave Father. I wish it could've been otherwise."

Jinn folded her arms across her chest. "I can't believe you would leave him just to come here and tell us," she said softly. "We would've been okay. You should've stayed there and taken care of him."

The Summoner remained motionless and silent. In truth, he'd come to Stern for a much greater reason than to tell his siblings of their father's accident.

Erec snapped up from the armchair and walked to the boarded window. He stared through the gaps between the boards into the night beyond and said, "I want you to take Jinn and return to Tyfor tonight. I'll finish up our business here in the next couple days. You two can start back tonight."

Jinn began arguing, protesting the foolishness of night travel. Erec retorted in force, demanding respect. He'd already made the decision. The two shouted with such fervor that they didn't see Darr rise from the bed until he stepped between them.

"Stop it, both of you," he said in a tone that quieted his siblings in one swift stroke. "I'm not going to Tyfor tonight. I didn't come to Stern to tell you two about the accident. I have more to tell you."

While calm on the outside, Darr's words carried all the buried emotions he kept within himself. He imagined himself like Nidic Waq or Racall—speaking relaxed, yet propelling intense emotions to his listeners, forcing them to feel his passion. The Summoner had no idea how he managed to do this, but it worked. Erec and Jinn stood transfixed before him.

Darr motioned to the bed and waited for them to sit. "I told you about the firehound, and about the stranger who rescued me and our father. It doesn't matter if you believe any of it, but it happened. There is magic loose again, and it's because of the Soul Seekers."

Erec started to protest, raising his hands, but the Summoner silenced him.

"Wait, Erec, let me finish. The man who rescued me was Nidic Waq. Yes, the prophet. He gave me a task to complete, and I chose to accept it. He gave me this task because there is more to Spirit Summoning than any of us knew. He showed me—that's how he rescued me. Magic," he said and let it sink in. "I wouldn't have believed it a week ago. Even now, I still have trouble, but I think it can be done. Spirit Summoners can wield magic, and Nidic Waq chose me to help him right the balance the Seekers have upset."

Darr realized he'd been too eager in his narration. Jinn looked ready to break down in tears, and Erec sat tall and rigid, a pyre of rage prepared to explode.

"So tell me, Spirit Summoner, what is this *quest* the prophet sent you on?" Erec asked, not bothering to hide any of his disbelief.

Darr swallowed hard. He didn't want to tell them about the Devoid. Not yet. "The Sephirs...they're being drained of the Light that gives them their magic. My charge is to restore them to their proper balance."

Erec laughed, long and slow and without warmth. The Summoner watched in helplessness. His sister rose from the bed, staring across the room and hugging her shoulders protectively. Darr tried to go to her, but his brother jumped in front of him. His fit of laughter ended.

"This is all nonsense, little brother," Erec said, his eyes burning. "Nidic Waq is a madman. Any magic you might have seen him do was probably sleight of hand. He's an outcast and a fraud."

"I believe him," Darr answered, remaining calm despite Erec's agitation. "I've seen a lot of things in the past week, things you can't begin to imagine. Something is tearing apart this land, and Nidic Waq seems to know how to go about fixing it. It might be Soul Seekers, or it might be something else, but whatever it is, I'm doing what I have to in order to help."

"What? By using power forbidden by the Kings of Ictar?" Erec asked, spitting out the words like they were poison. "You'll be locked up in chains and thrown away, or worse, executed. I won't stand by and let some pretender haul you off and make you abandon your family."

Darr glared at his brother. "It's no different than what you're doing by going off to join the army."

Erec's face erupted into a contortion of disgust at the remark, but Darr held his ground. His brother took steps toward him, fists clenched. Jinn came up behind Erec, holding him back by the arm.

"I think we should hear him out, Erec," she said in a voice so flat it sent shivers down Darr's spine. "We should hear everything."

Erec spun about to rebuke his sister, but his sister's determination quieted him. Together, the two siblings turned to face their brother. Darr stood before them, preparing himself for what he knew he must do.

With precise and deliberate words, he told them about Racall.

* * * *

Darr left nothing out of his story. Both his siblings listened as he tried explaining his experiences in the Currents, limited as they were. He didn't know if Erec and Jinn believed him, but they didn't interrupt. Growing up in Tyfor had sheltered all the Reintol siblings from certain aspects of the land, and the Four Archons was one such subject.

"So they're like caretakers," Jinn said.

The Summoner bobbed his head excitedly. "I think so—

something like that. Racall said the Archons are 'the voice of balance' within the Sephirs. The Sephirs' magic is in their hands and they use it to direct nature."

When Darr finished telling them what he knew about Racall, Erec nodded his head and said they would talk about it more in the morning. He walked to the armchair and settled among its dust motes. He was asleep in moments. Jinn said nothing. She walked to the other side of the bed and curled up on her side, leaving the other side open for Darr. Feeling the weight of fatigue pushing down on him, the Summoner laid down beside her. He stared up at the ceiling for a time wondering if he should say something else. In the end, he decided there wasn't much more to say.

While he hardly ever agreed with Erec, Darr shared a different bond with his sister. If Erec didn't believe him about Nidic Waq and Racall, he'd feel no great loss. Jinn, on the other hand, had always been connected to him with a special kind of understanding. She wasn't a Summoner and had no innate knowledge of the Currents and the spirits, yet she'd always been receptive to Darr's burden when they were growing up. She could sense when he could hear the spirits and she'd ask questions about what it felt like. She could never truly understand the abilities of a Spirit Summoner, but she understood better than most.

When he looked over at her still form in the darkness, he wanted to reach out and comfort her, to reassure her about his reasons for coming to Stern. Darr lay silent and closed his eyes against his distress.

Beside him, Jinn whispered, "I believe you, Darr, whatever you decide to do."

A smile parted his lips. Jinn's support was sometimes all he needed.

Chapter Ten

"At first, Symdus took the Light from the Four Elements as they spread through the land. Within weeks, Symdus collected enough Light to add months to his lifespan. Unsatisfied with the slow process of collection, Symdus began siphoning the Light from plants, then from small living animals. His hunger grew exponentially as his lifespan increased. Those assistants, that remained with Symdus, became terrified of what he was doing, but they also feared his experiments might turn on them, so they kept their heads down."

~From A Current History of Ictar, as told by Nidic Waq

Two days passed and Darr heard nothing from Racall, neither inside nor outside the Currents. The Archon's silence disturbed Darr, but nothing could be done about it. He turned his mind to other things. His siblings had come to the city in the first place to see why their father's ale shipment was several weeks late.

"After arriving in the city," Erec said, "I expected the delay to be caused by the theft of the Water Sephir."

Darr shook his head. "I'm guessing that wasn't the cause."

Erec spat on the ground and said nothing.

"Father's supplier ran out on the business, leaving his clerk behind to clean up," Jinn said in the lapse of Erec's silence. "On our first day here, we spoke with the clerk and believed everything was going to get fixed. We gave him a small amount of our money up front to ensure a quick delivery."

Erec laughed, cold and quick. "That turned out to be a mistake," he muttered. "The clerk ran off with our money, leaving us with next to nothing here in the middle of Stern."

"How did you find this inn?" Darr asked. "Surely there was someplace better."

"We tried, but the entire city is in a state of crisis," Jinn answered. "No one wanted to barter with us. Everyone wanted coin."

From the comfort of the armchair, Erec grinned and said, "In one of the taverns, I heard about this place. The owner is a bit of a drunk, and so long as he gets a barrel of ale from our shipment, he'll be happy."

The three spent the next couple days scouring Stern for a new supplier of ale, one who would deliver across the Valimere and who had a reliable reputation. It proved to be a daunting task. With the Lourcient River in its current state, the businesses it supported were at something of a standstill. From one end of the city to the other, the population struggled with their daily activities. If something didn't happen soon to restore the river, Stern would be deserted.

The endless search for a new supplier, coupled with the unceasing arguments with Erec over Darr's quest to secure the Sephirs, made the days go by agonizingly slow. As they walked the damp streets, the two brothers debated back and forth over their beliefs concerning everything from the spirits and Summoners to family values. Jinn, for the most part, stayed neutral through the discussions, interjecting vague comments only when necessary.

In the end, they settled nothing except they'd found a new supplier. They were fortunate to find a reputable merchant who would make the delivery across the Valimere with little coin up front. He even agreed to pay off the innkeeper of the Blue Star with the promised barrel. Darr kept his ears on the Currents during the transaction. He didn't believe the man to be a dishonest sort.

They ate their supper in a nearly deserted tavern several blocks away from their inn. It rained hard outside. Perhaps everyone had gone out to collect rainwater. He didn't talk much with his siblings while they ate. With their business finished, Erec intended on taking Jinn home at first light. His brother no longer pushed for him to return home, but

Darr knew Erec seethed on the inside, waiting for the opportunity where he could knock him senseless and carry him all the way back to Tyfor.

Darr had more trouble reading Jinn's feelings on the matter. They'd spoken earlier in the morning, and Darr had found Jinn didn't care so much about magic or Nidic Waq. Her concern centered on Darr's beliefs about his situation. His newfound abilities were more complicated than he'd perceived, and while Darr agreed with her, there didn't appear to be another method. As their last few hours together wasted away, Jinn looked sad.

With their meal finished, they returned to the Blue Star. Darr sat in the dusty, old armchair while his brother and sister packed their things. His visit hadn't been the most pleasurable, but he loved Erec and Jinn fiercely. He knew they both looked out for him. With them gone, he'd be alone in Stern until Racall returned.

Every night since the Archon's departure, Darr had gone into the Currents and searched for him. He tried calling out to the spirit creature, but his voice didn't carry in the Currents like it did in the physical world. One other option remained, but the thought of it terrified him.

Darr chewed at his lower lip and stared across the room at Erec and Jinn. The bright flame of a candle danced on the table beside the bed, sending up shadows across the walls. Jinn glanced over at him with a questioning look.

"What're you thinking, Darr?" she asked.

Darr relaxed and gave a faint smile. "I have to try something, and I want you two to watch over me for a moment. Just watch. I'll only be gone for a second."

"Gone. Where are you going?" Erec asked with skepticism thick in his voice.

The Summoner didn't answer. He closed his eyes and breathed into his stomach, his mind and body calmed. Carefully, he opened his ears to the voices of the spirits, and...

...he entered the Currents in a smooth, soundless rush.

The wisteria light of the spirit realm spread out before him, laced with the blues and yellows, reds and greens of the Four Elements. The beauty of the place radiated so much awe it made him want to cry. His brother and sister were there, mirrored by the Light giving them life. Darr wanted to reach out and touch them, to feel what they were feeling, but he resisted the temptation.

He quieted his mind and expanded his senses further, yet another lesson he'd learned from Racall. In doing so, the forms of Erec and Jinn receded into the wisteria light, leaving him alone with the fuzzballs of illumination that were the spirits. They danced and swirled all about him, their voices faint and indistinct. Darr prepared to reach out to them. How should he address them?

—Welcome, Darr Reintol—

—Welcome, Summoner of the Archons—

—Welcome, Walker of the Currents—

The voices startled him. Racall had taught him how to shut out their voices until he was ready to hear them. Somehow, his preparations had failed.

"Hello," *Darr greeted, though he remained wary.*

The spirits swirled around him, their listless forms coalescing all about his insubstantial body.

—Do not fear us Summoner—

—Your fear is not necessary—

—What do you require of us—

—What do you desire—

A faint tugging sensation pulled at Darr's mind, a warning perhaps. Emotions welled up inside him, and he fought to push them down. He couldn't panic now.

"I'm looking for the Archon of Earth. Where can I find him?" *Darr asked.*

—Him—

"Yes, where can I find the Archon of Earth?"

—Everywhere—

—In everything—

The *spirits began to spin madly about him. Fragmented images tumbled into Darr's mind. Mountains and trees and shooting blades of grass. Boulders rose out of rich soil and flowers and other plants sprouted from choking overgrowth. He saw rotting tree trunks fresh with green moss, and rockslides plunging down mountains, flattening grasses and trees only to renew them.*

Darr gasped in shock. In all of these images, he saw Racall. The spirits were showing him the ways in which Racall spread the magic of his Sephir out across Ictar, his physical presence by the loosest definition. The Summoner struggled against the images flooding into his head, trying to find an end to the web the spirits wove into his own Light. The images didn't stop, they increased in intensity and frequency. Darr's emotions rose to the surface.

"Please, stop," he cried in panic. "This isn't what I meant."

The spirits didn't hear him. The white pinpricks of light came swarming out of the ether. They touched him, weaving their minuscule bodies in and out of his own Light, a repulsive sensation. They were feeding off his emotions, and in turn, he began to feed off theirs. The memories and emotions of the spirits poured through his mind and soul, and in doing so, he had difficulty remembering anything about himself.

The calming hue of the Currents, and the spinning white lights of the spirits, were all he was aware of. He could barely remember why he'd come here. Did he have a family? Did he have a purpose? What was his name?

His questions no longer mattered. He gave in to the memories and emotions of the spirits driving him onward. He reveled in their wisdom and in the countless lives they shared. He danced with them, swirling about the ether as they did. The Summoner shared all his feelings of exhilaration and joy and...

...horror.

He froze. Something clicked in his mind, a tugging sensation. The spirits closed in tight, choking off his suspicions. Something was wrong, but he'd fallen too far into the Currents to figure it out. He couldn't even remember his own name. Yet, another name had been preserved in the depths of his mind, a name he knew would free him. But he mustn't speak it. He must will it.

—Racall—

A jolt of certainty coursed through him as he uttered the name, an utterance he made with only his Light. The spirits crowded over him in mad defiance, but their efforts were in vain. Wisteria light gave way to green and a massive shape exploded between the Summoner and the spirits. The ethereal forms scattered in every direction across the Currents. Darr's memories cascaded down into his head, returning him to himself. First and foremost, he heard Racall's lesson that the spirits were not to be trifled with for they would make him one of them.

Racall's broad shape materialized out of the green light, reflecting a number of emotions Darr didn't know the Archon possessed, worry and relief.

"I hope you have learned a valuable lesson, young Reintol," he said in the familiar harmonized voice.

Darr was still shaken from his experience. "I should've taken greater care when I approached the spirits. How did I reach you? My voice was so strange."

A trace of satisfaction radiated out of the Archon. "You are learning, Summoner. You are learning how to navigate the Currents as you are meant to."

Racall motioned towards a light spot in the spirit realm. The forms of Erec and Jinn appeared before them, their Lights unchanged since Darr began his journey into the Currents.

"It is time to return, young Reintol. You have found what you came here for."

The Summoner looked back at his brother and sister, and he drew his mind out of the Currents...

...he heard the sound of a blade drawn from its sheath.

Darr's eyes flickered open. Erec stood protectively before Jinn with his sword held before him. The Summoner knew he'd only been in the Currents for what seemed a moment, but Erec's instincts were faster. In the span of a few seconds, Racall had materialized in the center of the room, robed and hooded.

"Darr, get up!" Erec yelled.

The Summoner leapt to his feet and stretched his arm out to his brother. "Put your sword down. This is a friend. This is Racall."

The Archon reached up and pulled back his hood. Jinn and Erec gasped, likely from the sight of the giant's strange green eyes. Darr couldn't help but smile in recognition of their shock. It didn't seem that long ago he'd reacted the same way.

Any fears Erec might've possessed vanished. He stepped towards the Archon in challenge. "You say this creature is a friend, Darr, but he appeared out of thin air," Erec stated with his sword held high.

Racall's leaden gaze weighed down on Erec. "My appearance here has little to do with whether I am a friend or not. Appearances can be deceiving, so take care to judge accordingly." The Archon looked past Erec. "Hello, little Jinn," he said warmly. Jinn smiled and rose from where she crouched beside Erec.

The Archon started to walk towards Darr, but Erec took another step forward, coming between them. "You still haven't answered my question. How did you appear here out of nothing? Nobody uses tricks like that unless they're using magic."

"I am sorry, young Erec. I did not realize you had asked a question earlier," Racall said, his tone smooth and calm. Darr knew his brother must be burning up inside. "And I did not use magic to get here, nor did I appear out of thin air. Perhaps your brother has not told you yet, but I came here from the realm of the spirits. I came because your brother summoned me."

Darr stared wide-eyed. Racall made the last few steps to the bed and seated himself. How had he managed to summon Racall when he hadn't been trying?

"Racall, do you mean that voice I used...?"

The Archon raised his hand, silencing him. "Now is not the time for questions about your training. All I have given you is enough to set you on your way. The rest will come so long as you remember the lessons I have taught. Your timing in finding me could not have been better, for tonight I have discovered the location of the Sephir of Water."

"Is that where you were?" Darr asked, stepping around Erec in the process.

Racall nodded. "There are great shadows masking the Currents. I could not look for the Sephir there, but nonetheless, I located it. It is here in Stern, but deep within..."

"Wait, you can't be taking this seriously!" Erec sputtered. He stood within a few feet of Racall, his gestures threatening even with his sword lowered. "This has gone on too long, Darr. I don't care if magic is real or not. I don't care if there are spirits or Archons or whatever. You're coming home. Now. Tonight. We're leaving this city, this creature, and all this madness behind."

Darr started to object, but Racall turned toward his brother, calm in the face of Erec's rage. "Your anger is unwarranted, young Erec. It will take you down a path to your destruction should you follow it too far. It will push away everyone and everything you hold dear, leaving you stranded and incapable of ever returning."

A ripple in the Currents washed over Darr, a peaceful sense of reservation Racall brought out in Erec. His brother relaxed his shoulders and nodded his head, a meek child before an adult. Racall looked over his shoulder at Jinn standing motionless on the other side of the bed.

"Do you see, little Jinn over there? She is so composed and perceptive. She reflects the discipline you require, and you would do well to learn something from her. It is restraint, not anger, you require if you would be a Cortazian warrior."

The Archon returned his gaze to Darr. "Now, young Reintol, the Sephir of Water can be found several miles within the mountains backing the city. Not up their slopes, but inside their core."

Darr shook his head. "I thought you said the Sephir was still in Stern."

"It is, in a manner of speaking. In the waterway passage running beneath Dacon Fortress, the Sephir waits at the very source of the Lourcient River." Racall rose from the bed. "We must hurry though. I have arranged for the gates and dams of the passage to remain open, but only for tonight. We must go now."

Without the slightest hesitation, Jinn walked to Racall, looked up at his massive frame, and said, "I'm going too."

"No, you're not," Darr said, giving her no flexibility.

"Yes, I am." Her large green eyes revealed her determination in the matter. "I must see this for myself if you want my support."

"I don't care about your support, Jinn. I want you to be safe."

His sister shook her head. "If what you say is true, I won't be safe for a long time, if ever. I won't be able to accept what you're doing until I see it for myself."

"Me either." Erec strode forward, a stern look on his face that made Darr cringe. "Besides, if I let you go off alone, I'm going to feel guilty when you get hurt."

An awkward silence fell between them. Darr, now completely aghast, hoped his siblings would realize the danger they were putting themselves in. The Summoner cast his desperation to Racall with the wish he would put an end to this madness.

The Archon disposition was as cheerful as ever. "I suppose it is settled, except for the young Summoner there. He will change his mind. We must leave immediately though—four bodies travel slower than two."

Racall turned and opened the door, ushering Erec out first. Jinn rushed to her pack to retrieve her long knife before following. Darr remained behind, his eyes frozen with helplessness on Racall. The Archon nodded his head in understanding from the doorway before he waved his hand to motion the way out.

Darr reluctantly followed.

Chapter Eleven

"As his hunger increased, Symdus began draining the Light from the lesser races of Man, Elf, Dwarf, and Ogre. When he couldn't find enough Light to satisfy his needs, he began feeding on his own kind, and when he couldn't find enough by himself, he created Soul Seekers, elementals created from the Light itself. The Soul Seekers ravaged the landscape, searching out life of any kind to steal Light for Symdus to add to his own. This final act was Symdus's undoing."

~From A Current History of Ictar, as told by Nidic Waq

Rain fell in sheets from the dark skies over Stern. Miniature streams ran down the hill from Dacon Fortress into the canals crisscrossing the streets. A calm fell over the city, save for the constant spattering of rain, and the trickling of running water. For the first time in weeks, Stern was at peace.

It wouldn't last, not if Darr failed to find the missing Sephir. Feeling the bitterness of his thought, Darr shook it away.

The Summoner followed behind Racall's substantial form with Jinn at his side. They walked up Stern's cobblestone thoroughfare while Erec trailed behind, his cautious apprehension obvious to Darr. The four kept an even pace, growing ever closer to Dacon Fortress, the one time home to the Cortazian Kings. In the darkness of night, the stronghold and all its formidable walls and battlements were visible. Torches burned from the heights, their distant lights marking where soldiers kept watch. The structure took on the appearance of a massive stone cube, the city's vigilant sentinel. Somewhere at its peak, the Glass Tower rose, the altar room of the absent Sephir of Water, but in the cloudy blackness of night the tower's framework was invisible.

"Darr, what do you have to do when you find the Sephir?" Jinn whispered, leaning close.

The Summoner stared and shook his head. "I'm not really sure."

His sister gave him a startled look. "Have you asked Racall yet?".

"Well, kind of, but he was more intent on teaching me about summoning. So I guess it has something to do with that."

Jinn didn't look convinced. "It doesn't seem like a time to be guessing."

They continued in silence, leaving Darr to contemplate his situation. Nidic Waq had sent him, not Racall, to secure the Sephirs. Perhaps Racall and Nidic Waq believed he'd find whatever magic he possessed when endangered, but that didn't seem right. Something about Racall's presence went beyond being an instructor and guide. It had to do with Darr learning to summon and with whatever awaited them at the source of the Lourcient.

The Archon glanced back over his shoulder, catching Darr's eye with the movement. He smiled reassuringly before turning his attention back to the road.

The four approached the high wall fronting Dacon Fortress and turned down a side street leading past one of the many surrounding vineyards. It took several minutes to cross the sprawling field, but at its far boundary, they came to a channel cut much deeper and wider than the others.

Along here, the Lourcient River flowed from deep within the mountains and through the city to the Hondor Falls. An iron grate had been removed where the artery connected to Dacon Fortress, allowing entrance into the darkened passage beyond. Racall led them to the channel's edge and found a spot where metal brackets were hammered into its side, likely for workmen.

Without hesitation, the Archon climbed down and splashed ankle-deep into the stagnant water. Jinn shrugged and followed. She landed with a splash. The water came up to her knees.

Up the high wall of the fortress, the gaze of a lone patrolling sentry landed on Darr, his grim face outlined by the hazy light of a torch. The sentry watched him for a moment, turned, and continued his patrol heedless of the intruders below.

"What do you suppose that was all about?" Erec asked.

Darr shook his head. "I'm not sure. I bet Racall knows something."

"You know, you rely on that creature a lot for someone who's supposed to be doing this quest on his own," Erec muttered.

Darr ignored him and climbed down into the channel with his brother behind him, and in moments, the four stood reunited in what remained of the Lourcient River. Racall led them into the monstrous passage beneath Dacon. He took them forward several more paces onto the passage burrowed into inky blackness, until they came to a narrow alcove barely illuminated by the ambient light. The Archon worked with something for a moment. A spark appeared, and the acrid smell of burning pitch filled the air when two torches sprung to life. The alcove where the torches waited turned into a staircase, winding up into the fortress above them.

Racall handed a torch to Jinn and Darr while Erec glowered at him and said, "Pretty convenient–those torches laying down here in the dead of night when normally this place is underwater. If I didn't know any better, I'd say this Archon is leading you into a trap, Darr."

"Erec!" Jinn rasped, her face knotted in anger at the accusation.

Darr tried to quiet Erec, but his brother shoved him aside. "I saw the guards up on the walls. They knew we were coming. So tell me, Archon, what're you up to?"

Erec scowled up at Racall, but the Archon remained immovable and without emotion. "I have told you once before, young Erec, but we are here to take back the Sephir of Water and restore it to the Currents. I have made the Divine of Stern aware of what is going on, and they have made the arrangements that will allow us access to these tunnels." Before Erec had a chance to respond, the Archon turned his back and continued down the tunnel.

Darr looked back at his brother, wanting to question his rationale, but instead he followed after Racall with Jinn at his side. Erec stood rooted in place.

"This is nonsense," he yelled. "Sephirs and magic and the Divine—the Divine of all people should know there's no magic anymore. They'd never sanction this. I'm telling you, Darr, he's leading you into a trap."

The Summoner stopped walking. Surrounded by the halo of light from his torch, he turned towards Erec's shadowy form and said, "No, Erec. He's not leading me into a trap. I'd know it if he was. Now, you can follow us, so we can prove you wrong, or you can go back. Either way, I don't care."

With a curt nod, Darr turned and continued down the passage. A moment later, Erec's footfalls splashed through the water to catch up.

The waterway of the Lourcient was a masterpiece of Dwarf engineering, built during a short alliance with the Cortazians during the Aeon Wars. The retractable locks and dams built into recesses within the rock amazed Darr. The mechanisms were hundreds of years old, but still in use today, all controlled from within the safety of Dacon. An enemy could never gain control of the Lourcient River unless they gained control of the fortress, and no one ever had. Though someone had managed to steal the Water Sephir.

The little company navigated their way through the locks, all of which had been opened for their passing. In the near dark and slick with moisture, the dams were their most formidable obstacle, but Racall knew of hidden footholds that allowed climbing. After nearly an hour of travel, the passage lost its unnatural, manmade appearance. The walls were no longer smooth from the hands of bricklayers, but smoothed from the power of the river itself. Menacing, jagged stone overhangs drooped from the ceiling signaling their arrival inside the mountains.

"Racall, what do we have to do to get the Sephir back?" Darr asked. As he awaited an answer, his hand fidgeted at his sides.

The Archon sloshed through the water, but his voice echoed clearly against the passage walls. "I was wondering when you were going to ask. I warned you not to let your fear rule you."

Darr remained patient, letting the spirit creature slow his march long enough to pace himself alongside the Summoner and his sister. Erec still trailed several feet behind, brooding in the shadows.

"As we traveled through the Valimere, I told you about the Four Archons' relationship with the Sephirs," Racall said.

Darr thought it over. "Yes. You said the Archons were the voices of balance within the Sephirs. Nothing is more important to them than holding back Chaos."

Behind them, Erec let out a long sigh. Racall ignored him. "That is correct. But sometimes, the Archons are forced to destroy in order to maintain. A windstorm must sometimes destroy a thriving forest, or an earthquake will sometimes swallow a valuable water source. This is why the Four Elements all have a counterbalance found in another element, to ensure one element cannot grow stronger than the rest."

"What does that have to do with the theft of the Sephir?" Darr asked, a twinge of annoyance in his voice.

The spirit creature smiled and walked ahead. "Every force of life and magic wears a second face, and the Archons are not exempt from this rule. We carry dark urgings within ourselves that allows us to destroy and corrupt when it is necessary. For the most part, our destructive sides are kept controlled and repressed, though sometimes they break free.

Sometimes they are summoned." Racall's tone grew deeper and ominous. "We call them Ovids."

Darr grew quiet. The spirits had already begun to whisper warnings of the deadly creature into his mind. The Ovid they would face was born from the Water Sephir. That's why Racall was with him. Earth was the natural counterbalance to the element of Water.

"Summoned?" Erec asked, his tone skeptical. "Who would summon such a creature? The Soul Seekers?"

Darr remained silent. He still didn't want to tell his siblings about the Devoid. Not only did it stretch his already unbelievable stories further, but he wasn't quite sure he believed it himself. The Devoid was too much of a myth to accept as real.

"Whether it was the Seekers or someone else, is that what waits at the end of the tunnel, Racall? An Ovid?" Jinn asked.

"Yes. The Ovids steal the Light from the Sephirs, its magic included. All of the Sephirs are under attack, but the Sephir of Water's theft demonstrates just how bold the Ovids have become."

"Incredible!" Erec blurted out in a fit. "I can't believe you're buying into all of this too, Jinn. You're gonna be sorry when none of this turns out to be true, and I have to save both your tails."

Jinn stopped and turned, facing Erec in defiance. She marched up to him, holding her torch before her. "You had your chance to turn around and go the other way, but you're still here. I don't know what you think you're planning to prove by going any further, but it isn't going to be what you expect. I don't think it will be what any of us expects. So for the last time, be quiet."

Erec looked like he might explode in anger, but somehow he managed to restrain himself. He stood before Jinn's small, stubborn frame, nodding in obvious defeat, and motioned the way forward. Together, they fell into line behind Darr and Racall.

Darr smiled at the heated confrontation between his brother and little sister. For as far back as memory served him, Erec always believed he knew the best course of action in any given situation, and Jinn always put him in his place. Erec listened to her most of the time. Darr figured it had something to do with Jinn's role as the youngest child or because she was the only female in the family.

Darr didn't often get away with standing up to Erec.

They trudged on and the torches grew short, threatening to leave them in darkness. How they would get back without their light remained a puzzle Darr didn't want to decipher. The waterway passage continued to wind onward, a never-ending tunnel into the center of the mountains.

A rumbling from the spirits interrupted their trek. He couldn't make out their words, but their emotions were clear–repulsion and aggravation.

"Racall," Darr whispered. "What's going on in the Currents? The spirits are so angry..."

The Archon answered but Darr couldn't see his face anymore. "Ahead of us, the unbalance between the elements is great. The Ovid of Water is near."

The torches died out soon after Racall's grim proclamation, but the four travelers weren't left in complete darkness. From around a slight bend in the passage, blue light bathed the stone in its soft glow.

Racall turned to Darr and his siblings, whispering quickly, "We will be expected. Prepare yourselves for anything."

Darr reached for his long knife, not knowing what else to do. He found Erec beside him, eyes hard. Jinn stood at his other shoulder, her fear buried deep inside her, but it echoed out into the spirit realm. The Summoner gave them an encouraging smile before looking back for Racall's reassuring presence.

Chapter Twelve

"The massive amounts of the Light Symdus consumed corrupted his own Light, twisting his physical shape into something unimaginable. Seeing their master stray so far from their original purpose, Symdus's remaining assistants revealed his location to the Elder Council. Foreseeing the destruction of their world, Caeranol confronted Symdus with the intention of disabling him."

~From A Current History of Ictar, as told by Nidic Waq

Darr stared into the dark, empty space previously occupied by Racall. Although, it wasn't quite empty. Something blended into the rock of the cavern and looked to be a part of it while retaining an impression of separateness.

"Racall?" Darr called out.

–I am here, young Reintol–I have taken this form so we can fight against the Ovid–

The Archon used the Currents to communicate. It didn't appear Racall had a mouth to speak with. He looked like a rock-hewn statue of a man with tremendous arms and legs, and a thick torso. This new form would've eclipsed his old shape. Strangely, his face appeared somewhat similar to Racall's despite its lack of features.

"Darr?" Erec called out behind him, and the Summoner turned back. Erec held Jinn behind him, her protector first. "What is that thing?"

Darr shook his head, and his gaze fell on Jinn. "It's Racall. I think he transformed himself so he can fight against the Ovid."

"Darr..." Jinn began, but her voice lifted into a yelp.

Racall moved, the rock of his body turning and twisting. Erec looked ready to scoop up Jinn and retreat back into the passage.

"It's all right," Darr soothed, stepping in front of him. Erec's gaze remained fixed on Racall, as if daring him to make an aggressive movement. "His speech is limited to the Currents in this form, and only I can hear him. Erec, I promise you that this is Racall. He won't harm us."

His brother watched him, judged him. Erec's priority had always been protection when it came to his siblings. The concept of Racall had to be difficult for him. This new world of magic and spirits forced him to put less trust in his instincts, and more into Darr's.

Finally, Erec relaxed, and Darr gave him a faint smile. He turned back to Racall. "What do we do when we get to the Ovid?" Darr asked.

Racall looked down at him but said nothing.

Erec stepped forward and grabbed Darr's shoulder. "What did it say?" he demanded. Erec's forcefulness was growing thin.

"We'll just have to find out when we get there, Erec," Darr said and shook Erec's grip off his shoulder.

With his arms folded in front of him, Erec leaned in and said, "I don't like all this game playing. We shouldn't go any further until we know what to expect."

When Darr looked up again, he did so with certainty. "That's the thing, Erec, I don't think anything is going to prepare us for what will happen next."

Behind them, Racall shifted in a soundless movement that belied his body of stone.

—*Time to go, young Reintol*—

Exuding an air of dominance over the entire passage, Racall proceeded around the bend in the tunnel moving towards the source of the blue light.

Darr steadied his gaze on Erec. "We have to go now," he said.

This time when Darr turned, he didn't look back. He followed Racall into the pale light of the passage. Jinn and

Erec trailed behind them. Whatever awaited them would likely change all their beliefs about the world, but Erec would be changed the most.

As they rounded the final turn in the passage, the temperature dropped by several degrees. Darr shuddered in response. Before them, a large rounded cavern spread out, its sides worn smooth, but stalactites hung menacingly from the ceiling. Residual water from the Lourcient River lay motionless on the floor, and ice ran thick along the far end of the cavern, rising high up into a frozen waterfall.

Across from them, fixed into the ice, the source of the blue light blazed, a shining cobalt star that obliterated every shadow in its path.

Darr walked to Racall and said, "The ice. That's why the river has stopped."

The Archon's head bowed. *—Yes—And that—*

A flicker of shadow caught Darr's eye, movement from the base of the frozen waterfall. A dark form crouched before the intense blue light. Whatever manner of creature it was, it turned towards them and rose to its full height, blocking the light with its lanky build.

Darr gave a quick glance behind him. Erec shielded Jinn where they stood in the cavern entrance. When the Ovid approached, Darr recoiled within himself. While shorter than Racall, the monster gave the impression of being bigger with its gangly arms and legs. Thick rows of dark purple hair jutted straight back from its head like saw grass.

"Racall," it rasped. Its face was a grotesque mask of features—with the eyes of a snake, and the flattened snout of a lizard, but altogether the face of a woman. "You brought me a Sssummoner. How nissse."

Darr's legs locked beneath him, overcome by sudden fear. The Ovid intimidated him more than the cindercats that prowled the Valimere. The creature slid effortlessly through the water, ooze dripping off its body as it closed the distance between them.

"Darr!" Erec cried. Erec charged through the water, his sword arm raised, letting go a tremendous cry from deep within his lungs.

The Ovid stopped and raised its arms before Erec got close, clasping its clawed fingers in the air. Darr shielded his face as the creature slammed its arms down like a hammer. In a monstrous roar, the water around it exploded into a geyser that nearly reached the cavern's ceiling, billowing outward with an ear-deafening roar. An impossibly tall wave rose before them.

Darr gasped for air before the wave engulfed him and sent him spinning backwards into the dark.

* * * *

For one endless moment, Darr drifted in icy blackness. The water closed about him, suffocating and blinding him. He groped through the darkness unsure of which way he would find air. The spirits whispered with sudden clarity, and Darr drove himself where they willed him. He surged upward through the rippling surface, gasping for breath. Erec crouched several feet away, drenched and visibly shaken. He held Jinn in his arms while she coughed the water from her lungs.

Darr sloshed through the waist-deep water, struggling to reach his brother and sister. From out of the corner of his eye, he saw Racall. Darr turned and froze, awed by his presence. Unharmed, Racall had withstood the wave unleashed by the Ovid of Water. With his powerful arms braced to attack, the stone giant charged.

The Summoner shook off his hesitation and hurried to Erec's side where Jinn had lapsed into unconsciousness. "Is she okay?"

Erec cradled her and shouted over the roar of the settling water, "She hit that back wall. What is that thing?"

The Summoner stared at his brother incredulously.

"That's the Ovid!" he exclaimed.

Erec stared at the Ovid and Racall, his jaw hung open. Darr shook his head in frustration—his brother still couldn't accept the truth. The Summoner brushed at Jinn's forehead. He wished he could stay with her, but he got up and started after Racall, .

The Archon of Earth stood before the Ovid, towering over it. The Ovid didn't cower. "Your little friendsss injure easssily," it hissed.

—Go back to where you came from— Racall ordered through the ether of the Currents, his emotions forceful and cold.

One of the Ovid's gangly arms whipped out of the water, swiping across Racall's chest. Darr cringed as bits of rock flew away from the blow.

"You go back," it hissed.

Racall fell back a step and the Ovid attacked without restraint. The creature jumped on top of the Archon, raining thunderous punches down on his body with a quickness beyond human means. The Archon fell to his knee, and the Ovid beat him down further while crawling over him like a lizard. Wicked blue light appeared at the Ovid's fingertips, and thick layers of ice began to coat Racall's body. Darr cried out in desperation, unsure of what else to do. The battle was quickly growing out of control, and the Summoner still had no idea what Racall had intended for him to do.

With an explosive clap, Racall's arm shot out from beneath him and connected with the Water Ovid's forehead. The creature sailed through the air, then its scaled body skimmed out along the water's surface before sinking out of sight. With a strained motion, Racall rose to his full height. Patches of silver ice covered his body. The Archon shook off his mantle of ice and glanced where the Ovid had landed. When he looked back at Darr, his gaze suggested defeat.

—I am weaker than I thought—Help me, Summoner— Bring your Light to mine—

"How?" Darr pleaded. "Tell me what I'm supposed to do."

Racall couldn't answer. The Ovid rose out of the water beside the Archon and kicked one of his stone legs out from under him. Crippled, Racall suffered a fresh onslaught as the Ovid hacked away at him with a vicious whipping of its arms. There was no doubt in Darr's mind that Racall was losing this battle. Once he fell, there would be little hope for him and his siblings.

Darr's thoughts raced. Why doesn't Racall use his magic? Why doesn't he use his command over the Element of Earth to crush the Ovid?

The Summoner took a steadying breath...

...and plunged himself into the Currents.

Darr didn't seek the help of the spirits on this venture. Through the wisteria light of the spirit realm, the blue flare from the Sephir of Water blinded him. His mind focused and the light cleared away. The Ovid and Racall fought before him, their battle captured in both worlds. Outside the gates of Stern, when Darr reached out and touched Racall, he'd seen the Currents and the physical world overlap like this.

The Summoner slid to Racall's struggling form. Carefully, he placed the shinning white aura of his hands upon the Archon. His own Light mingled with Racall's, and together they spread out into the physical world.

Disgust raged out of the Ovid in waves. Too late...

Darr cried out and jerked upright, then collapsed to his knees. The lights of the Currents flooded across his eyes, overlapping his sense of the physical world. His consciousness merged with Racall's.

Darr got to his feet, and Racall stood with him, a stone pinnacle of destruction. Together they picked up the Ovid by its sawgrass head and flung it against the nearest wall, smashing it with a dreadful crunch. Darr twisted his head in the Ovid's direction, watching the Current's light dance around its mangled form. He urged Racall towards it.

The Archon complied, charging through the water as if it

were a mere puddle. Blue light spun wildly around the Ovid's arms in an attempt to defend itself, but Racall and Darr were quicker. The Archon clamped his massive fist around the Ovid's throat and heaved it up against the wall. Darr gritted his teeth, and Racall's other fist exploded into the Ovid's chest like a massive stone hammer, then he tossed the creature away.

Darr perceived everything through Racall's omniscient connection to the Currents. The Archon stood motionless, an immutable wall. Erec stared in shock at the spectacle unfolding around him while he cradled his still unconscious sister. Darr turned his gaze to the Ovid as it struggled to its feet, the blue light enshrouding its form growing dim and hazy. Darr urged Racall to finish it.

Green light shimmered all about the Summoner's arms, and Racall raised his hands high. A rumbling shook the passage, followed by a deep sigh issued from the cavern floor. A knot of triumph exploded inside Darr as a monstrous stone spire burst out of the water beneath the creature's crumpled form. The Ovid's cry, filled with hate, echoed across the cavern. It tried to escape, but Darr closed his hands into knotted fists. Racall obeyed his command and sent the spire upward, closing all about the Ovid before sinking back down into the earth. The creature spit and hissed as it drowned in the rock, wicked blue light emanating from the fissures.

With a final cry and a sickening crunch, the Ovid's body was crushed into oblivion. The rock spire sunk under the water, burying itself beneath the tons of rock below the cavern. In the Currents, the blue light encompassing the Ovid scattered into the wisteria landscape.

In a swift, hazy motion, Darr's link with Racall fractured and separated. The Summoner took a deep breath to steady himself. Being in the physical world and the Currents simultaneously had been more taxing than he expected. He felt disjointed from his body, like his mind were a glove trying to fit on a hand far too large. Nausea swept through him and he collapsed to his knees.

Above him, all he saw was Racall's familiar smile.

Chapter Thirteen

"When Caeranol confronted Symdus, he found a mere shadow of the elder he once knew. Worse, the hunger for the Light engulfed Symdus, and the man who once hoped to conquer death became like death itself. Symdus had ceased to be, and the Devoid was born in his place."

~From A Current History of Ictar, as told by Nidic Waq

Darr didn't know how long he drifted through nothingness before a spark of light flashed before his eyes. Water rushed into his mouth, and he struggled to rise from where he'd fallen, spitting and coughing, struggling for air. Darr rose to his feet and looked around. His breath steadied. Not much time had passed, he guessed. No one had moved since he'd collapsed.

Still hazy and shaken, he hurried back to Erec and Jinn. His sister lay unconscious, but Darr worried more about his brother. The color had drained from Erec's face as he held his sister, and it took several tries calling his name before he responded.

"Are you okay?" Darr asked him.

Erec shook his head. "What in chaos happened?" he asked trancelike. "That creature and Racall...and you, Darr...you stood there the whole time, but you were a part of it."

The Summoner smiled, surprised by his brother's state of shock. "We'll talk about it later, okay. Look after Jinn for a minute."

Darr's perceptions became clearer, and he turned to search for Racall. The Archon stood near the frozen waterfall, reverted back to his familiar human form. He approached Racall and noticed the brightness normally shining on the Archon's face was gone despite his broad

113

smile. He looked tired.

"Well done, young Summoner. You have done very well, and I must say you have learned all you can from me. The rest you must do on your own."

"I'm not sure I know what happened."

The Archon laughed softly. "Think on it. You will understand."

The comment frustrated Darr, but Racall wasn't in a position to answer questions. It appeared he had trouble standing. The Archon shuffled on stiff legs to where the Sephir of Water lay encased in ice. Darr walked towards it also, shielding his eyes from its intense blue light.

When they were before the Sephir, Racall reached up and pulled apart the thick ice enclosing it. The Archon removed it, and held it out to Darr. The light was so bright, Darr had trouble deciding the Sephir's size or even what it looked like.

"This waterfall once fed the Lourcient River," Racall said. "Once you return the Sephir to its altar, the waterfall will be restored to its normal state. Take the stairs at the front of the passage–you will be met by one of the Divine, a good man named Herdas."

"A Divine? Isn't a Divine going to want to know how I got the Sephir back? What about the laws forbidding magic?"

"Do not worry, young Reintol," Racall soothed. "This particular Divine knows well his place as a servant of Caeranol. He cares less about rules, than about maintaining balance. He will take good care of you."

Though still wary about receiving help from the Divine, Darr accepted the Sephir and squinted against its glare. Lightweight and irregularly shaped, the relic fit in the cup of his hands. He tucked it against his body to screen his vision and looked back up at Racall.

"You're not coming with me, are you?" he asked.

The Archon didn't smile. "No, Summoner. You must go on alone now. Perhaps, young Erec and little Jinn will accompany you. Having a brother and sister along on this journey would strengthen you like nothing else."

The Summoner glanced back at his brother and smiled. "Yes—maybe. I wish otherwise. You've been a good friend."

Racall nodded. "I will always be your good friend, young Reintol. I am always in the Currents. Let me know if you need anything."

"I will," Darr said.

The Archon's familiar smile flashed one last time. "Goodbye, young Summoner."

Racall's body shimmered, and his flesh turned back into stone. In a grating rush, his body melted into the floor of the cavern, uniting with the earth once more.

Darr stared into the empty space for a moment before turning his attention to Jinn. The Summoner tucked the Sephir of Water inside his tunic. The heavy cotton obscured its blinding light, but it provided enough luminescence for him to make his way to his siblings. Jinn still lay cradled in his brother's arms. Erec's haunted look troubled Darr, but Jinn's condition distressed him further.

Darr crouched down beside his brother and shook him gently on the shoulder. Erec flinched and looked up with a mix of emotions on his face. No words passed between them while the Summoner checked Jinn's body for injuries. She didn't appear to be bleeding, and aside from a slight bump on the back of her head, she looked to be okay. There were dangers associated with blows to the head and long spans of unconsciousness. He called her name and rubbed her hands, trying to generate some warmth while Erec sprinkled water onto her face. After a few moments, Jinn's eyelids fluttered open, and she jerked awake.

"Where is it?" she asked, her face panic-stricken.

Darr shook his head and placed his hand over hers. "It's all right. The Ovid is gone. The Sephir is safe."

Darr helped Jinn back to her feet. "Where is Racall?" she asked. "Did the Ovid..?"

Darr shook his head. "He's gone back to the Currents.

He's safe."

Erec stood motionless beside them, his expression vacant now. He looked lost and confused, more so than Jinn.

Within a few minutes, Jinn had recovered enough to walk. "You have the Sephir? Show us, Darr." She planted her feet, refusing to move.

Reluctantly, the Summoner pulled the Sephir free from his tunic, bringing his other hand up in the same motion to shield his eyes. Jinn and Erec did the same when the Sephir's light exploded into the cavern. After a hasty examination, the Summoner returned the relic to his tunic.

Darr led the way back through the waterway passage. Questions tumbled from his siblings' lips as they retraced their steps, and Darr answered patiently with whatever knowledge he could muster. He revealed everything he knew about the Currents, leaving nothing out this time. Erec held firm to his belief that the return of magic could mean nothing good, but he seemed less skeptical now.

"I wish I could've spoken with him before he left," Darr said without attempting to hide his frustration. "In some ways I feel like I made the right decision by connecting with Racall in the Currents, but I don't know if I could do it again."

"Better for all of Ictar if you couldn't," Erec muttered.

Jinn rolled her eyes and nudged her oldest brother. "I don't think it matters how you did it. What matters is that you did," she said. "Isn't that what Racall told you?"

Darr wasn't certain anymore. "Sort of, I guess. He said I already knew."

Jinn shrugged. "So what made you go into the Currents? What made you reach out to Racall?"

"Racall was losing the fight with the Ovid," Darr answered. "He told me to bring my Light to his, and the Currents were the only place I could do that."

Jinn nodded. "And as soon as you touched, Racall had control over his element again, isn't that right?"

Darr widened his eyes. "That's it! Racall's an Archon, but in his physical form—and Nidic Waq summoned him. Ah ha!"

"Slow down and make some sense," Erec said, his voice laced with frustration.

Excitement buzzed through Darr. "Nidic Waq summoned Racall into physical form so he could guide me. This allowed Racall to use only a fraction of his magic in the physical world, but that wasn't enough to defeat the Ovid. I needed to do the rest. By combining my Light with Racall's, together, we accessed the full power of the Earth Sephir."

Racall had been trying to teach him this lesson all along. Summoning meant bringing Light from the Currents into the physical world.

"Maybe you're right, Erec," Darr said, breaking the silence between his siblings. "Maybe magic is too dangerous a force, but how else are we supposed to fight the Soul Seekers and the Ovids? They both have use of magic that is destroying Ictar. I think they're much more dangerous than what I'm doing."

His brother shook his head. "I don't think you know for sure. You don't have a clue about the consequences of this summoning business. I'm willing to concede there might be Seekers out there. Now that Racall is gone, you have to rely on yourself. So what happens the next time you're threatened?"

Darr agreed with him. " Those are good questions—but I have to rely on Racall's lessons. I think he's prepared me well enough."

"That's not good enough, Darr," Erec said fiercely, his eyes hot in the dim light. Jinn reached over and put a hand on Erec's shoulder, but he took a step back from her.

"I think what Erec is saying is he doesn't want you to get hurt by relying on something you don't understand," Jinn said, "...and something he doesn't fully understand either."

In silence, they crossed the dams and locks underneath Dacon fortress, making good time shuffling their way through the passage. The hard lump of the Water Sephir rested against his chest, its muffled glow lighting their path. In a few hours, the river would be restored. It was strange such a small relic could accomplish such a tremendous task.

When they finally reached the passage entrance, daylight shone in through the iron grating, heralding the morning hours. With the coming of dawn and the change of guard, the grate blocking the passage had been put back, but the stairs leading up to the fortress weren't more than a few feet from the entrance. None of the Reintol siblings could be sure exactly how long they were within the tunnel, but they were exhausted from their trek.

Darr took the lead up to Dacon Fortress. The steps were slick with moisture, and the narrow space lacked any kind of handhold, but the three were too desperate for rest to do anything but struggle their way up. The stairs ended at a short landing after winding around several times. The Divine who would meet them was nowhere in sight.

They gathered on the landing, huddled in front of a narrow wooden door in the light of the Sephir.

"Now what?" Jinn asked.

Darr shrugged and eyed the door. "Maybe we should open it. The Divine might be out there."

The Summoner reached down for the handle, but Erec stayed his hand.

"I wouldn't if I were you. We don't know if there are guards out there or not, and besides, they might not be aware of our presence anyways. If you walk out there, you might have a lot to answer for walking inside the fortress walls with the Sephir of Water in your possession."

Darr relaxed his grip on the handle and slumped his shoulders, compliant to Erec's skepticism. He leaned on the wall behind him and it moved. The Summoner jumped back in surprise, alerted now by the slow grating of stone on stone. The wall adjacent to the door slid away on a hidden hinge, opening backwards into a darkened passage beyond.

The hazy orange glow of a torch appeared, followed by the wizened face of an old man composed of deep winkles and billowing white hairs. His robes were white and heavy, bending his small frame over into a slight hump.

"You must be Darr Reintol," he said in a dry and raspy voice.

The Summoner nodded, though he was hesitant. Then came a slight nudging sensation came from the Currents–the spirits whispering the identity of the man before him. "You're Herdas," Darr said.

A smile crossed the man's lips beneath his shaggy beard. "Good, good, yes. You're a true Spirit Summoner, just as Racall promised. I confess, I had my doubts, but now I see everything I've been told is true." The Divine touched his long white hair. "You have the Sephir."

Darr reached into his tunic, squinting his eyes in preparation. In a blinding blue flash, the Summoner brought the Sephir out from underneath his shirt. The Divine didn't flinch from its light. He stared at it in awe. Then he reached out to touch it, almost lovingly, but stopped.

Herdas withdrew his hand and cleared his throat. "It's hard to believe, seeing it again after being gone these past couple weeks. But I had faith Caeranol would have it returned. I thank you, Summoner." Herdas looked at Erec and Jinn and nodded gratefully to them before turning down the darkened tunnel that he'd come out of. "We must go now, to the Glass Tower."

The Summoner returned the Sephir to his tunic, and looked over at Jinn and Erec, hoping to see the same excitement on their faces that he felt. Both looked amazed, but neither spoke. Herdas ushered them into the narrow tunnel and slid the stone slab closed behind them. With torch in hand, he led them along the passageway through the walls of Dacon Fortress.

"The Archon, Racall, explained to me your need for haste and discretion," the old man whispered, but his voice was clear in the little passage. "I haven't told the governor of the Sephir's return, or of your journey into the waterway passage, but, someone will say something about your presence below Dacon last night. When that happens, many questions will arise. I'll make sure you'll be gone before that happens."

"Why would the governor have a problem with us bringing back the Sephir?" Jinn asked.

"Because rescuing stolen Sephirs isn't something Spirit Summoners normally do. The governor would be more inclined to believe you were the ones who stole it in the first place. Even if the governor did believe your story, your time would be wasted in the celebration he'd undoubtedly throw."

A glimmer of despair crept through Darr. How could he secure the other Sephirs if the governments entrusted with their care didn't trust him enough to find them?

"Herdas, is it like this everywhere?," Darr asked.

The Divine turned his head slightly, a puzzled look on his face.

"Am I going to have to crawl around through tunnels like this to restore the Sephirs because the people who protect them don't trust me to do it?"

The Divine shook his head. "No, Summoner. You'll come to see the race of Man is the most closed-minded of people when it comes to magic and the Sephirs. We Cortazians have little understanding of such things, even in the northern territories. The further you travel through Ictar, the more you'll see how integrated the magic of the Sephirs has become. Not all of the Divine seek to keep magic out of the hands of men. Some of us see it as inevitable."

The Summoner smiled grimly at the Divine's words. What would Herdas do if he knew Darr had control over the Sephir's magic? Perhaps the Divine knew of a Spirit Summoner's potential to reach into the Currents and harness the power of the Four Elements. Still, the Divine had authority by order of the Kings of Ictar to contain the forces of magic that threatened Ictar. Did that entail a potential threat from the Summoners?

Herdas kept them moving along the dusty passage. He took them up several flights of stairs and down long corridors. Darr believed they should be well within the heights of Dacon Fortress by now, yet they continued to climb upwards.

Herdas chose his path without deliberation and brought them to a halt at the end of a tunnel. He pressed on the wall in front of them, and the slab slid open into a brightly lit room. Two stuffed couches sat in the center of the room before a small hearth. On the opposite wall, a mattress squatted low to the floor, and the only ornate piece of furniture in the room took up the far wall, a massive desk.

"Welcome to my quarters," Herdas said, his face reflecting a small amount of pride. "While you're here, this will be your home. After Darr returns the Sephir to the Glass Tower, the three of you can rest here. No one will look for you here. I lead the Divine in Stern."

Darr nodded in understanding, smiling. "Thank you, Herdas. When will we be able to leave again?"

"You can rest until sunset. I'd prefer it if you left the city under cover of darkness. Now, if you'll excuse me, I'll clear the hall of the other Divine so we won't be disturbed this morning."

Herdas bowed slightly and departed through a door beside his giant desk, making sure to shut the door behind him. When the door closed, Erec turned towards him.

"Are you sure we can trust this Divine?"

Darr looked back at Jinn and she shook her head. When he returned his gaze to Erec, a look of pure sincerity graced his brother's face.

"The spirits are calm right now," Darr said. "They would've alerted me if we were in danger. I'm sure of it."

Erec gave a sort of half smile before turning away. Jinn stepped around both of them and walked to a small window behind the desk. Outside, the sky lightened.

"Do you think we'll get some kind of reward?" Erec asked. "We could send money to Father, he could really use it now with all of us gone."

Darr stared blankly. The thought had crossed his mind when Herdas had mentioned the possibility of the governor celebrating the Sephir's return, but there had never been a guarantee of a reward. And while Erec's intentions were good, Darr hadn't embarked on this journey for fame and wealth. Were his reasons for coming any less selfish?

Herdas came back through the door, leaving Erec's question hanging in the air, unanswered.

The Divine beamed with excitement. He looked from one face to the next, settling finally on Darr. "We're ready now," Herdas said. "The tower awaits you."

Chapter Fourteen

"Knowing there could be no undoing what Symdus had unleashed upon himself and the world, Caeranol struck out at the Devoid using all his considerable magic, but the Light expanding within the Devoid gave it unlimited strength and resilience. Having possessed Symdus's body, the Devoid could manipulate the Currents in the same way its host once could. Caeranol barely escaped with his life."

~From A Current History of Ictar, as told by Nidic Waq

Darr had only seen the Glass Tower once before, as a boy on his first trip to Stern. His father brought him to the center of the city where the thoroughfare connected with the larger vineyards. On a clear, bright day, father and son had gazed up at the monstrous Dacon Fortress and the shining jewel at its peak—the Glass Tower. His father told him how the Dwarves had constructed it by intertwining glass and iron to build a home for the Sephir of Water. As a boy, the tower inspired wonder and magic, a bright star fallen from the sky and set down on top of the fortress.

Now, as Darr stood within the sacred tower, he felt much more than wonder or magic. The Glass Tower sat outside the confines of time or the material world. To Darr's perception, he was within the Currents.

The Glass Tower rose from Dacon Fortress's highest tower, screening away the city of Stern and the surrounding land with its frost-etched glass. The mountains beyond the city were nothing but a dark smear. Enclosed by its walls and ceiling of glass and girders of polished iron, the tower looked small, yet it gave the impression of having vast space. They entered through a staircase in the floor, surrounded by stone and mortar one minute, and the next encased in a room not unlike the insides of a waterfall.

Jinn and Erec huddled close to the stairwell, both their faces reflecting awe. Neither said anything when Herdas nudged his way past them and came up alongside Darr. The Divine gestured to him, pointing to a metal stand that stood in the center of the room.

"We won't be disturbed, Summoner," his dry voice whispered. "Go. Return it to its altar."

Darr drew the Sephir from his tunic, so fragile in his hands. The intense light flared hungrily, as if the Sephir sensed its altar. Within the Currents, emotions of exhilaration and joy began to pour outward from the spirits, followed by whispered urgings to go forward. The Summoner quieted them. He took several steps across the translucent blue tiles making up the floor, like walking on water.

The altar was a foreign object. It had a round base like a barrel and it rose waist high into an obelisk, ending at a point. Runes and other undecipherable markings were etched along the surface of the smooth, glittering metal.

Darr reached out with the Sephir of Water in both hands. He took a quick glance over his shoulder at Erec and Jinn, their faces unreadable. Herdas nodded his head in encouragement. Gently, Darr placed the relic down against the four-cornered point of the altar thinking to balance it there...

...and both Sephir and Summoner were joined in the Currents.

When the Water Sephir connected with its altar, a dam broke, its magic surged out into the Currents. The presence of an Archon pervaded his senses, but it wasn't Racall. Like the connection he'd shared with Racall, he saw everything the Archon did. The magic of the Sephir diffused itself throughout Ictar. Ground water surged upwards through soil, nurturing the roots of plants. It froze glaciers that had melted and given way to floods, healing and controlling the natural flow of water. Swollen marshes receded to their natural state, and the evaporating moisture began to rise to rain down on dry lands.

Finally, in a burst of power from the Sephir, Darr and the Water Archon dove down into the depths of the waterway passage. They circled within the cavern where the source of the Lourcient River had been turned to ice. The Archon gathered in its magic, and in one swift pulse, the spirit creature liquefied the frozen waterfall.

In an explosive rush, the Lourcient River surged into the waterway passage.

The Archon's presence became separate from him.

–Thank you, Summoner–I am in your debt–

"Who are you?" the Summoner asked, his question spilling out into the wisteria glow of the Currents.

A soft blue light appeared before him, its color coalescing out of the ether until it had formed a body out of blue sparkle, small and feminine.

–I am Ariswa–I am the Archon of the Water Sephir–

The Archon came closer to him, her presence fluid and light, and Darr knew her in the same way he'd known Racall when they joined. As a nurturer and a healer, Ariswa exuded wisdom and agelessness. She adapted to change with barely a thought, moving along at whatever pace she set for herself, at one with her element.

Ariswa reached out to him, the blue sparkle of her fingertips brushing across the white shimmer of his face. They touched, and a shock of memory and emotion rushed through Darr. While the images were indecipherable, they made him feel needed.

–The service you have provided, Darr, is invaluable– With the Sephir of Water secured once more, the devoid seeking to envelop both our world and yours has weakened–

Ariswa pulled her hand away. Sadness poured out of her.

–A long journey awaits you, and this has been but its shortest leg–The days ahead will hold little joy for you–You *will face uncertainties and doubts–You will see the many faces of death and destruction, and you will want to run away–*

The Archon's words upset Darr. Nidic Waq and Racall had both told him his journey wouldn't be easy, but Ariswa sounded more honest. She didn't shade the truth of things.

The emotions flowing from Ariswa changed, her sadness replaced by determination and pride.

–There is always hope–

She reached out to him again, and this time, four blinding white lights erupted across his vision, obliterating any trace of darkness.

–The Chosen, Darr Reintol–They are out there and they are waiting for their destiny–

The importance behind the Archon's words confused Darr. "Who are the Chosen? Where can I find them?"

Ariswa laughed, a light feeling that warmed him despite his confusion.

–Such questions matter little right now–The answers will come to you, but for now, you need only worry about the next Sephir–

Darr moved towards the Archon, but Ariswa's body of blue sparkle spread apart.

–You have made us all proud, young Summoner–You will do well in the days ahead despite the challenges you will face–

Darr couldn't stop the Archon from leaving him. The questions and statements she'd posed to him were intriguing, but he believed her when she said the answers would come. Like Racall, Ariswa wasn't prepared to give him any concrete explanations. He'd learn what he needed to learn when the time came.

–We are forever in your debt, Darr Reintol–

Ariswa's final words. The Summoner knew the time had come to return to the physical world. The Currents and its mysteries would be waiting for another day...

...When Darr opened his eyes to the Glass Tower, the bright light of the Water Sephir had dimmed, replaced by a soft glow. The Sephir hovered a finger's width from the top of its altar. It had the texture of a rough-hewn crystal plucked straight from the ground, but its shape was vaguely round, like an orb. With its blue surface, clear and unblemished, its shape imperfect. Regardless, the Sephir gave the impression of perfection.

Darr found it to be the most beautiful thing he'd ever seen in his life.

At awe, the Summoner turned to Herdas and his siblings, but the entire fortress trembled as he did so. Horns blew in the city below, but from the height of the Glass Tower, they sounded far away.

The rumbling from below the fortress grew thunderous, shaking them all.

Herdas's face glowed with excitement. "You've done it, Summoner," he said. "We must leave now, the governor will be here soon. Those horns are warnings for the floodgates. The Lourcient River has returned!"

* * * *

As the Lourcient River awakened, Stern's populace amassed in an uproar on the streets below. Darr and his siblings watched from a window in Herdas's quarters. The old Divine had left them several minutes before. With the river's apparent return, the governor would go to the Glass Tower, anticipating the Sephir's return. With hundreds of citizens rioting before the entrance of the waterway passage, it looked as though many of Stern's citizens believed the same.

The people below fought with the soldiers, yelling for the governor and demanding information. From the deep rumbling underneath the city and the sound of the warning horn blowing in Dacon, no one could deny the state of the river was changing. The guards below forced the citizens away, ordering them to return home, but the people persisted.

Don't run away from what you believe.

Darr heard his mother's voice, the memory brought back with startling clarity while watching the people below. He'd been quite young when his mother had told him those words, but he remembered her as if it happened yesterday. Her body small and her face round, like Jinn's, her hair brown and dark and curled about her face.

He didn't remember what had prompted the words, but he remembered being afraid. He remembered feeling uncertain. His mother had found him, comforted him, and told him—Don't run away from what you believe. Face it, head on. The people of Stern embodied his mother's words. They were certain, and they believed with their hearts, in the return of their river. He wasn't sure he could remain in a situation when logic told him to turn away.

Another quake shook the fortress, and Darr steadied himself on the window sill. The locks and dams within the passage were keeping the river's massive flow in check, but before long, they wouldn't be able to hold it. The engineers would have to release the river or risk damaging the system. What would happen when they opened those locks? He'd seen the amount of water released when Ariswa had freed the river.

The guards along the edge of the waterway passage forced people back in a rush, desperate to get them clear. From out of the passage entrance, an explosion of water erupted, blowing its iron grating out of the fortress walls and sending it flying over the heads of the rioters, dead leaves in a gusty wind. The water of the Lourcient River surged down the channels cut throughout the city, overflowing onto its streets as it raced steadily for the city walls where it would become the Hondor Waterfall.

Below, both citizens and fortress soldiers, picked

themselves up from where the river's eruption had knocked them down. They danced in the streets as the river's channels overflowed around them. Their streets were flooded, and undoubtedly, some of their homes, but the people of Stern had their river back.

And they would never know why.

It was rewarding enough to watch them for a little while longer.

Chapter Fifteen

"A war against the Devoid and its Soul Seekers broke out. The massive, shining cities of the Ancients fell one by one, and as their population dropped away, their enemies grew stronger. The Elder Council tried to fight against the Devoid using relics both spiritual and scientific, but nothing could penetrate its defenses."

~From A Current History of Ictar, as told by Nidic Waq

After it became evident Stern's population would be celebrating for some time to come, Darr and his siblings settled themselves in Herdas's quarters and went to sleep. The old Divine stopped in sometime around noon and told them not to worry about the governor. No one suspected anything about their presence. Too tired to ask more, Darr rolled over on the couch and slept.

In the late afternoon, Darr lifted his head and looked around the room. Jinn slept soundlessly on the low mattress, and Erec stood motionless, staring out the window at the shadowed cityscape below. Darr threw off his blankets and rose from the couch. Herdas had left plates of food on his desk. He grabbed an apple and walked to stand near Erec.

Darr took a bite, chewed, and asked, "Are they still celebrating down there?"

His brother nodded. "I don't think it will end for a while." Erec looked over, his dark eyes serious. "You know, I'm sorry for what I said this morning–for implying you should do this for the glory."

Darr dipped his head in shock. Erec rarely took back his actions, let alone apologize for them. "Thanks. If I'm being honest, I wondered the same thing about sending help to Father."

Erec smiled. "When I saw those people out there, they

were so happy. I know there are bigger rewards..."

The Summoner almost laughed out of pure astonishment, but he didn't want to offend his brother. "It's nice to see that you're broadening your horizons," Darr said.

"Don't get me wrong," seriousness crept back into Erec's tone, "I still don't agree with what you're doing. Magic is an outdated tool...but maybe in your hands, it'll do better. It did some good here in Stern."

Erec turned back to face Darr and took a deep breath. "That's why I'm coming with you. I've got to watch your back because I know you won't, and you can't rely on those spirits all the time."

Darr didn't want to see his brother endangered, and more, he knew his brother had doubts about the entire effort. Erec's life would be changed irrevocably by going any further. His brother wasn't open-minded, and he wouldn't accept a change in his beliefs easily. Darr studied the determination in his brother's face, and he remembered something Racall said to him earlier. He would find strength from his brother and sister. Perhaps the Archon knew something about Erec that Darr didn't.

"Are you sure about this?" the Summoner asked. "Things will never be the same afterwards."

Erec nodded. "I know, but I think I can handle it."

"Well neither one of you is leaving me behind."

Both brothers turned towards Jinn. She hopped up from her bed, but Erec shook his head in protest. "You aren't coming," he stated resolutely. "Father is still alone back in Tyfor and none of us knows what his condition is. You have to go back. One of us has to."

Jinn stopped in front of Erec, pointing a small finger into his chest. "Don't talk to me about obligation. You were the one ready to take off and leave us all to join the king's guard. It was your obligation to stay, yet you chose to follow your heart." Erec's face darkened, but Jinn didn't back down. "We don't hold it against you, Erec, and you shouldn't hold this against me. I saw just as much as you did down in those tunnels, and I think I have a right to see where all of this goes. Besides, who's going to keep you two from killing each other?"

Darr raised his eyebrows and a smile twitched on his mouth. Jinn would be the most understanding when it came to his abilities. He could talk freely with her about the Currents and the magic in ways he never could with Erec. It concerned him that he'd be putting her in danger by allowing her to come along. She possessed little experience of the world outside of Tyfor and no fighting skills. Then again, neither did he. Hopefully, between his summoning abilities and Erec's adequate swordsmanship, none of them would be in too much danger.

Darr raised his hands between his siblings, diffusing the fight before it erupted.

"Jinn can come," Darr said.

Erec flung his arms up. "You're insane."

"Jinn's right," Darr continued. "She has a right to be here, and I think we need her. If the two of us go alone, we'll end up arguing and fighting the whole time. I think since we started this together, we should end it together."

Erec bit his lip and nodded solemnly, holding back whatever almost came out of this mouth. "Okay, but I don't like this. Now I have to look out for the both of you."

Jinn and Erec started bickering again, but Darr left them alone. He stalked off towards Herdas's desk and the food that waited for them. After a few moments, his siblings dropped their argument, more interested in their hunger than their fight. The three gathered around the desk and ate the meal the Divine had left.

Outside, the daylight waned, yet the sounds of celebration continued. When sunset finally arrived, Herdas returned to take them out of the city.

* * * *

Herdas and a few of his trusted guards had carefully arranged their departure. He dressed them in the white robes of the Divine, and had their packs taken down to the base of Dacon. No one suspected who the Reintols were while they made their way through the fortress. Anyone looking at them would see nothing out of the ordinary, only a few Divine on an evening stroll. They reached the fortress gates with no interference, but the guards on duty might upend their plans. Herdas explained to the gatekeepers three of his order were being dismissed to Darlholme. With nothing more than a casual shrug, the guard pulled the gates opened and released them into the night. Darr breathed a silent sigh of relief.

The little company made their way down the hill leading from Dacon, taking back roads in order to bypass the celebrating crowds. The channels cut through the streets now flowed with water. Darr smiled. At the edge of the city, they found horses and fresh supplies waiting for them. The three mounted up, and with Herdas leading on his own horse, and his guards flanking them, they rode down the city thoroughfare towards the walls.

"It wasn't an easy matter revealing the Sephir's return to the governor," Herdas explained to Darr. "He's a very strict man and doesn't like secrets taking place within his city, not to mention within his fortress. Suffice to say, he was very pleased to see the Sephir had been returned, though he realized it couldn't have gotten there on its own. The crowd at the base of the fortress distracted him for a time, but it didn't allow me to escape his attention altogether."

A knot formed in the pit of Darr's stomach and he asked, "So what did you do? What did you tell him?"

The Divine smiled. "I told him the truth. I told him a Summoner came to me with the Sephir. This Summoner had found the means to locate it and had defeated the enemy who had taken it. When he asked where this Summoner could be found, I told him he'd already left–a very crafty fellow, that Summoner."

"The truth?"

Herdas laughed. "I had much explaining to do. The governor didn't think Summoners were capable of doing much more than hearing voices. I told him there are some that can do a little more."

Darr caught the hidden meaning in the Divine's words. Herdas was aware of a Summoner's potential, but Darr decided not to ask him about it. The answer he might get worried him.

When they came to the city walls, the portcullis raised at their approach and the guards were blind to the four Divine passing underneath Stern's walls to the plains beyond. Herdas led them a short way past the gates and brought his mount to a halt. He lowered his cowl, his billowy white hair sticking out in all directions.

The Divine smiled warmly and said, "Thank you for everything you've done, Summoner. Your service to Ictar will never be forgotten, even if your name can't be known." He nodded in thanks to Jinn and Erec before fixing his gaze on Darr once more. "Keep your robes on until you reach the Lourcient River. We don't want any stray eyes to fall on you. Do you know which direction to head?"

The Summoner nodded. "To the Dwarves. They protect the Sephir of Earth."

Herdas nodded. "Yes. You'll have to make your way to the city of Arcnor, deep within the Dwarf territory. I know the distance is great, but you'll do fine, Summoner."

Darr turned away, but then turned back. "Herdas? Could you do me a favor?"

The Divine nodded agreeably.

"My father, Hydle Reintol, was injured in Tyfor before I left for Stern. I wasn't able to stay and help him back on his feet. Could you send someone in my stead to help him and tell him Jinn and Erec have come with me?"

"Of course," the Divine said. "I'll send someone tonight in fact, a young man among my order who's used to running errands to far places. Don't worry about your father. He'll be informed."

Darr smiled and said, "Thank you."

Jinn and Erec also gave their thanks. Darr replaced his cowl, and gave a final wave to Herdas. With his brother and sister beside him, they rode down the hill towards the Lourcient River.

* * * *

They did as they were told and kept the robes of the Divine on until they were well out of sight of Stern. They reached the dark banks of the Lourcient within an hour of leaving Herdas, its powerful waters churning strongly through the night, falling from the heights of Stern's wall at the Hondor Falls and winding through the plains back towards the Valimere Mountains. A sense of peace came over Darr when he heard the rushing water. A few days ago he'd passed by these plains and the river had been nothing more than a debris-clogged creek. Now the Lourcient's place in nature had been returned, and the balance within Ictar had been strengthened.

Erec found a spot close by the river secluded by a copse of hemlock. They tethered their horses, discarded their robes, and wrapped themselves in blankets within the shelter of the trees. For a time, they spoke about what had transpired the day before with the Ovid and the Archon, Racall. They talked about the revival of the Lourcient, and how strange it was Darr's magic had brought it about. The Summoner didn't tell them about his connection with the Water Sephir and its Archon when he touched with the altar. There were some experiences, he sensed, he needed to keep to himself.

After a while, Jinn drifted off to sleep, leaving Darr and Erec alone with the sound of the Lourcient River to remind them of the outside world.

"It's a beautiful night for being so late in the fall," Erec said. He looked up through the canopy of hemlock limbs to the black sky beyond. "It's warm..."

Erec's voice trailed off, leaving them surrounded in uncomfortable silence once more. His brother was attempting to make peace, to say something encouraging. He knew Erec well enough to read into his words and movements. He understood how his seemingly insignificant gestures were really meant for the emotions he couldn't bring himself to display.

"Thank you, Erec," Darr told him, smiling.

"Thanks for what?"

The Summoner shifted, stalling in order to choose his words carefully. "For coming along and watching out for me, and for being a big brother exactly when you should. You'll see things I may not, and I respect you for that, whether you're right or wrong in the matter."

For a moment, it looked like Erec might lash out, but he grinned and shook his head. Darr breathed a silent sigh of relief. With Erec, he could never tell what kind of response he'd get.

* * * *

Darr recognized the vision of the towering castle, the gardens of indescribable beauty, and the walls of stone and thorns surrounding them all. He'd seen this landscape before in his dreams, though when and in what context, he could't recall.

The Summoner wondered whether he dreamed the experience, or if he somehow drifted through the Currents in his sleep. His thoughts scattered instantly upon having them. The familiar images became clearer.

Gardens surrounded in thorns rose up, their beauty filling every one of his senses. The wall of thorns emerged in sharp contrast, wicked and piercing, twisting along the border of the garden. They appeared far away and non-threatening. As a spectator, Darr observed the flow of images, a hindrance to nothing. Next came the massive single-towered castle, a dark obelisk shrouded in ivy, pitched in defiance against the sky.

The elders appeared, men whose wisdom Darr sensed instinctively. They gathered along the paths winding through the garden. They spoke in low tones while two men argued on the front steps of the castle.

Darr walked along one of the paths, no longer a spectator but a participant, his own ears two of the many straining to hear the conversation between the two arguing men. He edged his way along the periphery of the gardens making his way towards the lone spire, trying to make out the voices of the arguing men. After a moment, the men came into view through a break in the shrubbery—one dressed all in black, the other in regal white.

The whispered words of the two men were indistinct. He strained his ears harder. "Prolonging of life," was all Darr heard.

The man in black erupted with anger as he began arguing vehemently with the regal-looking man. His words became distorted, but strength and fierceness radiated from both men. When it ended, the man in black wheeled about and stormed off through the gardens.

When the man in black approached the wall that marked the barrier of thorns, he turned and fixed his gaze, filled with hate, on Darr.

The Summoner gasped in shock and stumbled backwards. He braced for the impact of the ground, but nothing came. He opened his eyes a pinch and saw nothing but black. He stood upright, but no ground lay beneath his feet or sky above his head to determine where or in which direction he stood.

A voice called out, a gentle urging of his name. Darr

looked in the direction of the voice, and Erec appeared before him, his features clear. The Summoner blinked in confusion. Erec gave him a sad smile. He turned and walked away. Darr called out to him. When Erec didn't stop, the Summoner ran after him. His brother's pace was faster somehow. Darr rushed ahead, intent on catching his brother, but Erec receded further into the dark.

In the moment before waking, Erec vanished into the all encompassing black, leaving Darr to ponder what had happened.

Chapter Sixteen

"Even in the face of such catastrophe, Caeranol had a plan. Using power unique to the Ancients, Caeranol forged a talisman called the Azlude that would erode the Devoid's defenses. Along with a handful of his most powerful elders, including his apprentice, Damon, Caeranol confronted the Devoid a second time. The Azlude worked exactly as it should have, but the onslaught of magical power released by the Devoid in its defense was unimaginable. The energies obliterated Damon and several other elders. The Azlude, while indestructible, was not immune to the Devoid's deceptive magic, and it disappeared from the battlefield, changed into something else entirely. Caeranol remained alive, protected from the Devoid by the spirits for reasons he didn't understand."

~From A Current History of Ictar, as told by Nidic Waq

Darr woke sore and disgruntled. For the last few hours before dawn, he spent his time staring up at the stars and thinking over the images of his dream and what they might mean. When morning appeared, the images lost their edge and faded into the ether. By the time Jinn and Erec awoke, it didn't matter anymore.

"So how are we getting to Arcnor and the Earth Sephir?" Jinn asked over their breakfast.

Darr wasn't sure when he answered. "The easiest route would take us west through the Ruk Mountains and into Kurflin. It seems like the most obvious approach."

"Obvious, yes," Erec said, "and that's exactly what the Soul Seekers would be hoping for. The road to Kurflin is just that, a road. It's wide open and anyone would see you coming for miles, especially the Seekers."

"We could take a boat from Dis," Jinn joked, her mouth askew with sarcasm.

Darr laughed and shook his head. "Those boats don't take buttons and lint as currency," he said. The joke wasn't a good one. Avoiding the Soul Seekers on their way to the Earth Sephir might not be possible.

"We could go to Conra for help," Erec suggested in seriousness. "Conra knows the way through the Barricade Mountains and the lands beyond. With his guidance, we could reach the Dwarves in a week."

"But Conra doesn't leave his cabin anymore," Jinn said. "We'd have to go through the swamps to get to him and we don't know the way."

"Yes I do. I remember the way from when Father took me a few years back."

Darr could tell right away that Erec wouldn't be backing down. He'd made it clear that he would protect his siblings. If going in search of Conra might keep them out of the sights of the Soul Seekers, his brother would steer them that direction.

"How sure are you?" Darr asked his brother.

Erec didn't appear uncertain when he answered. "I know the way. I remember it clearly."

At his side, Jinn looked doubtful, but Darr trusted his brother. "Fine," Darr said. "We'll go find Conra. It'll be good to see him again anyway."

With cold, but favorable weather, Erec led them in single file. They rode along the river until they found shallows suitable to cross. Once they reached the southern side of the river, Erec took them east towards the coastline. They didn't push their horses any harder than they needed to, and rested them when necessary.

"I wish we could've seen Father before leaving," Jinn said during a quiet stretch in the morning.

From the front of their procession, Erec said, "I do too, Jinn, but the old man's always been good about focusing on what's right in front of him. He's got Arn to help him and the store to keep him busy. He probably won't even remember where we've gone once he gets back into the swing of things."

Darr doubted Erec was right about that, but he knew his brother was only trying to comfort Jinn. Although, maybe there was a way to check on the old man. Racall had told him he could locate people through the Currents, but he didn't have the slightest idea how.

As they traveled the coastline of the Arktary Ocean, he made numerous endeavors to search the Currents while riding alongside his siblings. He dove into the spirit realm when they broke their conversations, but the attempts often left him empty-handed and disoriented when he emerged. He tried again when they stopped for the night, but the spirit realm proved too vast and uncharted for him to single out one man. Any contact with their father would have to wait.

After another day of steady riding, they reached the edge of the Lowlands of Deron. The lowlands were a huge, bowl-shaped valley sunk deep into the plains, its marshy depths hidden in fog and gnarled foliage.

Erec climbed down from his horse and began removing its saddle.

"What're you doing?" Jinn asked from atop her mount.

"We can't take the horses down there," Erec answered without looking up. "We'll have to strip them of this gear and set them free. If we send them east, towards Dis, someone will find them."

His brother had a point. Even if they got the horses through the lowlands, they wouldn't be able to take them into the mountains beyond. It would be best for the horses to simply send them away.

"How long will it take us to get through there?" Jinn asked, staring warily into the fog below.

Erec scanned the horizon beyond the murky bowl. The Barricade Mountains rose up as an impenetrable wall not more than a few miles away, though they looked far off. "It's almost noon, but I think we can get through today if we're quick about it. When Father and I passed through here, it only took us a day."

Darr's stomach tightened. "You're sure you know the way?" he asked.

Erec chuckled. "Of course. Now come on, we're burning daylight standing out here talking about it."

Darr and Jinn followed their brother as he picked a hidden trail leading down into the bowl of the lowlands. The fog enclosed them, shutting out a good portion of the light and giving them chills that couldn't be dispersed. Darr pulled his cloak tight about his body, but it didn't help. They could do nothing but shake with cold while still trying to maneuver through the slick terrain. The swamps of the lowlands spread out around them—glassy green pools of water lined with saw grass and twisted, dying trees. The landscape of the lowlands contained only mud and mire, slowing their pace considerably.

A couple of hours after they departed the edge of the lowlands, darkness fell so quickly it left them in mild shock. No one could tell how close they were to the edge of the swamp, but Erec continued to lead undaunted, picking out a path through the dim light. Jinn came up close to Darr, her small form pressed close against him as the darkness engulfed them.

Darr thought about his brother's words about the lowlands being more treacherous during the winter. He wouldn't want to consider coming down here then. The predatory nature of the place affected his senses. Animal sounds off in the distance would suddenly cut short when something bigger and stronger claimed its life. The surrounding swamp water bubbled in places, hiding creatures laying in wait to trap their next victim. Even the insects buzzing incessantly around him were predators coming to feed off the flesh intruding on their land. Darr tried to shut out the sounds and concentrate on the path in front of him, avoiding the feel of the mire altogether.

They followed Erec until it became too dark to see

anything except a vague outline of his body. Erec stopped in his tracks, and his head and shoulders slumped.

"We're lost," he said, not bothering to turn around.

Jinn's body tensed as she prepared to lash out, but the Summoner gripped her shoulder, holding her in place. He approached his brother calmly, keeping Jinn separated to prevent a bad situation from becoming worse. "Do you have any idea where we're at?"

Erec hesitated, then nodded. "I think so, but things have changed a lot since I came here as a boy."

"We need to make a torch," Darr said, keeping his voice steady. "We'll keep going for another hour. If we don't make it out, we'll have to stay here for the night."

"No, Darr, we can't," Jinn protested.

"I agree," Erec said flatly. "There are things in this place that will..."

Darr broke both their arguments off. "There are worse things out at night that will come looking for signs of life. Soul Seekers. I don't feel like attracting their attention."

Without waiting for a response, Darr cast about for a green branch. He found one, tore it down, and went through his pack looking for his flint and his knife. He cut a woolen strip off his blanket and bound it tight about the end of the branch, coated the end in sap from the tree, and used his flint to ignite it. A bright orange flame sprung to life, eating greedily at the sap covered blanket. The flame wouldn't last long. Darr passed the torch to Erec, and encased in the orange glow, he trudged through the lowlands once more.

They hadn't been moving more than a few minutes when they heard a hollow splashing sound, like a large stone dropped into a pond. Erec brought them all to a halt and they stared into the darkness of the swamp, waiting for the sound to come again. Nothing happened, so they continued onward. The splashing sound came again, this time much closer. Erec wheeled about, drawing his sword in one fluid motion.

Darr peered past the bright halo of the torch, but only shadow presented itself. Jinn looked too, her face intense with concentration.

"I think something's out there," she whispered.

The Summoner was nodding in agreement when the spirits whispered with gentle precision.

–Hurt you, Summoner–

–Get back–

–Bad things–

–Want to hurt you–

–Get Back–

The splashing sound came again, this time close enough to drench the Summoner and his siblings with the stale swamp water.

"Get back!" Darr screamed, realizing it was too late.

A nest of snaking tentacles came shooting out of the darkness in front of them. Jinn screamed out as both her leg and torso were caught up. A slimy tendril tightened around Darr's arm. Erec rushed over to them, but he fell face first into the mud with both legs snared. His sword and the torch flew into the dark.

In the dim light of the dying torch, something huge rose up out of the darkness before them, dripping and oozing the fetid water of the lowlands. Tentacles snapped wildly out from its corpulent body. It came into view, a giant, tooth-riddled maw split wide emitting an eerie cry.

Erec grasped for his sword, but the creature sensed his movement. It flung him about with uncanny strength, beating him against the ground, dragging him towards its jaws. Jinn freed her hunting knife and severed the tentacle around her waist. She launched herself forward and sliced through the tentacles on Darr's arm, freeing the Summoner so he could go to his brother's aid. The creature responded with a barrage of its whip-like appendages flailing across the clearing. Jinn fell away, stricken, and a tentacle wrapped about Darr again, squeezing tight.

The Summoner tried to connect with the Currents, but his concentration failed with every struggled breath.

"Darn crawlers," someone grumbled from out of the darkness.

An iron crossbow bolt flew through the air, whizzing mere inches from the top of his head. The bolt buried itself deep within the creature's body, and it cried out in pain.

Again the voice shouted out, "To chaos with ya!" And another bolt buried itself in the creature's bulbous form.

With a painful cry, the creature released the tentacles binding Darr and his siblings. With the same dunking, splashing sound that had brought it, the creature sunk back down into the swamp waters in retreat. Darr looked up dazedly from the ground and took in a huge gulp of air. Erec picked himself up from out of the muck, and Jinn lay in a tangled heap several feet away, muttering in indignation.

Two strong leather boots clumped down in the mud before Darr. He followed the boots up to a set of thin legs and waist, getting the make of the man who had rescued them. He didn't wear a coat or forest cloak, dressed only in woodsman garb. Darr looked up into the man's weather-browned wrinkled face, and saw something else—pointed ears and sharp eyes hidden slightly behind his shaggy gray hair.

"Fools," the Elf rasped. "What do you think you're doing traveling the lowlands at this time of night? And taking on a crawler no less. You're lucky I saw your light. That thing would've killed the lot of you."

The Summoner smiled at the old Elf. It would be interesting getting to know Conra again.

Chapter Seventeen

"In retaliation, the Devoid unleashed a sickness to disable the Ancients, making them easy victims for the Soul Seekers. The Ancients' population dwindled. Caeranol gathered his remaining brethren and barricaded them within a mountain range, temporarily shielding them from the Devoids. Using their knowledge of the Currents and science, the Ancients devised a way to depart their land, allowing them to be free of the Devoid's destruction. But where would that leave the lesser races of the land? What about the Sephirs and their Archons? Who would protect them from the Devoid's hunger?"

~From A Current History of Ictar, as told by Nidic Waq

Darr sat on the floor of Conra's cabin, wrapped tightly in a blanket while sipping a cup of ale. Beside him, Erec sat next to the stone hearth, a fire crackling within its open maw. The small cabin contained a table, a few chairs, and a small bed tucked into a nook in the corner beside the hearth. Shelves filled with odd trinkets lined the wall beside the kitchen. Darr stared at the strange objects and tried to decipher their origin without success.

Conra applied a healing salve to Jinn's shoulder in silence. The tentacles of the crawler had left a series of abrasions along her arm. The injuries were nothing major, but the Elf insisted on treating them. When Conra finished binding the wound with a fresh bandage, he got up with a wink to Darr and disappeared into the shadows of his kitchen.

For his age, the Elf appeared strong. Conra had to be nearly seventy years old, yet he lived alone on the fringes of the most dangerous country in Ictar. He'd dispatched the crawler with little more than a second thought, and despite his protests about his weakening eyesight, he led them safely through the Lowlands of Deron in near darkness.

At his side, Darr whispered to Erec, "I've only met Conra twice before, but he's so much stronger than I remember. He's a..."

"He's a survivor," Erec said with a nod, a smirk swelling on the side of his mouth. "To us, he was always just a friend of Father's, someone to share his history. But Conra's tougher than most anyone you'll ever meet."

When Conra reappeared from the darkness of the kitchen, he carried a tray filled with bread and cheese. They accepted their evening meal gratefully, grasping at handfuls of food as Conra set the tray down. The Elf collapsed into a wooden rocker beside the hearth and watched them eat. No one had said anything about what brought them. The journey through the lowlands had been too exhausting, and the hike across the plains too dark. Conra appeared pleased simply to have their company.

Conra rocked back and forth in his chair, causing an irritating creaking sound. Darr looked up, and found the old Elf smiling, a cat who'd cornered its prey.

"It gets pretty lonely out here in the winter time. It's good to get some company," the Elf said. "I'm glad your father sent you three down here for a visit."

Darr shifted uncomfortably and cast a furtive glance at Jinn, but she wouldn't meet his gaze. Darr cleared his throat. "Well, that's the thing, Conra. Father didn't send us. We came on our own."

The Elf crouched forward in his rocker, his face beaming. "Ha! I knew old Hydle wouldn't be foolish enough to send all three of you down here. Do you know what kind of trouble you could've gotten into? Don't you know what that crawler would've done to you, if I hadn't been around? You'd be at the bottom of those swamps, that's what."

Darr nodded his head in unison with his siblings under Conra's disapproving stare. They were all complacent in the scolding, even Erec, who normally wouldn't stand for being treated like a child. The Elf studied them for a moment longer, letting the intensity in his eyes speak for him. He relaxed and settled back into his rocker.

"Sorry I had to do that, young ones," Conra said, his tone soft now. "I can't have you all risking life and limb just to see me. You survived, and you learned, that's what's important. So how's Hydle doing anyway?"

Again, Darr found no words. He searched both Erec's and Jinn's faces for answers, but neither would provide what he searched for. How could he tell Conra what happened? Would the Elf believe him, and would it be wise to tell him everything? The Summoner stared up at Conra, searching for the words that wouldn't come.

"What's the matter with you three?" the Elf exclaimed, his face bereft of all amusement. "You all look as if you're at a funeral."

"A lot has happened," Erec whispered. "More than I believe."

Conra leaned forward in his rocker again, intrigue lining his sharp features. Regardless of the consequences, Darr took a steadying breath and told Conra the events that had brought them to him. The Summoner kept certain aspects of his story vague, especially where summoning and the Currents were concerned. For now, Conra should know the big details–the Sephir of Water had been rescued from an Ovid, accomplished because of an Archon sent by Nidic Waq.

"We're on our way to the city of Arcnor where the Earth Sephir is kept," Darr said. "We were hoping you could tell us how to get through the Barricade Mountains to save us some time."

Conra gazed into the air in front of him as he rocked back and forth. "That's quite a fascinating story," he said. "I'm not sure how much of it I'm supposed to believe."

"You can believe want you want, Conra," Erec said, his eyes burning with defiance. "I wasn't sure how much I was supposed to believe, and I'm still not sure. I know what I saw down in those caverns beneath Stern. It was horrible."

The old Elf nodded grimly and stood up. He walked stiff-legged to a nearby window and peered out into the night. "It'd be easy to write you all off as mad, but I've heard a lot of things about these Soul Seekers. Quite a few hunters pass through here, headstrong fellows who think they can navigate the Barricades. I give them what help I can and send them on their way, but I've heard things from them. The Seekers are black things that rip you to shreds and steal the life right out of you. I've seen things too. Outside on the really dark nights, it gets still sometimes, so still I can hear my own heart beat..."

When Conra paused, an unusual sense of dread settled over the room. I'm sensing his emotions in the Currents, Darr realized.

The Elf turned away from the window and sat back down. "As for the Barricade Mountains, you don't stand a chance of getting through them yourself. You'd be much better off going around. Take the pass at the Ruk Mountains west and go south through the plains of Kurflin. It's a much safer route."

Darr shook his head. "It'd take us almost two weeks to make the journey. We need to get to the Dwarf Borderlands quickly, and going through the Barricades is the only way we're going to do that."

"No, you're not." The Elf laughed. "The three of you are completely inexperienced. You'd be lost within your first couple hours. The snow doesn't come for another few weeks, but it's still pretty cold up there. You'd freeze before you'd ever find your way out again. I'm telling you, go west. Take the safe route."

"He's not going to help us, Darr," Erec stated, his face blank.

The Summoner wasn't willing to back down. "Conra, please. Just give us something to work with. Please give us some kind of help."

"What about your spirit friend, the Archon? Can't he help you? Or what about the prophet? Did he just expect you to find your own way?" The Elf stared at the three, his solid face revealing the fire creeping up within. "You three can't really be considering this?"

Darr kept his gaze fixed on the Elf's, his own fire rising up in defense. Something within the Summoner shifted, strengthening his emotions. It appeared Conra saw the shift as well.

A smile wormed its way across the corners of the Elf's lined face, devilish in the dim light. "Here's some good advice, young Darr. Get some sleep, so you're well rested for your journey west...across the plains."

Conra lifted himself out of his rocker without another word and plopped down amid the covers of his bed. Darr stared after him in astonishment.

* * * *

Midnight had passed when Darr woke himself up from a dreamless sleep, throwing his blankets off and sitting upright. His drowsiness was a fog inhibiting his senses, and he took a moment to let it fade. His siblings were sprawled out across the floor beside him, bundled in blankets and sleeping soundly. How he could endure this journey without them was beyond his comprehension. They were the links that tied him to home, to reality.

Conra's bed sat empty. The pungent aroma of tobacco smoke came from outside. His father smoked sometimes. The memory created a pang of longing so powerful his throat constricted and his eyes watered. Darr sighed, shaking away the nostalgia, and lifted himself off the floor, making his way over the sleeping forms around him. He wasn't sure why, but the urge to talk to Conra one more time couldn't be ignored. When he reached the front door, he pulled back the latch, opened the door, and slipped out into the night.

On the porch, he found Conra in a wide swinging chair, his gray head directed out onto the black wash of the plains beyond. The Elf held a pipe in his mouth, its bowl gleaming red in the darkness, but when Darr appeared, Conra removed it.

"You should be asleep, Boy," the Elf croaked.

Darr sat down in the chair alongside the Elf. Conra's gaze was on him, but Darr did nothing except look out at the night. Though he played at being aloof, he somehow aided both himself and Conra. His certainty was overwhelming. The Elf watched him for a moment longer before returning his pipe to his mouth, and together, they sat in silence for several minutes.

A question came to Darr, a faint whispering that directed which tone and intensity he should use. "What's the real reason you won't take us through the Barricades?"

For a long time Conra continued to stare out at the plains, his pipe still in his mouth more as an accessory rather than a tool. When at last Conra looked over at him, a wave of fear washed over Darr, its source unknown, but it vanished moments later, snuffed out in the night.

"Over the years, I've explored the Cortazian territories as no other has," the Elf began, his voice low. "I know every nook and cranny of the Barricades, and I know how far along the plains I've traveled by the layout of hills and trees. The Barricades are my last source of adventure, and they're starting to bore me."

Conra took a steadying breath. "Death has come for me, Darr, and it passed me by. It made me think about a lot of things."

The voice in the back of Darr's head warned him to remain silent even though the Elf's words startled him. He waited. After a few moments, Conra continued.

"Several weeks ago, I sat out here and watched the night. When I finally decided to go back to bed, that's when I saw the shadows. At first, I believed what I saw was nothing more than the swaying of the trees far off in the distance. I was wrong. There weren't any trees in that direction. Maybe it was a caravan of some sort, but it moved too easily to be wagons. I realized the shadows were much closer than I had estimated."

A breeze picked up a scattering of embers from Conra's pipe, but he ignored them. "My first impulse was to step back inside the house and forget what I saw, but I couldn't. I'd heard of the Soul Seekers, but I didn't believe the rumors to be true. This is my land, and I know it better than any. If something threatened, I needed to know what it was."

Conra bit at his lower lip before going on. "I slipped off the porch and crept into the tall grass, my Elven senses, and my huntsman skills, aiding me. I couldn't see the passing shadows anymore, but I sensed something close, and I ducked down into the grass and peered into the night."

A wave of fear washed through Darr, and this time, it wasn't easily dispelled. The fear wasn't coming from him, but rather, it came from Conra. Projected through the Currents, Conra's fear came unbidden and easily read.

"Stars lit the landscape," the Elf said. "I waited, but nothing presented itself, but my instincts were crying out to me there was something terribly wrong. And suddenly, the shadows I'd been stalking appeared less than a hundred feet in front of me. They moved like their bodies were carried on the wind. They were tall, at least seven feet in height, their bodies wrapped in tattered robes and cowls. Nothing of their features were visible. Their bodies were born of the darkness itself."

The bowl of Conra's pipe glowed red, and he breathed the smoke in deep before exhaling. "My whole body went cold. I looked up at the things. They didn't appear to be searching, but I knew better. They sensed me, and they were waiting for me to reveal myself. So I closed my eyes and shut out the image of them. I slowed my breathing to almost nothing and let my heartbeat adjust until it beat only as a muffled thump. I didn't let my eyes open. I knew if I did, my fear would give me away."

Conra took another steadying breath. "And then I was alone. The change came quick, like a clamp had been released from my throat. I opened my eyes and saw nothing. The shadows had disappeared, gone back to wherever they came from."

The old Elf exhaled in a soundless rush. Conra's face became more at ease, his muscles relaxed, his teeth unclenched. When he looked over at Darr at last, his eyes glistened in the faint starlight.

"That's why I didn't want to take you through the mountains," Conra whispered. "When those things came for me, I saw how dangerous this world has become. I'd never want to put you kids in front of that kind of danger."

Darr shook his head. "Conra, those black things are the same ones we're trying to put an end to. And sooner or later, we'll have to face them, but our chances of doing so are greater the longer we're out in the open. If we go through the Barricades, it'll shave nearly two weeks off our travel time. If we go along the plains, we'll be exposed to the Soul Seekers for that much longer."

Conra laughed, slow but sharp in the silence of the night. The Elf tapped out the bowl of his pipe, and rose to his feet, leaving Darr staring up at him. "That's probably why I'll take you through the mountains, Boy," he said, followed by a sharp cackle. "I don't know how you did it, but somehow, you made me face my fear. You held it up to the light, and I saw it for what it was."

Conra reached out and clapped Darr hard on the shoulder. "Now, go get some sleep. You'll need the rest for tomorrow." He turned and leaned against a porch post, ignoring Darr while he looked back out to the plains.

Darr watched him, wondering what in the world he'd done and how, but the voice in his mind had gone silent.

Chapter Eighteen

"The spirits of the Currents found something in Caeranol that no other living being possessed. He alone could walk in both worlds, not as a mere traveler, but as someone who could transcend his physical form and become a spirit creature. Unlike the Archons of the Sephirs, he would become an Archon of the Light, a champion to uphold the balance of life in a world succumbing to death."

~From A Current History of Ictar, as told by Nidic Waq

Warm daylight and the pleasant smells of fresh bread filled the cabin. Darr opened his eyes, refreshed and feeling better about himself for the first time in weeks despite Conra's haunting story the night before. He stood up from the floor and stretched. He walked stiff-legged to the table where Erec and Jinn sat before a breakfast of hot tea, fresh bread and fruit.

"I thought you were going to sleep the morning away," Erec said, a smirk turning his mouth on edge.

Darr brushed the hair from his eyes and shrugged, taking a seat alongside Jinn. Conra appeared a moment later, bringing in a blast of cool air from outside when he stepped through the front door.

"Lots to do today," the Elf said. "You better eat before we get started. Go on. Eat up."

Darr feigned ignorance and remained silent. Jinn shook her head. "Before we get started doing what, Conra?"

The old Elf snagged an apple from the table and took a bite. He chewed and swallowed before answering. "We have a lot of supplies to gather if we're going through the Barricades, so c'mon, let's get moving."

Erec slumped back in his chair. "I thought you weren't taking us," he said.

Conra set the apple down on the table and stared. "A man can change his mind, can't he? Now let's get a move on, Erec, before I change my mind."

Jinn and Erec appeared pleased with the Elf's announcement despite his forceful response. The decision meant they wouldn't have to fumble their way through the Barricades or risk being caught out on the open plains. With Conra's help, they would reach their destination faster than they could have hoped.

After breakfast, Conra put the three siblings to work. Supplies needed to be gathered–ropes and picks for climbing, and warmer clothing for the higher elevations. Spare water skins would have to be brought, not only for the higher elevations, but also for their trek through the Karahesian Wastelands. Darr and his siblings rebuilt their packs while Conra gathered dried foods, of which he had plenty since he rarely traveled anymore.

Midmorning waned into afternoon, but Conra, a meticulous survivalist, refused to leave anything to chance. He made sure to outfit himself and each of them with the necessary provisions that would keep them alive through the cold of the mountains and desolate wastelands beyond. Water skins were filled, extra foodstuffs were carefully stored, and warm blankets were fastened on top of each of their packs. Darr couldn't help but feel safer in Conra's presence with all the preparations he was making on their behalf.

They sat on the front porch before leaving, eating a quick lunch. "I wasn't much older than Erec is when I met your father," Conra said, followed by a soft laugh. "Your father was in Mertz on a supply errand and I wandered into the city looking for someone to help me haul building supplies south to build my cabin. Hydle was the first and last person I asked."

Darr swallowed a bite of apple and asked, "You worked together for a couple months, didn't you?"

155

Conra nodded. "Hauling all those supplies took almost a month, and Hydle stayed another month and helped me build. Yes, we had a lot of fun working together."

At hearing that, Darr no longer felt so bad about leaving home in exchange for the journey he'd always wanted. His father had done the same thing. When he looked back at Conra, the Elf had a distant look on his face.

"I haven't seen your father in over five years," Conra said with a sigh. "You never can get the past back."

The Elf dismissed himself and cleaned up their lunch. A wave of unexplained frustration washed through Darr when Conra left. Was he the source of the feeling? If so, why would he feel such a thing simply by remembering his past?

After securing his home, Conra announced it was time to go. He led them in a southerly direction towards the looming wall of the Barricade Mountains. Darr lost himself looking up at the gargantuan peaks. The foothills rose sharply, turning into sheer cliffs stretching hundreds of feet into the air to their jagged heights. The Barricades had less the look of mountains than the appearance of some monstrous wall created by the Elements.

No trail marked the way forward as they started up into the foothills. A slight parting in the trees led to the dark wall of rock ahead. It didn't appear there was any opening into the mountains. Darr mentioned his doubts to Erec and Jinn, but neither appeared bothered. Like him, they could only rely on Conra's navigational expertise. The slope grew steep and the climb became more treacherous as they had to grasp at roots and tree limbs to pull themselves further along. Still, the wall of the mountain appeared solid. Maybe Conra really didn't know his way.

When they reached the top of the slope, the Elf took them to the east through a narrow fissure in the Barricades wide enough to squeeze a body through. Conra looked back and beckoned them to follow before disappearing into the little fissure. Darr and his siblings stepped into the dim light of the narrow opening. A sliver of light shone from its opposite end.

Once they cleared the fissure, a land of stone ravines and valleys, cliffs and overhangs sprawled before them. Little foliage could be seen, and the only water Darr saw tumbled from on high and disappeared into the dark gorges below. The Barricade Mountains were a world composed of rock, with no rhyme or reason to their workings. Cliff ledges led upwards and spiraled onto distant peaks, others led down into its depthless valleys. Darr never would've been able to navigate his way through the mountains alone. The looks of confusion on his siblings' faces confirmed his realization.

Conra looked back and smiled, a reassuring presense. "Now, let's see if we can get out of this mess." The Elf scanned their surroundings for a few moments before leading them out along one of the rocky ledges.

Hardly any words passed between the three siblings for fear of interfering with Conra's observations. The landscape of the mountains provided little scenery, and their journey quickly turned into a tiresome march.

When they stopped for the night, Conra built a fire, from the wood that Erec had been collecting throughout the day, beneath a rock overhang.

"So, what do you think, Darr," Conra called out, meeting Darr's gaze. He finished throwing together a modest soup using a few roots and herbs he'd packed and settled back against the rock wall in the falling darkness to let it simmer. "You still think you could've gotten through here by yourself?"

Darr shook his hair away from his face. He poked at the fire with a stick, glad that they had enough wood to cook a hot meal and to ward off the evening cold "I would've gotten lost before we passed through that fissure. Thanks again, Conra. It means everything to us that you're here."

The Elf produced his pipe and lit it, sending a huge blue cloud of smoke into the air in the process. "I love these mountains. I love the challenge they present. Not many men can get themselves through here. I almost didn't on my first time around."

Jinn hunched forward, her green eyes shining. "You got lost here?"

"Well of course, Miss Reintol," Conra said followed by a laugh. "Everybody has to if they're ever going to learn how to get through. I got badly lost and almost starved to death right before I moved over here. I'd heard about the Barricades, and as a headstrong youth, I decided I'd be able to get past them. I was wrong, but fortunately, I had some help and a brilliant bit of luck. A trapper happened through and saw me wandering around half-crazed with starvation. He nursed me back to health and took me through."

"How come you never talk about your past, Conra?" Erec asked, his brown eyes intense as he sat back from the fire. "Father said you never told him what brought you here, only that you came from the Elven territories."

A long stream of smoke rose out of the old Elf's mouth. He looked at Erec as if in challenge for daring to ask. "I believe a man should be allowed to live with his past. Like young Darr over there, we all have secrets that bind us to our past and make us who we are. If we go around spouting off to everyone who asks what we keep from them, we lose who we are and what makes us special."

Erec stared in silence, oblivious. Conra sighed and said, "Like the three of you, I saw things in my youth that changed the way I saw the world. I didn't see something as evil as that creature you ran across in Stern, but I saw the Sephirs have power we can't comprehend and the Divine can't control." Conra swallowed hard and shook his head. "We're supposed to live in a world where we're safe without magic, but perhaps it's the other way around. Without magic, we're defenseless."

"Magic should be controlled," Erec said, his tone set the words in stone. "The Divine and the Kings of Ictar keep careful watch over the Sephirs to prevent their magic from ever being abused again. If magic is being used, it's because of lunatics like Nidic Waq who have no respect for the rules."

Heat rose into Darr's face at his brother's words. "Nidic Waq is a Summoner, Erec. I have the ability to harness the magic of the Sephirs like he does. Does that mean I have no respect for the rules because I'm a Summoner?"

Conra looked stunned by Darr's words, but he remained silent.

"You already know how I feel about your use of magic," Erec said, his eyes fierce. "If the Spirit Summoners start using magic, the Aeon Wars are going to happen all over again. The Divine should've foreseen this happening and enforced their rules by any means..."

Erec cut himself off, but Darr stared in open shock. Jinn refused to remain silent. "So what're you saying?" she asked in a dangerous tone. "Should the Divine lock up all the Summoners to prevent them from using magic? Should they kill them off so they won't be a threat? You're talking about your own brother!"

"I know. I don't know what I was saying, but I think the Summoners should be watched. What if the wrong person gets hold of the magic and we end up back where we were with the Aeon Wars? What if it ends up worse, and we end up getting thrown back into chaos? Did you ever stop to think where these Soul Seekers came from—where did they learn how to summon the Ovids? I don't think any of this would be happening if Spirit Summoners weren't allowed to..."

"Don't finish what you're about to say, Erec," Conra interrupted. Solemn and dark, the Elf's features looked wise beyond even his years. "The trouble with youth is you never think things through before you speak. And when you think to take them back, it's too late. I know you love your brother, and I'm not entirely sure what's going on, but I know you wouldn't wish Darr any harm." Conra looked back at Darr. "As for magic, it's an inescapable part of this land. The kings and the Divine think they can contain it by keeping a close eye on the Sephirs, but magic isn't like that. It's a part of Ictar, and I don't think anybody will ever change that."

"Somebody has to," Erec retorted. "Otherwise, we're all going to end up dead or worse."

"That's just the way life works sometimes, Boy," Conra replied. "If a river runs south, there's not much you can do to change its course. You can block it off, build a dam, but if it wants to, that river will break free."

"Well, I'm not accepting that," his brother said and jumped to his feet. In the glow of the fire, Erec stormed off into the darkness of the surrounding cliffs.

Conra raised his hand as Darr and Jinn both started to rise. "Let him go," he said. "Erec needs to figure things out on his own. He'll be all right. He's conflicted between what he sees with his eyes and what he thinks he knows to be true."

Conra checked on their soup, then poured steaming cups full of the concoction for his charges and himself. As the tension eased, the conversation turned back to the mountains again. Conra's words became a buzzing in Darr's ears as his thoughts wandered back to his confrontation with Erec. Darr understood his brother's reasoning, but enslaving the Spirit Summoners suggested Erec's beliefs were more rigid than Darr could ever imagine.

Darr sighed and stared off into the darkness after Erec. What could he do that would tell him he understood his doubts no matter how different their beliefs might be? He reclined against the wall of the cliff overhang while Conra and Jinn talked, concentrating on the night sounds around him and took deep breaths. Darr closed his eyes for only a moment...

...when he opened them, he'd slipped into the Currents.

Darr's deep state of relaxation had allowed him access. He used similar techniques to consciously listen to the spirits. Perhaps he was getting more accustomed to the

Currents, and in turn, passage between his world and theirs became like breathing air in and out of his lungs.

The spirits danced around the white aura of his Light, their whispers audible and encouraging him to make peace with his brother. Jinn and Conra still sat before him. Their Lights strong and shining, huddled before the swelling red aura of their campfire. He found Erec's Light standing some distance off. The Summoner flew to him, closing the gap between them in something short of an eye blink.

Now that he was there, Darr didn't know what to do. Erec wouldn't be able to hear him if he said something. What if he let himself feel what Erec did? Darr hesitated at first, contemplating the repercussions of invading Erec's privacy. In the end, his curiousity broke his wall of resolve. He let down his defenses, and Erec's emotions washed over him.

Feelings of self-loathing and remorse overcame Darr. Doubt and utter sadness were accompanied by flashes of his brother's memories. After a few moments, his brother's perceptions became indistinguishable from his own. Resistant, Darr rebuilt his defenses. He felt sick inside. He'd overstepped his bounds by searching Erec's Light, and yet, the spirits urged him to right Erec's perceived wrongs.

Nidic Waq and Racall both had been able to generate emotions within other people. Racall told him they weren't emotions pulled out of thin air, but emotions buried deep within a person, then pulled to the surface and made stronger.

He lowered his defenses once more, letting his Light open up to his brother. Erec's emotions and memories came rushing forward again, a torrent of regret and anger. The Summoner held his ground against his brother's feelings, resisting the force of the Currents to merge with Erec's Light. Darr filtered through the emotions, looking at the memories and the feelings they invoked in Erec, tapestries hung on his conflicted mind. Hidden amid the tumbled mass *lurked a memory of himself and Erec not more than a few years ago.*

They were swimming in a lake near Tyfor, but Darr went too far out in the waters and began to drown. Erec leapt in after him and swam to his aid, pulling him to the shore with no thought to his own safety. The entire time, Erec's only fear was that he'd lose his brother. No matter what their beliefs, the brothers shared a bond that inspired Erec to do anything for Darr.

Focused, the Summoner reached into Erec's Light and pulled the memory to the surface, an impossible sensation, like holding onto the wind.

Within the fraction of time allowed in the Currents, Erec's emotions began to change. His anger and self-loathing eased. Darr had brought some peace to his brother, that alone was progress. He relaxed his thoughts and retreated back to the dark night of the Barricade Mountains...

When he opened his eyes, Conra and Jinn still huddled before the fire, warming themselves against the chill. Darr said nothing about his encounter in the Currents. Jinn might understand, but , his summoning abilities were too new and untested with her. Several minutes later, Erec reappeared from out of the darkness. He sat down before the dying fire and stared at its red embers.

Only Conra spoke, "We have a long ways to go tomorrow, everyone needs to get some sleep."

It would be hard to do. Even after Darr closed his eyes, he still saw Erec's sad face.

Chapter Nineteen

"Caeranol watched the last of his people disappear from the world that had once been their home. Then he entered the Currents and took the full strength of the Light into himself. His body was absorbed into the land, but because the Light came freely from the spirits, Caeranol's humanity remained. Tasked with protecting the land from the Devoid, Caeranol went to work using his power as an Archon. He hid the lesser races from the Devoid, and he protected the remaining relics left behind by the Ancients. Then he confronted the Devoid one final time."

~From A Current History of Ictar, as told by Nidic Waq

They followed Conra along the mazelike cliffs and valleys of the Barricade Mountains. Despite his experience as a guide, Conra made a few wrong turns, forcing them to retrace their steps and start over. Darr spent most of the journey with Jinn. Conra was too focused on navigating to say much of anything, and Erec had slipped into a reclusive mood, trailing far behind his siblings. Jinn and Darr left him alone, talking amongst themselves about things other than Summoners and magic.

It wasn't until they came down out of the Barricades three days later that Erec came around again. The Karahesian Wasteland's blasted landscape sprawled out before them, and its bleak atmosphere would've shaken anyone.

"Ictar really is in a state of imbalance between the Elements," Darr announced.

Conra shook his head and grumbled, "What you see has nothing to do with imbalance." He didn't elaborate.

They settled themselves for the night on a cliff at the base of the Barricades. From there, the dry, barren earth of the wasteland stretched out to the sea. Long, winding cracks riddled the landscape from the scorching heat, like a large clay plate left in the kiln for too long. Darr couldn't see anything living.

Sitting before their fire they ate supper, while Conra was content to watch the landscape and smoke.

"Long ago, this region was filled with life," the Elf said in a hushed voice. "During the Aeon Wars, the races took to fighting using elementals created from the Sephirs. The forces of magic unleashed during the fighting left the Karahesian razed and empty of life."

"That's horrible," Jinn whispered, her shock apparent on her face. "How could the races have survived if they were doing such terrible things?"

The Elf looked over at her with sadness in his eyes. "They were negligent, Jinn. But they were also afraid of the power they used. If the Sephirs fell out of balance, chaos would return, so they took small pieces of magic to try to conquer their enemies. Hmph. Even with their small magic, they sure did make a mess of the world."

Darr and Erec listened from opposite sides of the campfire, eased back on their elbows while their sister and Conra talked.

"How do you know so much about the Aeon Wars?" Jinn asked, edging closer to the heat of the fire.

"I made it my business to know," Conra said. "The wars might be done and over with, but they've shaped this land, turned it into what it is today. I don't think we should forget the impact they've had on Ictar."

All three siblings nodded in agreement. Erec had mellowed since their argument in the Barricades. Maybe Erec had thought things over and come to different conclusions. Or perhaps, Darr's excursion into the Currents had done something after all.

The four slept soundly that night and woke early to the unnatural heat of the Karahesian. Even during the fall months, the wastelands were hot. Rain only fell late in the winter, and even that didn't change the barren land much. The Elf led them south out of the foothills, leading them in a direct line with the mountains both for navigation and to keep then shaded during the hottest hours of the afternoon.

By the time they stopped at nightfall, the temperature had dropped to near freezing. They had no wood for a fire, so they ate a cold meal and wrapped themselves in blankets and tried to sleep. The second day went along in much the same manner, but now the terrain began to descend. Darr scanned the horizon. Nothing but the Karahesian stretched in every direction except where the Barricades rose up to block his vision. It didn't look like they would be nearing the end of the wasteland any time soon.

When they stopped again that night, Darr's thoughts lingered on his father. He sat alone in the darkness of their camp, wrapped in his forest cloak and blanket to fight off the cold. Conra and Erec slept, but Jinn stirred where she lay on the ground beside him. She turned her head towards him, her face outlined in the white light of the stars. She sat up and shifted her body over to his.

"What's the matter?" Jinn whispered.

Darr shook his head. "I was thinking about Father. I wish I could do something to check on him."

"Can't you go to the Currents?"

"I've tried, but it's hard."

Jinn's gaze dropped. "I've been thinking about him too, but we all made a choice in coming here. I'm sure he's fine, probably just a little worried."

The Summoner reached out and hugged his sister. "Thanks, Jinn," he whispered back. "I guess I'm feeling like I should try to check on him."

She pulled away and looked him in the eye. "Darr, you don't have to do anything more than what's expected of you. You're still learning. Besides, didn't Nidic Waq and Racall warn you about spending too much time in the Currents? Maybe you should try to let things come to you rather than trying to go to them."

Jinn was right, of course. She was most of the time.

Maybe he should relax and let things take their natural course.

"I'll watch myself. You're right. I've been trying too hard."

Jinn smiled. "Erec and I, even Conra, we're all here to support you. You aren't alone in this. We may not have magic, but we have other qualities that will aid you."

Jinn turned and rolled herself into her blankets. Darr lay back, the hard earth beneath him. Thoughts of his father continued to force their way into his mind. Maybe Jinn was wrong. He needed to practice summoning in order to improve. Yes, Nidic Waq had warned him to use the Currents only as needed, but how could he help his friends and family if he didn't know how? He had the means, but he didn't have the experience.

The Summoner made up his mind. He wouldn't put his family in danger again. He would master the spirit realm until no doubt remained on its workings.

He slipped into the Currents in search of his father.

* * * *

Darr soared through the wisteria light, flitting between the Lights of people connected to the physical world while he listened to the spirits. Nothing new revealed itself. Every time he reached out to find his father, he was met with resistance.

—The Currents are not easily navigated—

—Shadows deceive us all—

The spirits were not encouraging. Worse, their words confirmed Nidic Waq's warning to be wary of the Currents. Racall had told him to be mindful as well, though he couldn't remember what the Archon had shown him. Darr suspected his presense might be doing more harm than good.

One more try, and then he'd retreat for the night.

He quieted his mind, letting his Light drift through the

spirit realm. The Lights of the physical world faded away, leaving the spirits to swirl around him. Soon, he quieted even them, and Darr was alone. He focused his thoughts, not on his father as he'd been doing, but on himself. If he couldn't break through the befuddled Currents to find his father, perhaps there was something about his own abilities he could learn.

For a long time, Darr paid close attention to his Light, noticing how it reacted to thoughts and feelings. He longed to make sure his father was okay, and some part of his Light resonated with that feeling. Is this feeling desire? Is my desire urging me to explore?

"Show me...Show me what I can't find..."

The feeling emptied out of Darr, leaving him hollow, though the urgency of the feeling remained. His Light folded inward, compacting down into his desire.

An aura of white appeared before him. The Light of another began to shine, cutting through the wisteria glow of the Currents. Darr struggled to reach out to this new Light as he continued to shrink down into himself. His concentration slipped, his mind lost its focus. The Light faded away, but Darr knew who it belonged to.

"Jinn."

Darr's Light unfolded, and he focused his thoughts back on the physical world. Jinn's Light, as well as the Lights of Conra and Erec appeared around him. Nothing appeared out of place. Darr drifted closer to Jinn's Light. What had he seen a moment ago? What was it about her that had drawn her to him?

Confused and exhausted, the Summoner let the matter drop. He'd explore what he'd seen another day. For tonight, his Light was tired, and he went back to the physical world.

* * * *

The four set out determined to reach Oasis by nightfall.

Darr trailed silently at the end of the procession. His mood had darkened since last night, having had no success in locating his father. He kept reminding himself of his inexperience, yet somehow that wasn't enough. He'd summoned the Archon of Earth for spirit's sake. Yet, every attempt at finding his father had failed. Last night's attempt had created more confusion for him.

When they stopped for lunch, Conra informed them they weren't far from the edges of the wasteland. The flats would end at the Valley of Kaehn within a few hours. There they would be able to find safety with the city of Oasis, if they could gain entrance. The Kurflinese were suspicious of strangers, especially those coming from the Karahesian. They would have to be careful about how they approached the city guards.

Less than an hour after they stopped for lunch, a stirring within the Currents came over Darr like a sickness growing in his stomach. Absorbed in his dark mood, Darr ignored the disturbance. When he finally noticed it, he didn't have to enter the Currents to hear the spirits. Darr tried to pick out one of the crowded voices, but he could sense upset and anxiety. Darr went back to his ruminations, but the spirits returned with their same jumbled messages. He listened again, wondering if perhaps he'd missed something the first time. Nothing had changed in their urgings, so he dismissed them once more.

A quick scan of the horizon revealed nothing out of the ordinary. The Karahesian's blasted landscape was the same, except to the south where it sloped downward and disappeared into a wash of yellow and green that became the fields of Kurflin. Ahead of him, Erec, Jinn, and Conra walked down the slope towards the valley ahead, but no one appeared concerned.

Maybe he'd lost his ability to communicate with the spirits since leaving Racall. Maybe his abilities were tied to the Archon, but that didn't make sense. He dug through his memories in search of a different answer.

While deep in his thoughts, the Currents ripped open. The feeling came swiftly then vanished, but Darr knew what it meant.

A deep rumbling filled his ears and the ground beneath him shifted enough to cause him to stumble. Darr called out to Conra just as the Elf looked back in surprise. Jinn and Erec turned also, their faces reflecting a mix of fear and curiousity. Darr put his ear to the Currents and waited. Racall had told him about elementals, how the weak points between the Four Elements could break and form them. He was supposed to be looking for those breaks, and he'd failed in doing so. Whatever was coming would be a direct consequence.

The rumbling turned to a roar, accompanied by tremors that shook the four to their knees. A knot formed in the pit of Darr's stomach. The hard surface of the Karahesian broke apart, separating the Summoner and his companions. Two silvery-black spears, surged upwards through the earth. A pair of claws appeared, like those belonging to sea crabs, only much larger. The killing appendages lifted high above the four before crashing down into the earth, pulling the rest of the monstrosity up from beneath. What surfaced was a crab, only it stood ten feet tall, armored in a shell of tarnished silver covered in wicked-looking spines. The creature's spindly legs didn't appear they'd support its weight, but Darr doubted that would slow it down.

The creature was an elemental, torn from the Light of the Earth Sephir.

"A scattercrab!" Conra yelled, his face bright with wonder. He traced his steps around towards Darr. "I didn't think these existed any..."

"Get away, Conra!" Darr shouted, running to push the Elf away, but the scattercrab moved faster. The creature rotated its body and drove one of its claws into the ground between them, sending them both flying. It rammed its other claw out towards Erec and Jinn, but they were both quick enough to dodge out of the way.

Ideas raced through Darr's head, fragmented solutions to the problem he'd caused, but there was no time. Erec made a desperate attempt to draw the scattercrab away, but the creature turned towards him. Conra fired a bolt from his crossbow, but it bounced away, succeeding only in drawing the crab back towards them. Darr and Conra sprinted away as the monstrous claws tore into the earth once more. Erec ran beneath the scattercrab when its back turned, forcing his sword upwards between its metal shell. With a loud clang, the sword impacted and shattered.

The crab shifted, aware now of Erec's presence beneath it. Jinn ran forward waving her arms, trying to distract the crab long enough for Erec to escape. She narrowly avoided a claw swinging over her head, giving Erec the chance he needed to leap to safety, but the crab caught him during his retreat. Its claw swung out, and with a thunderous clap, it sent him flying.

The sight of his brother tumbling across the flats was enough for Darr. The Summoner steadied himself...

...*He'd expected to find the scattercrab moving in the spirit realm like the Water Ovid and Racall, but the elemental's bright green aura stood motionless. Elemetals, it seemed, were timeless.*

Darr gazed through the wisteria light. He needed the Archon of Air and its permission to use its magic. Where would he find it?

—You worry too much, Summoner—

—Your fears eat you alive—

The words of the spirits were reprimanding, but helpful. Racall and Nidic Waq had been telling him the same thing from the beginning. But how could he overcome his doubts when he hadn't learned anything about himself?

—You have learned much—

—You have yet to utilize that knowledge—

The light of the spirits swirled around him. Darr calmed himself. In the Currents he was somewhat safe from what went on in Ictar. The scattercrab and time itself had no meaning here.

He fixed his gaze on the yellow star identifying the Sephir of Air. Its light flickered weakly. The Summoner flew to it with the thought of taking a single step.

He hung in the air before the golden light of the Air Sephir, and reached out to the pulsating light. The Light of his body mingled with the Sephir's. The Archon's mercurial presence came to Darr as soon as their connection was forged.

−You are the Summoner who traveled with Racall, are you not−

Darr concurred. "Who are you?"

−I am the Archon of Air−I was called Tamas by the Ancients−You are nothing like them−

The Summoner ignored the comment, even though it was odd. "I need your help. An elemental has escaped on the Karahesian, and I need your magic to neutralize its own."

Arrogance flooded out of the Sephir.

−I am aware of the scattercrab−What do you expect me to do about it−

Shock roared through Darr. Didn't the Archon care? "I need your help. Only the Element of Air can counter the imbalance that created the scattercrab. Isn't there something you can do to help me?"

−Not when you talk to me like that−

Frustration welled up. The Archon of Air acted nothing like Racall. It was conceited to the point of being rude.

A memory returned from when Darr first called out to Racall in the Currents. The spirits had dragged him down and tried to make him one of their own. Out of fear for losing himself, he'd called out to the Earth Archon, not by using his physical voice, but with his Light.

"I need..."

Darr stopped himself, hearing the words come from the part of himself that still perceived the Currents as a physical world. He concentrated. Light and mirrored images made up the Currents. Everything he perceived to be real only imitated the outside world.

Darr didn't breathe for there was no air. He didn't wet his lips for he had no lips to wet.

–Tamas, lend me the magic of the Air Sephir to counter that of the scattercrab–

The light of the Sephir flared once where it connected with Darr, sending golden tendrils snaking into the Light of his arm. The arrogance of the Archon lessened, turning to mild satisfaction.

–Well done, Summoner–Now let us see how well you handle that magic–

Darr examined the golden light where it flowed through his arm when he was expelled from the Currents...

...When he emerged, Darr clenched his right hand into a fist, fighting past the burning sensation in his arm.

As if sensing the magic he carried, the scattercrab turned on him. The creature let out a piercing cry and its spindly legs carried it forward in a rush of torn earth, its shining claws lifting high in preparation to crush him.

Darr stumbled backwards, cradling his arm against his body as electric fire coursed through his flesh and bone. When the creature was a few yards away from him, Darr thought fleetingly of running. Instead, he released the light from his arm, and the magic of the Air Sephir took shape.

The magic ripped the Summoner's arm forward with a sharp thrust. White bolts of lightning surged out of his flesh and slammed into the scattercrab, picking it up and throwing it backwards. The magic of the Sephir didn't stop. The lightning bolts surging from his arm tore into the crab, ripping off chunks of the metal shell. The scattercrab struggled and screeched, but the lightning pinned it fast to the ground, shredding it.

It's shell disintegrated and sand poured out of it, sending up clouds of dust. When the last bolt tore through it, the scattercrab was nothing but an empty metal husk atop a pile of sand. With the magic expended, Darr lowered his arm. Jinn and Conra's stares lingered on him until they were drawn to Erec who layed sprawled out, face down.

Colors and lines began to blur together and fade. Numbness filled Darr's ears, and he collapsed to the ground.

Chapter Twenty

"The battle tore the world apart from one end to another as Caeranol and the Devoid fought in both the physical world and the Currents. Caeranol won, though he could not destroy the Devoid, only disable it. Caeranol released the Light trapped within the Devoid, and using the Sephirs, Caeranol imprisoned the Devoid within a place of nothingness. Caeranol hoped the Devoid would wither away and die, with no life to feed it."

~From A Current History of Ictar, as told by Nidic Waq

Darr opened his eyes in a lazy flickering motion that left him dizzy. Conra crouched over him with a smile on his seamed, wrinkled face. Darr lifted his head, but Conra eased him back down.

"Careful now, boy. Don't want you hurting yourself again. Here, take this."

Conra placed a water skin against Darr's lips and poured cool water down his throat. The Summoner drank, gasping for air between gulps. When he finished, Darr slid himself up into a sitting position despite Conra's protests. Still light-headed, from his fall or from the magic, Darr wasn't sure. His summoning had taken a lot out of him, yet the particulars of the experience were still vague in his mind. He remembered nothing save the Archon of Air giving him the magic of the Sephir before being thrust from the Currents. Everything else he remembered as a blur of color and sensation.

"How do you feel?" Conra asked. "You've been out for almost an hour."

Darr shook his head. "I'm a little confused and dizzy, but nothing hurts if that's what you're asking."

Conra was emphatic. "I'm not surprised if your brain's a little rushed about," he said. "That was quite a light show you put on. When I heard you and your siblings talking about magic, I had no idea you were gonna pull a trick like that out of your pocket."

Darr had no idea either. He thought by going to the Archon of Air and asking for the magic of its Sephir, it would come into Ictar the same way Racall had, a physical embodiment of its element. Instead, Darr received its magic and was sent back to Ictar to wield it.

Darr started to speak, but Conra cut him off, his eyes bright. "I've never seen anything like that, and I've seen some strange things. The Summoners in Navda can't do what you just did, boy, do you know that?"

Darr gave a wan smile, hoping the Elf would sense he didn't want to talk about this particular subject. "I know, Conra. This is something I only recently learned, and I'm not too confident with it..."

"Incredible," the Elf exclaimed, slapping his knee. "I never would've guessed the way you three were carrying on. I didn't think magic could be channeled like that. Simply amazing. You were throwing lightning bolts at that crab for spirit's sake."

Conra's enthusiasm grew tiresome. Darr's thoughts were too muddled. Behind Conra, Erec sat upright beside Jinn, his face stricken. Bandages wrapped his torso.

"How's Erec?" he asked Conra, desperate to change the subject.

"Aw, he'll be all right," the Elf said, turning his head to look at Erec. "Your brother can take some punishment, that's for sure. That scattercrab knocked him a good one, making a pretty good mess of his back, but I patched him up best I could.."

Darr picked himself up off the ground, taking a moment to stand and make sure all his parts were working. His dizziness passed while he took measured steps over to Erec and Jinn.

"Are you okay?" Jinn asked, a mix of fear and concern

reflected in her eyes.

Darr nodded his head, silent before Erec's cold gaze.

"Jinn said you used magic." Erec breathed the words like a curse.

Darr nodded. "Yes. We can talk about it on the way to Oasis. Do you feel up to the walk?"

Erec's expression told him 'no', but he bowed his head and tried to stand. Darr gave him his hand and levered him to his feet. Erec still needed Darr's support in order to walk.

"Conra, how far to Oasis?" Darr asked, his brother's weight bore down on him already.

The Elf scanned the horizon and the sky. "I'd say we have about two hours before we reach the Valley of Kaehn. Another hour after that. If we hurry, we can make it before nightfall."

Jinn and Conra split the contents of Erec's pack to distribute the extra weight since he could no longer carry it. Satisfied with their new burdens, the four set out.

With the sun setting behind the mountains at their backs darkness fell quickly. If not for the moon and starlight to guide them, they would have had to camp another night out in the open. Conra led the way across the fields of the valley, taking them straight for the walls of Oasis. From where it sat between the edge of the valley and cliffs of the Barricades, the city took on a forbidding look. Towering walls stretched out of sight into the east, hiding the city behind it like an overprotective guardian. Faint torch light glimmered dully from battlements, marking the only signs of life. Darr looked at the walls and saw only paranoia of the outside world.

As they approached the city's gate, Darr saw there would be no getting in. No foot traffic moved through the gate this late at night, and a handful of soldiers guarded the walls both above and below—the militiamen of Kurflin. It would take a civil war before regiments of Cortazian soldiers patrolled Oasis, a free city in the minds of the southern territories.

Darr slowed his pace, but Conra hissed at him and told

him to keep up. The Elf slipped his hand into his pack and pulled a dark scarf free. He rolled it up and tied it around his head.

"What're you doing?" Jinn asked in a near whisper.

"I'm hiding my ears. The Kurflinese aren't very friendly to Elves."

They walked up to the city gates, and two of the guards moved toward them, an intimidating pair in their black uniforms. Darr looked up at the shadowy forms of several other soldiers watching from atop the walls. One of the approaching guards lowered a wicked looking pike, blocking the gate, while the other walked towards Conra.

"Oasis is closed to visitors for the night," the soldier called out, his voice stern.

Conra kept his composure and walked forward a few paces. "We're in need of assistance, sir," he called out. "My friends here are the children of an old friend. We were hunting crater fox up in the Barricades. Young Erec there had a nasty fall, and we were closer to Oasis than home, so I brought them here. He needs medical attention."

Another soldier appeared from the gate house, a bear of a man. While his features appeared frightening, he had a kind voice. "Coming down out of the Karahesian on a night like this—you gave the men quite a fright, what with all the talk of Soul Seekers."

Conra stood his ground and gave a disarming smile. "I assure you, we're not Soul Seekers." He opened his arms in submission.

The soldiers eyed them for a moment, as if assessing the situation. He grunted and coughed. "This is tricky business. No one goes into the city after dark. However, I can see your friend there is in need of help. We can't have fellow Kurflinese dying outside our walls, now can we?"

Conra thanked the solider, who in turn grunted and signaled to the guards on the wall to raise the portcullis and open the gates. The guard with the pike didn't move, his suspicious gaze beating down on Darr while he helped Erec along. Even though he was grateful for the kind soldier, Darr didn't like the way this country felt.

They passed through the gate and found themselves on the main thoroughfare which ran to the city's south gate. Ramshackle buildings jammed together stood guard over narrow streets and alleyways. A beast born into captivity, Oasis was oblivious to its own imprisonment.

Conra led them quickly down the street, pushing past groups of revelers from the taverns when he had to and avoiding them when he could. Erec had trouble moving his legs, forcing Darr to carry most of his weight and pull him along. They needed to find an inn soon or he would pass out.

Time dragged on, but eventually, the noise of the taverns fell away and the street opened up into a wide central square. A large, gated mansion sat in the square's center, heavily guarded and lit by torches. From its appearance alone, it might be home to a king. The entire common area and surrounding establishments were clean and quiet.

"This is the Black Square, the political center of Oasis," Conra explained. "A Cortazian governor lives under heavy guard in that mansion. He never leaves. The Kurflinese might have accepted the king's ruling governor, but they don't abide by his rules. Things are going to get ugly here before too long." The Elf motioned towards a gathering of lighted buildings on the east side of the square. "We should be able to find an inn here, but I'll probably spend everything I have on a room. It'll be worth it though. We'll be safe and well fed."

Picking his way across the star lit square, Conra took them towards the closest inn, the Red Wyvern. As the old Elf had promised, the establishment was clean, well maintained and cost a fair amount of coin for a room. Darr thought the amount too much, but he couldn't complain.

The innkeeper led the way down the inn's north wing, up a narrow staircase and down another hallway. They struggled in their effort because Erec could no longer hold himself upright. When they reached the end of the hall, the innkeeper unlocked their room and opened the door.

Their room had by far the most grandiose decor Darr had ever seen. Waxed wooden floors gleamed and a fireplace of iron and stone took up most of the left wall. Two doors stood open on the far side of the apartment leading to a bedroom on one side and a private washroom on the other. A pair of glass-paned doors led to a balcony looking out over the Black Square.

Conra hadn't rented them a room—he'd rented them a palace.

"I figured you all could use a place like this to rest," the Elf said, scratching his gray head. "There won't be anyone bothering us here. All we need to do is rest and relax and forget about...whatever it is out there."

Darr wheeled on him. "This is too much, Conra. We don't need all this. It's probably not too late to switch rooms."

Conra put up his hands and shook his head. "Go on, enjoy it. What's life without a little indulgence now and then. It might be good to have a memory of this place when we're stuck out in the cold somewhere."

Darr stared in confusion. "You mean, when *we're* stuck out in the cold—Jinn, and Erec, and I. You said you were going to take us as far as Oasis."

"Of course, of course. What was I thinking? Anyway, take the room and enjoy yourselves. I don't want to hear another word about it." Conra turned to speak with the innkeeper, closing himself off from anything more Darr had to say.

Resigned to Conra's generosity, Darr and Jinn hauled Erec into the apartment's interior and settled him on one of the couches. Their brother didn't appear aware of his surroundings or anything going on around him, but he looked pleased to be at rest. Once Erec was settled, Conra went about starting a fire in the hearth.

While they waited for the fire, Darr and Jinn stepped out

onto the balcony and the cool night air. Together they looked out on the Black Square.

"You really scared me today, you know," Jinn said in a near whisper, her face bowed down and hidden.

"You mean with the magic?" Darr asked.

Jinn nodded and raised her head, her green eyes startling. "I didn't know it would be like that. I've always believed what you said about the Currents, but I never believed...I didn't think magic existed like that..."

"I didn't either," Darr said, cutting her off. "And it scared me too. The whole thing scared me senseless. It's like I told you earlier, I didn't know what I was getting myself into when I went to the Currents, but I had to do something. This is as strange for me as it is for you."

"No, it's not." Jinn's gaze was both intense and afraid. "In some ways, you still know what you're doing. You're still aware of your actions when you go into the Currents. You know when you're talking to the Archons or spirits or whatever. Erec and I don't know what's going on until after the fact. We only see you exploding in light, and we don't know if this is the last time we'll ever see you."

Darr couldn't speak. He hadn't thought about his summoning like that. He'd spent all his time trying to include Erec and Jinn in the happenings of the Currents, but they could never truly be a part of it.

"I'm sorry," he told her. "I wish I could make you understand things better."

"You don't have to apologize," Jinn said. "Just try to remember no matter how hard you try to explain things, it's never going to be enough. There are some things that Erec and I aren't going to be able to understand." She reached out and placed her hand over his. "But I'll always love you, Darr."

The Summoner smiled and promised himself he'd take fewer risks with his magic in the future.

Conra called from the main room, summoning Jinn and Darr in from the cold. A feast awaited them that would've fed them three times over.

"Where did you get all of this, Conra?" Jinn asked, her eyes huge as she surveyed the food layed out on a serving table. Roasted chicken and potatoes, fresh vegetables and fruits, a variety of cheeses and breads, and two pitchers of ale.

Conra laughed softly. "I asked the innkeeper to put it together. He was happy to bring it up to us considering the amount I spent on this place."

Darr couldn't comprehend how Conra had managed it all, but he decided to fill his stomach and simply be grateful. Conra, Darr, and Jinn gathered before the giant fireplace, warmed now by its heat, and they helped themselves to the meal. Erec stirred from his rest, aroused by the smell of hot food. He couldn't find the strength to rise from the couch, so Jinn brought him a plate and fed him.

They were finishing their meal, wrapping up the leftover food and saving it for the morning, when a stirring within the Currents sent shivers along Darr's neck.

Jinn stopped lighting the candles in the apartment and asked, "What's wrong with you? I can tell something..."

"Quiet," Darr rasped.

The spirits said nothing, but they were uneasy. No, it wasn't unease. It was anticipation, like the way he would silence his thoughts during a thunderstorm.

Conra rose to his feet, reached for his crossbow, and clicked an iron bolt into place. Erec tried to rise, but Jinn pushed him back, telling him he'd be no good in a fight. She pulled her long knife free and eased herself before her brother, his protector this time. Uncertain, Darr looked at Conra, but the Elf only shrugged.

Darr reached down for his knife and hesitated. The knife wouldn't do him any good he sensed. He probed the edges of the Currents, trying to get a feel for the disturbance without actually submerging himself in the spirit realm. Something grew closer, almost inside the room. With careful steps, he walked to the door and placed his hand on the intricately wrought knob, turning it to pull back the latch.

He managed a quick look over his shoulder at Jinn who mouthed the words "be careful". Darr looked back at the door and threw it open to the hallway beyond.

Nidic Waq stood there, towering over him.

Chapter Twenty-One

"At peace, the world of the Ancients slowly began to heal. The Sephirs grew strong once more, and the Four Elements swallowed up the destruction caused by the Devoid. Over the course of many generations, the races of Man, Elf, Dwarf, Ogre, and Dragon emerged from the hiding places Caeranol had made for them. At first, they congregated and intermingled, but they were wary of their new world."

~From A Current History of Ictar, as told by Nidic Waq

Nidic Waq slid into the room like a wraith, his tall frame wrapped in a tattered black cloak. His physical features remained unchanged, though he looked darker and more forbidding. Darr hung onto the door for dear life. Nidic Waq's ominous presence filled the room.

The prophet's green eyes scanned the room, his wide mouth set into a flat line. It appeared as though he would become a focal point for them all to stare at in silent horror.

"Hello, Conra. Jinn. Erec," Nidic Waq said, his gaze met each of them as he said their names. How clever, Darr thought. He learned their names by listening to the spirits.

"Hello, Darr," the prophet said at last.

A connection formed with Nidic Waq in the Currents, though Darr hadn't felt it on their first meeting. It was a bond similar to the one he'd shared with Racall.

Darr rose to his feet, his uneasiness with the situation beginning to fade. He closed the door and moved around Nidic Waq towards Conra and pressed lightly on the Elf's shoulder, prompting him to lower his crossbow. Reluctant, Conra did so. It seemed too many strange things had happened for him to lower his guard completely. No matter how dark an impression he made, the prophet wouldn't harm them. Nidic Waq's emotions told Darr as much.

"What're you doing here?" Darr asked.

Nidic Waq's faint, mocking smile appeared. "I have come to see you, of course. You and your friends. Do you think I might have a seat and some of that ale?"

"You might as well," Erec blurted out. Though he lay injured on the couch, Erec looked ready to leap up and throttle the prophet at the first sign of trouble. Not that his attempt would matter all that much.

Nidic Waq ignored him and walked over to a seat across from Erec. The prophet removed the tattered black cloak he wore, revealing his familiar white robes, burned through and shredded in spots. Whatever Nidic Waq had gone through to get to Oasis, it'd been a struggle. Darr poured a cup of ale, his mind racing as to why the prophet had returned. Did it have anything to do with the scattercrab, or something more?

Darr handed him the cup and Nidic Waq lifted it to his lips. The prophet took his time. Darr stepped away, uncomfortable, and sat down next to Erec, encouraging Conra and Jinn to do the same. Maybe once everyone was sitting, the tension would ease.

Once they were all seated, the prophet set his cup on the floor and turned his attention to them. Darr sat before Nidic Waq, worried that his siblings and Conra had no idea of the man's capabilities. There wasn't anything he could do for them.

Darr found Nidic Waq's stare on him. "You've grown much since I last saw you, Summoner," the prophet said, his voice smooth despite his worn down exterior. "You've made progress. Not much, but progress nonetheless."

Darr's anger boiled to the surface, but he calmed himself and said, "I think I've done very well considering all that's happened."

"You *have* done well," the prophet said, "but not exceptional. You've taken unnecessary risks and placed yourself, and those you travel with, in danger. However, you've overcome your difficulties and day-by-day, you master your summoning abilities. You aren't the ignorant youth I met in Tyfor."

Darr eased himself back into his seat and glanced sideways at Erec. His brother watched the prophet with all the consideration he'd give a venomous snake. Conra stared in wonder, but it didn't appear he would be saying anything.

"What happened to you?" Jinn asked, fearlessly breaking the tension. Darr respected her for it. "It looks like your journey was as dangerous as ours."

Nidic Waq examined his robes without interest. "Yes, Jinn, my journey here was not a flight of luxury by any means. Would you like to hear?"

She nodded her head, and a half-smile creased the prophet's face. "After I left your brother in Tyfor, I went to Darlholme to advise the Cortazian King in his preparations for sending his army south to the Triker Forests. On my first night after leaving the outpost, the Soul Seekers found me. My objective at that point in time was to meet Darr when he came down out of Cortaz, but I couldn't risk bringing the Seekers to him. So, I led them into the mountains west of the Barricades and made my stand there. I defeated them all, but by this time, Darr had already restored the Water Sephir and was on his way into the Barricades. The obvious choice was to intercept him when he came out at Oasis."

"Why did you have to find me at all?" Darr asked. "And why couldn't you use the Currents to track me?"

Nidic Waq's smile fell. "Had you been paying attention when I first spoke with you, the Currents are in a state of confusion, making it nearly impossible to locate anything in Ictar from within the spirit realm."

Darr shallowed hard. The state of the Currents was why he couldn't locate his father. He'd exposed Conra and his siblings to the dangerous scattercrab without any reason for it. He'd taken unnecessary risks and put his desires before his own good sense, nearly costing them everything.

"The lesson has been learned, Summoner," Nidic Waq

said. His pale green eyes narrowed. "I didn't come here to teach. I came here to tell you the rest of a story. All of you. It's time you understand what it is we fight and why."

"Why wait until now, Prophet?" Erec asked, his features dark. "Why wait until we're so far from home before telling us the rest of your story?"

"Because it will not matter—your minds are already decided for other reasons."

Nidic Waq turned away from Erec's angry glare and straightened his frame. The crackling fire in the hearth pervaded the silence as Darr and his friends waited for the prophet to start.

He began by retelling the history of the Ancients, how they rose to power by learning to live in harmony with the Sephirs. He explained how they reached an apex in their learning, leaving an avenue that only one man, Symdus, dared to explore, and how that avenue had led to the creation of the Devoid.

Darr might've imagined it, but the room darkened at the mention of the name. A chill numbed his body. He was glad his siblings and Conra finally knew about the Devoid, but somehow it felt more real as a result.

Nidic Waq continued by telling how Caeranol had attempted to destroy the Devoid, then of his inevitable failure. Following the sacrifice Caeranol made by becoming the Archon of the Light, the prophet concluded his story of how the Devoid had been imprisoned, and how the Ancients had fled.

"I always wondered what happened to the Ancients," Conra whispered.

Erec rolled his eyes. "I don't believe it. You just can't accept the fact that they're gone. They fell prey to their creation, and that's that."

"Erec!" Jinn exclaimed, her eyes filled with disgust. "Just accept maybe there's something you don't know."

Darr worried more about what Nidic Waq might do to his

brother. The prophet sat motionless in his chair, his stare disturbing as he looked at Erec.

"History does change with the teller," Nidic Waq said. "The Ancients are gone from Ictar. How and why? I suppose it doesn't really matter. But there's one thing about their story that matters considerably."

Erec's scowl grew long. "What's that?" he asked.

"That the Devoid be erased from Ictar."

Nidic Waq explained how Caeranol hid the remaining races during the imprisonment of the Devoid, and how their reemergence had led to the Aeon Wars. Lastly, he told of the creation of the Divine by Caeranol to ensure his promise to the people of Ictar would never be forgotten.

Nidic Waq sat motionless for a long moment before lifting his head up slightly, emphasizing his wide features. "Caeranol promised to send the Chosen of the Light, four people selected by the spirits, for the spirits alone would be the first to detect the Devoid's return. These four would possess Lights infused with Caeranol's magic, delivered to them by the spirits, allowing them to use talismans and magic to defeat the Devoid."

The prophet shook his head. "I've been searching for the Chosen for some time now. The magic laying within their bodies should've made them easily identifiable, but the Devoid's manipulations in the Currents prevents both myself and Caeranol from doing so. Even in its prison, the Devoid can make alterations to both the physical world and the Currents."

Nidic Waq's eyes brightened, and his gaze settled on Darr. "But something unexpected happened recently. A Summoner, stumbling through the Currents, somehow reached out with a part of his Light and connected with the Light of one of the Chosen. Thanks to you, Darr, Caeranol located the first of the Chosen."

Darr's stomach lurched. Who had he revealed to Caeranol as the first of the Chosen? He remembered that venture into the Currents in search of his father, seeking out something hidden, and he'd found...No.

The corners of Nidic Waq's mouth lifted, and his stare shifted from one face to another, settling on Jinn.

"The burden you bear now is great," Nidic Waq said quietly. "Jinn Reintol, you are the Healer of the Light, the first of the Chosen who will deliver Ictar from its shadows for good."

Chapter Twenty-Two

"Fearless, a man named Wyntol Ictarus set out to explore the new world left behind by the Ancients. The maps and charts he created led to fame among all the races, and they honored him by naming the new world Ictar. At the time of his death, Wyntol revealed artifacts he wished to give to all the races. In his travels, he'd found the Sephirs left behind by the Ancients who once protected them."

~From A Current History of Ictar, as told by Nidic Waq

Nobody in the room moved. Jinn had become a focal point, a statue hewn from granite, still and unchanging.

There is so much more to know, Darr thought to himself. Why Jinn? Why now? What is it she must do and will she be safe?

Why not me?

This last thought disturbed him, but before he could think on it, Jinn stood up and walked to her room. Without a backwards glance, she disappeared into the darkness and closed the door behind her.

Erec struggled to rise, but Nidic Waq advised, "It'd be best if you let her be for the night."

"What would you know, prophet?" Erec shot back. "She's my sister and all of this is nonsense."

"What you think to be best for Jinn is tainted by your anger," Nidic Waq replied, his tone firm. Erec's face turned bright red, but he said nothing. "Let her be. Let her make her own choices, just as you have made yours."

The prophet rose up before them, his presence filling the entire room. The man no longer intimidated him. The truths he'd revealed this night were far more threatening than anything physical about him. Isolation would follow the prophet anywhere he went because of his knowledge.

"I'll return in the morning. For a little while longer, our paths shall be the same." Nidic Waq turned for the door. As he passed Darr, he whispered, "I'll talk to you then." The prophet stepped through the door and into the halls of the Red Wyvern.

As soon as the door closed, Erec shot Darr an accusing look. "What was all that Chosen nonsense? Did you know about this?"

Darr shook his head. "No. I knew nothing about it until tonight."

For a brief moment, Erec appeared to contain himself before erupting in anger once more. The words blurred together as Darr's thoughts centered on Jinn. He worried for her, and for whatever task Caeranol had set for her. He wished he'd never brought her and placed her in this kind of danger

He wished it'd been him.

The thought disturbed him for the second time. He worried for Jinn without a doubt, but in the deepest part of his soul, he believed he should've been the first of the Chosen. Nidic Waq had sent him to help the Soul Seekers and restore the Sephirs.

Erec continued to yell and Conra tried to calm him down. Darr saw without seeing, and his vision blurred. His thoughts drifted and spun away.

* * * *

Darr's dreams were disjointed images of Nidic Waq and Racall, of his family and Conra, and his mind's rendering of the creature called the Devoid. He woke tired and stiff, but as soon as his eyes opened, he could feel Nidic Waq's presence in the Currents, waiting close by.

The early morning light outlined the bodies of his brother and Conra. Erec slept on the sofa, his face free of distress for the first time in days. Conra looked as if he might have melted into the chair across from him. The door to Jinn's bedroom remained closed. Now, the harbinger of doom, Nidic Waq, waited outside to bring some new disturbance to their lives.

He sighed. Nidic Waq wasn't responsible for the truth of things. The events conspiring against them had been set in motion long ago. Nothing could be changed. All he could do was accept his place.

Darr rose from his chair and made his way to the door, keeping his movements light and undetectable. In the hallway, Nidic Waq stood motionless while Darr shut the door. The prophet's shredded robes were replaced with fresh ones. He'd left behind his rundown appearance from the previous night, but Darr eyed him assertively.

"I apologize for my harsh words last night," Nidic Waq said, his face confirming his sincerity. "You've contributed much to this journey and you've done well. Had it not been for your attempts to navigate the Currents, the first of the Chosen would still be unknown to us."

Darr smiled but said nothing. Nidic Waq continued. "Despite everything, I admire your will to succeed, but I cannot stress enough the dangers compiling against you. The further you travel, the harder it will become for you to avoid using the Currents. The journey ahead will require more of your attention not only to the physical world, but to the Four Elements connecting in the Currents. You could have discovered Jinn without allowing the scattercrab to break free."

"How?" the Summoner asked.

Nidic Waq shook his head. "Since Stern, you've been oblivious to the balance of the Four Elements in the Currents. I can read it in your Light. Racall told you to be mindful of imbalances and to stay far from them. In the days ahead, I will show you how to heal these imbalances when you find them, but you must learn to look for them."

Darr recoiled inwardly, ashamed at his failure. Nidic Waq

reached out and gripped his shoulder, reassuring him.

"I'm sorry, Summoner," the prophet said. "I know you're doing your best. I want you to be safe. While it's good Jinn has been revealed, there are still three more Chosen to locate. As for the Soul Seekers, they're ready to crush the Dwarves at any moment. The defense the kings and I have made will soon be rendered ineffective because the Seekers' numbers are increasing far too rapidly. That means the Devoid knows of our plans to stall the Soul Seekers, or worse, it knows of the Chosen."

"What does that mean for Jinn?" Darr asked.

"It means you must protect her and yourself. Once you cross into the Triker, you'll find the Seekers at every turn."

Darr hesitated but spoke before he could think better. "Why wasn't I named one of the Chosen? Why does Jinn have to bear this burden?"

Nidic Waq rubbed at his beard, and said, "I cannot begin to understand why the spirits selected Jinn over you. Something about her was required and that is all I know. While each of the Chosen are infused with Caeranol's magic, he doesn't make the decision as to who inherits that magic. The spirits are the ones to decide."

"Shouldn't he still know who they are?"

"Yes," Nidic Waq replied. "However, the Currents are so badly distorted he can't discover where the magic was dispersed. Worse yet, the spirits aren't able to tell him. It's as if they've forgotten, and the only way that can happen is if something very powerful is disrupting them."

Darr's throat tightened. "Does the Devoid know where the Chosen are?"

Nidic Waq nodded. "It's a possibility. Regardless, we must act swiftly and find the other Chosen before the Devoid can put any of its knowledge to use."

Darr thrust his fear into the back of his mind, burying it under Nidic Waq's words. "I should go wake the others," Darr said and turned back towards the door.

"You're as important as the Chosen," the prophet said in a soothing voice. "I don't know how you were able to reveal Jinn as one of the Chosen, but some part of you knew how."

Darr looked over his shoulder and asked, "What does that mean for me?"

"It means your journey hasn't changed. The Devoid is held in check by the Sephirs' power alone, and without them, it will break free of its prison completely. The Chosen cannot defeat the Devoid unless balance is first restored to the Sephirs. But there's more at work here, for Caeranol told me before I spoke to you in Tyfor you were tied to the Chosen somehow. It appears now you are to discover them somehow."

A buzzing tingle shot down Darr's neck. Excitement or fear, he couldn't be sure. The Devoid would be defeated, not because of his acts directly, but because of his journey. He wasn't out for the glory of ridding Ictar of evil, but that wasn't entirely true. He would prove to himself his skills as a Summoner were worth something.

"Thank you," Darr said. "I'll do my best."

Nidic Waq's stare bored into the back of his head. "You'll do well, Darr Reintol. Now go and wake your friends. Talk to your sister–she needs your support. When you're ready, meet me outside. I'll have provisions ready for the next leg of your journey."

Nidic Waq's presence in the Currents faded to nothing more than a whisper, but Darr didn't turn back to watch him go. He walked into the room and woke Conra, telling the Elf to help Erec up and make sure he could travel. Conra went to Erec at once, leaving Darr to wake Jinn.

The Summoner rapped on the door into his sister's bedroom, and after a moment, he stepped inside. Jinn no longer slept, but she remained in bed, her body stretched out flat beneath the covers while she stared up at the ceiling. She didn't appear to notice him when he sat down next to her on the bed.

"How're you doing?" he asked, feeling stupid for asking. Jinn didn't answer, her eyes were focused on an imaginary point above her.

Darr reached for her hand and grasped it. "I want you to know you have my support," he told her. Jinn blinked and her lips moved slightly. "I don't know what you're supposed to do or how you're going to do it, but I want you to know you'll have me to help you through it, just as you've helped me."

Jinn tilted her head towards him. "Thank you," she whispered.

Darr smiled and asked, "Are you up for moving around? Nidic Waq is waiting for us whenever we're ready."

His sister raised herself up and stretched. "I suppose so. I don't know what's expected of me, though. I'm not sure where I'm going or what to do when I get there."

Darr shifted his body. "Start by listening to Nidic Waq. I know he's difficult and intimidating sometimes, but he has an enormous amount of pressure on his shoulders. He's looking out for all of Ictar and doing his best to protect it. He knows what he's talking about. I would know if he was lying."

"I believe you," Jinn said. "If you have faith in him, then I will too."

"Then we'll figure all this out as we go," Darr said, forcing an encouraging smile. "You're coming with me anyway. We'll discover our fate together. There's no point in sitting here and worrying about what might happen next."

The two siblings looked at each other, and the connection between them grew stronger. Did the magic they command somehow bring them closer? Jinn's magic was a mystery, but it had to be strong if it could defeat the Devoid.

"Thanks, Darr. I'll be along in a moment."

The Summoner squeezed Jinn's hand and got up from the bed. Relieved that his conversation with Jinn had gone well, Darr still faced one more obstacle. He had to talk to Erec. His brother would be difficult, but that was no surprise.

In the main sitting room, Conra and Erec sat on the couch while the Elf applied a healing salve to his back. Darr got a good look at the wounds left by the scattercrab. His brother had endurance, and the courage it took to deal with the pain testified for his strength. Darr waited patiently while Conra wrapped Erec's back and ribs with fresh bandages.

"Do you think you'll be able to walk?" Darr asked.

"Does that mean you're still going?" Erec asked, his voice filled with defiance.

"Why would I change my mind?"

Erec cocked his head like Darr had spit in his face. "You can't really believe all that talk last night."

Darr shrugged. "I don't believe it." He waited until the confusion appeared on Erec's face. "I don't believe because I know. I heard it all from the spirits when Nidic Waq told the story. Everything he told us is true. Now you have to decide how that's going to affect you."

Discomfort washed over and replaced Erec's confused look. Without listening to the Currents, Darr sensed the emotional battle roiling within his brother.

"I'm sorry," Erec whispered, hanging his head. "I might be angry with you and fearful of the danger you're putting yourself in, but I'm not. I've seen the things you can do."

Despite his surprise, Darr remained calm and concentrated on Erec's words. "Then what is it? Why do you resist so much?"

When his brother lifted his head, the glare of anger burned in his eyes again. "Because I don't believe in this quest, and I know I should, but something inside won't let me. My heart tells me this is all wrong. We shouldn't be fighting this battle with magic..."

There it is, Darr thought. Erec's misgivings all centered on using magic. It wasn't that he didn't believe there were Soul Seekers or the Devoid. The conflict came from his belief that magic was wrong no matter what form it took. The way of the sword had always been Erec's answer to everything.

Now, at a time when physical strength served no purpose against their enemy, he had no idea what to believe in.

"I think I know what you're trying to say," Darr said. "I want you to know I don't think any less of you for what you believe."

"I don't expect you to think one way or another about what I believe, but..." Erec smiled. "I'm glad you don't look down on me when your beliefs conflict with mine. I'm glad we can still be friends despite our opinions."

"Well spoken," Conra said in a mere whisper.

"Enough of this." Erec propped himself up with a low groan and stretched. "I'm well enough to walk today, but don't expect me to carry any weight. I'll leave that to you, little brother."

Erec gave him a playful shove and laughed when it caught Darr by surprise, nearly knocking him off his feet. The Summoner righted himself and flipped his hair out of his face. He shot his brother a mocking sneer.

When they were finished teasing each other, the brothers went about preparing their things. Jinn appeared from her room looking refreshed. Darr smiled at her as she went to work packing, impressed with her courage. Conra acted oddly quiet, saying little during their preparations. It appeared he had something on his mind, though the Elf would talk when he was ready.

When they were starting downstairs, Conra finally approached Darr. Erec and Jinn had already gone down the hallway. The Elf called Darr back before he stepped out the door.

"You know, I've been thinking about all this business with the Devoid and the Chosen and what not, and I think I'd like to come with you," the Elf announced.

When they first met, Conra had been stubborn and irritable. As they traveled together, and Conra became more interested in magic, his attitude had changed. Darr wasn't sure why, but he believed it must have something to do with his request to come with them.

"I'm not sure I understand, Conra," Darr said. "I didn't think you wanted to come this far, let alone go to the edges of Ictar,"

Hesitation flashed across the Elf's face, but he forged ahead. "I know, I know, but I've been meaning to return to the south for years now. And I'm interested in you and the magic you command. I know I'm old, but you won't find a more experienced tracker than me. I don't think I could return home without seeing where all this business leads."

Darr bit his lower lip. Conra was a good friend, and Darr couldn't imagine the Elf backing down on anything. They were headed into dangerous country, lands they knew nothing about. Nidic Waq wouldn't be with them forever, and Conra's skills as a tracker and survivalist would come in handy.

"You're sure about this?" Darr asked. "Nidic Waq says we'll be in much more danger once we cross the Dwarf Borderlands."

Conra chuckled. "Do you think I got to where I am today by avoiding risks? Darr, I welcome the adventure."

A smile spread across his face and he nodded his approval. "I guess we should be going then."

The Summoner turned and walked out the door with Conra a step behind.

Chapter Twenty-Three

"Against Wyntol's wish for the races to share the Sephirs, the Aeon Wars began. The wars continued over the next millennia, crisscrossing Ictar like a disease. The five races fought over the Sephirs in relentless battles, sometimes to protect them and other times to exploit their power. Early on, the races discovered magic forcibly pulled from the Sephirs had many uses. They could augment their physical abilities or create elementals capable of vast destruction, but magic such as this upset the Four Elements and threatened returning everything to chaos. The races used their newfound power cautiously."

~From A Current History of Ictar, as told by Nidic Waq

As promised, Nidic Waq stood alone in the shadows of an alleyway beside the Red Wyvern, hidden from all who passed. Darr wouldn't have been able to find the prophet had he not sensed him in the Currents. He brought his companions before the prophet, who gave everyone, including Erec, a perfunctory nod. His gaze lingered momentarily on Conra.

Doubt rumbled through the Currents. "Conra would like to continue on with us," Darr said. "His experience as a tracker will be invaluable, and he's proved himself a loyal friend."

Nidic Waq's face lacked emotion when he eyed the Elf. "After all you've heard last night, you accept the dangers that lie ahead?"

Conra grunted and shrugged. "I've been ready for anything for the better part of seventy years."

"This journey would be better suited to those who are younger," Nidic Waq said. "The trials ahead will undoubtedly test your endurance."

"I'll take experience over youth any day of the year,"

Conra snapped. "I may not be able to move as fast as I used to, but I'll manage just fine."

The seconds ticked by while the prophet looked down at Conra as if in evaluation. At last, he nodded and welcomed Conra, then went about distributing food and supplies from a sack he carried. He'd also found a replacement sword for Erec, though how he'd done so in a military state like Oasis couldn't have been easy.

When he was finished, Nidic Waq discarded the sack. How the prophet planned to support himself without provisions was a mystery. Then again, Nidic Waq had taken care of himself this long without a pack, and he seemed to be doing just fine. Once everyone was ready, Nidic Waq turned and led them into the city.

Oasis had a much different look during the day than it had the previous night. Buildings stood proud and cared for along the busy road. The merchants and townspeople they passed were indifferent to them, but not unkind. Once they reached the end of the thoroughfare, they were required to pass through an inner wall, Oasis' main defense. Like Tyfor, the farming communities outside the inner wall appeared cared for and stable. The city's fortifications encased the farmland as well, running west to the mountains and east to the ocean. The Kurflinese lived within a cage.

They reached the southern walls of Oasis shortly after midmorning. The soldiers standing guard at the gate might've questioned them had they known they were heading into the Dwarf Borderlands, but Nidic Waq gave the name of a town to the west. The guards let them pass without incident.

For the remainder of the day, the company of five traveled south across the plains. The low, blunt peaks rising up before them marked the Dwarf Borderlands. They kept their conversations to a minimum, and stopped to rest only twice.

Nightfall brought them to the bottom of the rolling

foothills leading up into the Borderlands where they made their camp. The night air felt crisp, but pleasant. Not long after the company had settled down around a low fire and prepared supper. Erec and Conra talked politics regarding the Kurflinese, and Darr and Jinn talked of home. Nidic Waq remained silent, wrapped in his white robes while sitting before the fire.

They were finishing their meal when Nidic Waq leaned towards the fire, illuminating his wide features.

"I want you all to know about the journey in the days to come." Darr managed a sideways glance at Jinn and found her staring vigilantly at the prophet. "We'll be taking Fenihks Pass into the Triker. The route is difficult, but navigable. It should take us two days to reach the other side. Afterwards, I'll take you only as far as the town called the Crossroads before heading west for Jacova."

"So how do we get to Arcnor?" Jinn asked.

"We'll be met within the Triker by friends who'll show you the way," the prophet replied in a gentle tone.

Conra hunched forward and asked, "Why are you taking us through Fenihks Pass? There are safer routes into the Triker."

"The Seekers are still hunting me," Nidic Waq said. "It will be easier to slip past them on the less traveled paths."

Erec laughed. "It'd be easier to go without you then."

"If you can find the Soul Seekers before they find you, then yes, you should go without me." Erec started to say something but Nidic Waq interrupted. "Keep in mind, Erec, you won't be able to detect their presence physically. You'll have to rely on your brother's skill to navigate the Currents for any kind of warning, and by the time he's able to figure out what threatens, the Seekers will be upon you."

Darr suppressed his urge to dispute Nidic Waq. Though navigating the Currents had become much easier, the spirits had failed to warn him of the Seekers in the Valimere. A feeling of deep cold had given the only indication, and that'd been too paralytic to help.

Nobody had anything to say after the prophet finished. One by one, they rolled themselves into their blankets and went to sleep. Darr thought briefly of who would stay up to keep watch. Out of the corner of his eye, he saw Nidic Waq, his solitary form outlined in firelight.

* * * *

The second day went much like the first as Nidic Waq led them up into Fenihks Pass. Compared to the path they took through the Barricades, the terrain might as well be an open field, but their trail oftentimes disappeared amid the winding defiles.

They camped for the night at the top of the pass beneath a massive rock structure resembling a bird stretching upwards in flight.

"The Ancients took shelter within these mountains when the Devoid first started its hunt for them," Nidic Waq said at a slow point in the evening. The sun had just set but it was too early to sleep. "An old legend of theirs told of a bird that could revive itself after death. They named the pass after the structure above us, seeing in this image their own perseverance. After the departure of the Ancients, the name of the pass and its legend survived, passed down by the races of Ictar."

Conra hunched forward and said, "The Ancient's have left much for us to examine."

"It's amazing to me the amount of influence they've had on the races," Nidic Waq replied. "Their stories have passed into Ictar's history, surviving even the catastrophic violence of the Aeon Wars. It's a comfort to know some things aren't subject to the dictates of time and change."

Nidic Waq lapsed into silence once more. There had to be more to the story of the Chosen of the Light, but the prophet wouldn't be telling them anytime soon.

On the third day, as they descended out of the Borderlands, the rocky slopes merged with the towering pines of the Triker. As usual, nobody wanted to talk. Fear of the Soul Seekers was likely the cause.

Around noon, the low peaks of the Dwarf Borderlands disappeared behind them. The massive trees of the forest rose up, and the path ahead stretched into darkness interspersed with thin shoots of daylight. No wonder the Seekers had chosen the Triker as their first target.

When the way forward became too dark to navigate, Nidic Waq brought them all to a halt within a broad clearing illuminated by the fading daylight. They settled down and wrapped up in blankets to keep warm since Nidic Waq forbid any kind of fire. A half moon shone down from above giving a small measure of comfort from its light.

"I haven't been forthcoming about Jinn's role as the Healer of the Light," Nidic Waq said, his quiet voice breaking the silence. "I prefer to focus on the journey at hand, rather than on the trials ahead. You've all been patient, especially you, Jinn."

Darr, Jinn, and Conra hunched forward so the prophet wouldn't have to spread his voice. Erec sat outside their circle, avoiding the conversation.

Nidic Waq's features were barely identifiable when he began. "Because of my service to Caeranol, I'm privileged as well. When Caeranol established his covenant, he left only a few details as to what was required of each of the Chosen. There will be four, each with a specific role in defeating the Devoid. The Healer of the Light will carry a talisman called the Moonstone. I'm not entirely sure how this magic is to be implemented, but it will be one of four necessary components."

"What does it do?" Darr asked, curious as to the nature of the magic his sister would wield.

Nidic Waq didn't immediately answer. "The Moonstone is a relic from the time of the Ancients, but its true origins are unknown. Its power allows the user to break down the physical effects of magic and disperse it back to the Currents."

The light of the moon outlined Jinn's features. Her face masked whatever she felt, and Darr refused to venture a look into the Currents to check on her.

"So how do I find this Moonstone?" Jinn asked, her tone strong but quiet. "What do I do until I find it?"

Nidic Waq's voice turned stern, but not cold. "You do both by staying alive. Along with Caeranol's covenant, the Divine were charged with protection of the talismans that would bring the fall of the Devoid. Only they know how and where to retrieve the Moonstone, and until you find the Divine who will show you the way, you must stay alive."

"How are we supposed to locate this Divine?" Conra asked.

"The Divine who holds the answers you seek will be near the Sephirs," Nidic Waq answered. "Caeranol knew the Sephirs would be threatened when the Devoid returned, and he placed his Divine accordingly. When it's time, the Divine will find you."

Herdas, the Divine who helped them in Stern had been sympathetic and understanding of Darr's trials. He knew why the Sephirs needed restoration. Was Herdas one of Caeranol's Divine? If so, had they missed something important from him?

"Be silent." The words rushed out of Nidic Waq in a hiss.

Darr froze, listening to the Currents. Whatever Nidic Waq sensed was undetectable to him. At his side, Jinn held herself rigid. Erec and Conra started to move, but another hiss from Nidic Waq halted them.

"Do you feel it?" Nidic Waq asked, his voice so quiet Darr could barely hear.

Within his own Light, Darr went cold. He focused, searching for the source of the feeling. Nothing physical accompanied the sensation, like when the spiritual realm had torn open, except this feeling came without the spirits. Numbing cold, endless and unfeeling.

Three black shapes emerged into the pale light of the clearing, detaching themselves from the shadows of the trees around them, darker than ink spilled on parchment. They stood upright, wearing tattered robes and cowls, and the silvery glimmer of hooked claws dangled at their sides. Their faces weren't visible, only the depthless void of their cowls.

The Soul Seekers had found them.

Nidic Waq rose to his feet, his forbidding appearance equal to that of the Seekers. The black creatures didn't move, but they watched. Darr knew better. They were waiting to strike. Nidic Waq took a step back, putting himself before his charges.

The prophet motioned Darr and his companions to stand. "The Seekers are created from the Light of the Currents," Nidic Waq said. "They are bound to the physical world only by their robes. Cut through their robes, and the binding fails. Be quick about it, for they're fast and ruthless enemies."

Erec rose to his feet and drew out his short sword. A moment later Conra, with crossbow held ready, appeared beside him. Jinn stepped behind Darr. They both had hunting knives and no other defense except for the men protecting them.

Terror roared through Darr. He couldn't fight the Seekers with a knife. On impulse, he established a connection with the Currents, hoping to summon anything to aid in his defense.

The spirits cannot help you here, Darr. Nidic Waq spoke to him, his words drifting through the space of the Currents. *The Seekers aren't part of the Four Elements and they aren't subject to the same rules. They can attack you both here and in the Currents. Be patient. Help is on the way.*

Before Darr could relax his mind, Nidic Waq threw his arm wide and released a bolt of white fire from his outstretched hand. The air crackled and the fiery bolt rushed forward, incinerating the middle Seeker.

The two remaining Soul Seekers rushed aside, missing the white fire and vanishing into the dark. Erec stumbled backwards in an effort to protect Jinn, while Conra fired a bolt from his bow into the darkness. Nidic Waq dove to the side, his fingertips glowing in the moonlight as he bore down on one of the Seekers as it reappeared. The last Seeker's liquid motion dispersed into the shadows of the Triker and was lost.

Darr dropped instinctively, missing the slashing claws of the Seeker as it charged into the clearing. Conra fired a bolt pointblank but it only tore a hole in the creature's robe. From out of nowhere, Erec dashed up behind the Soul Seeker, his sword tearing away at its back. The creature stumbled away and flung its arm around, knocking Erec square in the chest and sending him flying. He didn't stay down. By the time the Seeker had turned around, Erec tore into it again, dodging blindly past its claws.

Darr ran to Jinn's side and pulled her back to the center of the clearing. Conra shouted out a sudden warning and Darr found the other Soul Seeker racing for him. The Summoner froze, anticipating the end.

A massive axe soared down before him, and a stout figure rose up. In one swift motion, he lifted the axe and brought it down again. The blade split the Soul Seeker down the middle, and robes and all, it erupted into a cloud of ash. Darr fell backwards in shock, crouching protectively over Jinn when the clearing lit up with the white fire commanded by Nidic Waq. The prophet stood before them as the ashes of the last Seeker exploded around him.

"Is it over?" Jinn asked, her voice shaking.

"Not yet," the man who'd saved them said, his voice deep and powerful.

A Dwarf, marked by his stocky build and dark skin. Another Dwarf appeared from out of the forest, this one taller and leaner than the other, but his complexion unmistakable.

"There are more heading this way. We must be quick," the newcomer whispered. He came up to Darr and Jinn, offering his hand and lifting them to their feet. "It's a pleasure to meet you, Darr Reintol, but we can talk more once we are safe. My name is Feywen Dery and this is my friend, Lacdur."

Nidic Waq emerged beside them with Erec and Conra a step behind. "How close are they?"

"Close enough to see our teeth," Lacdur grumbled, his eyes intense.

Feywen glanced over his shoulder and said, "Grab your things and let's go."

Darr and his companions snatched up their packs. With Nidic Waq behind them, the company chased after the Dwarves into the Triker with the Soul Seekers in pursuit.

Chapter Twenty-Four

"From within the Currents, Caeranol watched the races fight amongst themselves. The spirits had tasked him with maintaining the balance between life and death, but Caeranol did what he could to protect the races from themselves. His reach within the physical realm was short, so he relied on the Currents to prevent the most brutal atrocities from taking place."

~From A Current History of Ictar, as told by Nidic Waq

Darr and his companions followed Feywen Dery through the black trees of the Triker. The Summoner didn't know where they were going, and he wished he knew more about the man with whom he trusted his life. Nidic Waq's faith would have to do.

Jinn looked back at him, her round face outlined by shadows and small fragments of light. Darr couldn't communicate with her, so he focused on keeping his senses sharp instead. Tree trunks whipped past them, blurry shadows in the night, and their footfalls were soft from the thick padding of needles on the forest floor.

Several times, Feywen stopped and brought them to a halt. He would stand still for several moments as if searching for something. Sometimes he would send Lacdur on ahead while he waited in silence with the group. It appeared Feywen and Lacdur communicated through sign language, but Darr couldn't be sure. Every time they stopped, no more than a few minutes passed before Feywen led them onward.

They ran for more than an hour before they finally stopped. The Dwarves found an outcropping of boulders with a crevice on one side that opened up into a small cave. Feywen and Lacdur kept their eyes on the trees around them while they shuffled their charges inside. When Darr and the others were under cover, Feywen whispered something to Nidic Waq before racing off into the night with Lacdur.

The small company sat motionless and silent within their hideaway. Nidic Waq guarded the entrance of the cave, an immutable presence facing out into the night. Erec and Conra retained their loose confidence, rooted in their mutual need for physical excitement. Darr sat with Jinn huddled next to him, her small frame tense, like his own. He'd been completely unprepared for this last encounter with the Soul Seekers.

Midnight approached when Feywen and Lacdur returned, their bodies bringing in a blast of heat from their overworked muscles. Lacdur dropped down and drank from an ale skin. Feywen sat down in an empty space along the cave wall away from anyone else.

"They're gone," Feywen said after a moment's rest.

A collective sigh brushed through the little cave, but Darr thought it might have come from him alone.

Lacdur stopped drinking and set the skin aside, wiping his hand across his mouth in the process. "They put up a pretty good chase. Had to lure them halfway to the Borderlands before we could ditch them and head back."

"So we're safe?" Darr asked, wanting only one answer.

Feywen nodded his head. "We will be safe enough for tonight. The Seekers think we went north into the Borderlands, and they'll not turn back tonight."

"How's that possible?" Conra asked. "You had to have left some kind of trail."

"They *can't* find us, Elf," Lacdur said, his voice rough and reprimanding. "The Seekers don't see things the same way as you and I. 'Aos—I don't even think they can see."

Feywen interjected, "Lacdur and I have been studying the Soul Seekers for almost...four months now..." He paused, took in a deep breath. "We know them better than anyone else in Ictar, except perhaps Nidic Waq. We've been tracking their movements and patterns in an attempt to prepare a better defense. Very soon, we'll report back to the generals in Jacova so they can make use of our information."

"What do you mean, they can't see?" Conra asked again.

"The Seekers are creations of magic thinly contained in vestments of the physical world," Nidic Waq answered. "They embody the primal force of death, and as such, they merely seek out life and consume it."

"So how did you avoid them?" Erec asked.

Lacdur laughed and said, "We tricked them. We outdistanced them, then we doubled back far away from where they could sense us. They're shadows chasing shadows now."

Darr couldn't imagine the courage it'd taken the Dwarves to test the Soul Seekers.

"How did you two get involved in this?" Darr wondered aloud.

Feywen leaned back into the cave wall, his features cloaked in the deep shadow. "That, my friend, is a long story. I'm afraid tonight is not the night to tell it, but just know I do this for personal reasons, Lacdur as well. These are the respects we pay to our king." The Dwarf hesitated a moment before adding, "And my father."

"What's that supposed to mean?" Erec blurted out.

Lacdur slammed his hand down on his knee, his features agitated despite being saturated in the dark. "It means exactly what it means, Boy."

"Feywen Dery is the son of Gyrot Dery, the late King of the Dwarves," Nidic Waq interrupted, his voice calming. "He's been kind enough to take you all to Arcnor, so I'd let the matter rest for now."

No one said a word after that. That didn't keep Darr's mind from racing. How could the son of a king be traipsing through the woods rather than ruling his nation? Furthermore, why did they refer to Gyrot Dery as if he were dead? Darr had heard stories of the Dwarf king, a peacekeeper known across Ictar. News of his death would've traveled fast.

"We'll be protected here for the night," Feywen said. "We should all get some sleep."

One by one, with the exception of Nidic Waq, they rolled themselves into their blankets. The cave provided no room to stretch out, so they were forced to lean up against the rough rock walls. Jinn and Conra fell asleep easily enough. Lacdur and Feywen also managed to get comfortable. Darr sat awake for several minutes before Erec leaned into him.

"How are you doing, little brother?" Erec whispered into his ear.

Darr shrugged. "I'll be all right. What do you think of all this?"

"I think we should be careful in this forest. I wouldn't want to fight those Seekers again."

Darr smiled to himself. Erec didn't back down from fights. It appeared he'd learned a bit of caution. "What do you think of Feywen?" the Summoner asked.

"He seems like he knows what he's doing," Erec replied. "Lacdur as well, but if he keeps talking to me like I'm a child, I might have to show him I'm not one."

"I don't think that's a good idea," Darr whispered. "He looks like he could crush a bear."

Erec snorted. "We'll see." He scuffed his boot against the ground before saying anything more. "I want you to know, I believe you now. Even after seeing the Ovid, I really didn't think there were Seekers. I thought they were only a ghost story."

"Don't worry about it," the Summoner said and meant it.

Darr sensed relief coming from Erec, but the feeling didn't come from his instincts or the spirits. For a moment, he was a part of Erec's Light, feeling his exact emotions. Darr concentrated on his breathing and broke off the connection. He wanted to explore the sensation, but it felt too intrusive. He needed to exercise caution in the Currents, otherwise he'd unleash another elemental on his friends.

They shifted their bodies away from each other and wrapped up in their blankets. Darr smiled to himself, thinking it wasn't such a bad idea having Erec along after all.

* * * *

Morning came, and with it, stiff joints and cranky demeanors from the members of the little company. Feywen and Lacdur were gone, probably off scouting for the journey ahead. Nidic Waq was absent as well, but his disappearance wasn't surprising. The Summoner and his companions stretched out their limbs and moved around the small cave, but no one was willing to go outside.

When the Dwarves returned, Feywen announced they'd found no trace of the Seekers. When Darr asked if they'd seen Nidic Waq, he received only blank stares.

Feywen took a seat near Lacdur, giving Darr the opportunity to see the Dwarves closely for the first time. Tall and lean, Feywen's build matched Erec's, his eyes cobalt blue shining out through the smoothness of his face. With a lighter tone skin color, Darr thought he might look unusual for a Dwarf, but he admitted he hadn't seen many Dwarves. Lacdur had more common Dwarf features–compact, but heavyset body, and skin so dark it almost looked like charcoal. Intense hazel eyes peered out from his face, making him look more animal than man. The Dwarves weren't unusual looking, but Darr found them fascinating.

Nidic Waq appeared in the opening of the cave a few minutes later, his tall form blocking the daylight beyond.

"The way south is clear," the prophet announced. "No Seekers will threaten us today." He waited for a nod from Feywen before stepping back out into the Triker.

"How can he know for sure?" Jinn asked in a whisper, but Darr shook his head.

Lacdur, though he didn't seem to be listening, answered Jinn's question. "The Seekers don't often show themselves in daylight," he grumbled. "The summoning that brings them here is tied to darkness. Even in these trees, the Seekers won't appear until dusk at the earliest."

Feywen finished his breakfast and jumped to his feet. "We leave at once," he announced. "The journey to the Crossroads will take us almost three days, and the light goes quickly within these trees. We'll be traveling all day, with one stop to rest. We must reach another safe haven like this one by nightfall, and Lacdur knows of one, but it's a great distance from here."

He looked from face to face, waiting from a nod of understanding from each of them. "Let's depart then," was all Feywen said.

The Triker Forest enfolded them. The branches overhead created an impenetrable barrier, allowing only small threads of brightness down on their path. The forest dipped and rose as they traveled, gentle folds in the terrain, but everything looked the same. Not to Lacdur, it seemed, who led unswervingly even though a trail wasn't visible.

Around noon, Lacdur brought them to a halt in a small clearing with a natural spring at its center. They gathered around the water, sitting on rocks while eating their lunch, letting the sun warm their faces. Nidic Waq kept his tall frame hidden in the shadows of the forest.

Their lunch was nearing completion when Lacdur announced, "You Reintols have got quick feet. We're making excellent progress today."

Feywen cleared his throat. "Since we have a little time," he said, "I am a Dwarf prince, the only son of the Dwarf King, Gyrot Dery. Over the summer, my father was killed. This has been a closely guarded secret for the last few months, and until recently, it wasn't public information."

"But why?" Conra asked, his voice distressed.

Feywen furrowed his brow. "Growing concerned about the threat of the Soul Seekers, the three kings of Ictar—Ariel Forn, Lendor Terwin, and my father—met secretly to discuss the threat. After much debate, they decided to travel to the Tower Castle and seek out the guardian Archon, Caeranol."

"I thought the Tower Castle was only a fairytale," Erec said. Darr cast a glance at Nidic Waq who scowled in anger.

Feywen didn't appear bothered by the question. "That is precisely what I thought at first. From the accounts I received, the kings took a ship and sailed to the lone island holding the Tower Castle. They found the island covered in miles of thorny brush, but inside they found a perfect garden, tended and infused with life. At its center was the castle."

Images flashed through Darr's mind, reminding him of his dream of the two arguing men. He'd seen a tower surrounded by gardens surrounded by thorns.

"Inside the castle," Feywen continued, "they were met by Caeranol himself, for only within its walls was he able to appear to them. He showed them many things about the Seekers and the Devoid, and the Chosen of the Light. The Chosen would be found, but until then, they'd have to hold against the tide of Seekers. He warned that if the Elven city of Exed fell, the Devoid would free itself. The kings were instructed to do everything possible to keep the Seekers occupied while he searched for the Chosen."

Feywen settled his gaze on Darr. "Caeranol told the kings he would find someone to aid them, a boy who would find the Chosen of the Light and restore the Sephirs."

Shaken, Darr looked over at Nidic Waq. The prophet gazed back. Distrust welled up inside Darr, and he asked, "Why didn't you tell me?"

"I didn't think you were prepared," Nidic Waq answered, his face bowed deep within his cowl. "It was hard enough convincing you of the importance of restoring the Sephirs. I couldn't fathom your disbelief had I told you of your connection to the Chosen."

Darr shook his head, letting the sting of betrayal sink in. Nidic Waq had offered him a way out of Tyfor, and he took the chance to leave. Perhaps the real betrayal came from himself.

"I didn't mean to upset you, Darr," Feywen said after a moment. "They were told to trust in Caeranol and bestow on him their faith that his covenant would be fulfilled."

Feywen let the tension ease for a moment. "The kings left the Tower Castle, but outside they were attacked by Soul Seekers. At the end of the fight, my father's broken body was among the fallen. When I returned to Jacova with my father's body, the Dwarf Elder Council quickly decided his death would have to be kept secret for fear of spreading panic. My father's body would lie in state, and the people would be told he was ill."

Feywen eased forward and sighed. "I did not agree with this tactic, but until I was crowned, the council was in charge of the affairs of the state. So Lacdur and I left Jacova in order to better understand our enemy. When we departed, the council judged me unfit for kingship, and by leaving Jacova, I had forfeit the monarchy. Some time after, my father's death was quietly disclosed and the council took leadership of the Dwarves."

Conra shook his head and said, "I can't believe they did that to you."

Lacdur grunted, almost a laugh. "The Dwarf Elder Council has been looking for an excuse to dissolve the monarchy for years. They prefer a democratic approach. 'Aos—some democracy. The council is nothing more than a bunch of old men who think they know what's best for everyone else."

"With the Seekers getting so close, how are they going to protect Jacova?" Jinn asked, concern highlighting her features.

Feywen shook his head. "I really don't know. Brenan Jase is Chief Councilman, providing leadership in place of my father. He's a good man, but he led the arguments allowing the council to dissolve the monarchy. While I believe he made the decision with the intention of helping the Dwarf people, Jase may have made the move for reasons I cannot fathom."

"He's a snake," Lacdur grumbled, but Feywen didn't respond.

"Regardless, Jase leads my people now," Feywen continued. "I've talked with him several times since Lacdur and I left. He knows almost as much as I do about the Seekers, but I don't think he puts that information to good use. He's trying to ignore the dangers we face, but he's keeping in contact with the Elves and the Cortazians. He knows what happened to my father, and I doubt Jase would disobey one of his final wishes."

Feywen Dery, the once-prince of the Dwarves, Darr thought. What kind of man was he to stick to his principles though it meant losing his place among the Dwarf nation? It made him a man of discipline and integrity, but sheathed in iron.

"We had better be leaving," Nidic Waq announced from within the shadows of the trees.

Lacdur jumped to his feet, complaining about how long they'd been resting. The other members of the company gathered their things, falling into line behind Lacdur. Jinn came up beside Darr and patted him on the shoulder.

"Are you all right?" she asked.

Darr didn't want to answer. "Just thinking things through."

"Well don't think too hard," Jinn said. "What Nidic Waq did wouldn't have changed things, would it?"

Jinn gave his shoulder a quick tight squeeze. A gesture of support. Jinn followed after Erec into the trees, reminding Darr of how much he admired her for her optimism. He didn't think he would've been as brave had Nidic Waq told him everything about his quest on their first meeting.

* * * *

An hour before sunset, Lacdur led the company into a gorge carved between a line of twisted cedar, their shelter for the evening. So long as they stayed low and quiet, they wouldn't be found by any wandering Soul Seekers. They had more space than the cave from the night before, but that didn't make them any more comfortable. Tree roots stuck out of the soil all around them, and the air in the gorge was damp and cold.

The company settled down and attempted to get comfortable. Lacdur and Feywen offered to share the watch during the night. Erec offered to help, but Lacdur silenced him. He had no experience detecting the Seekers. To Darr's surprise, Erec rolled into his blankets without further comment.

Darr wrapped up in his blanket and his eyes grew heavy. Someone's fingers brushed lightly on his shoulder. The black shape of Nidic Waq rose over him, though he knew who it was from the touch alone.

"Come with me, Darr," the prophet whispered and turned away.

Darr wouldn't ignore him outright even though he wanted to. He'd have to deal with his anger another way. Darr crept after the prophet's swaying black shape. They walked to the far side of the gorge, a spot partially illuminated by a filament of moonlight. Nidic Waq took a seat on a moss-covered log and motioned Darr to sit beside him.

"I wanted to talk with you before we travel any further south," Nidic Waq said in a hushed voice. "After tomorrow, the Seekers will be at hunt where the shadows of the forest run deepest. We must be on our guard, if we're to avoid them."

Darr started to speak, but Nidic Waq interrupted him. "I want to apologize. I never intended to deceive you, but certain things had to be kept secret if you were going to listen to what I had to tell you. It seems I'm manipulating you, however I take the actions I must because you're a necessary component in all of this."

Darr nodded as if to agree, though he was reluctant to accept the prophet's methods for getting what he wanted.

"The reason I've brought you out here tonight is to check on your progress with your summoning. You undoubtedly have questions and concerns, and I want to be able to help you while I can."

"I want to know why summoning is ineffective against the Soul Seekers," Darr said without hesitation.

Nidic Waq leaned closer before answering. "The Seekers are made from the Light. The Light is a primal force, bestowing both life and death. From this force, the Devoid creates the Soul Seekers, beings with no rational thought that can be easily directed."

Nidic Waq eased himself closer. "Because the Seekers are an extension of the Light bonded to the Devoid, they can cause interference in the Currents. This is why you feel so cold when they're around. This feeling carries into the Currents as well, creating disruptions that will prevent you from calling out to the Archons. Worse, these disruptions could leave you stunned in the physical world. Now, this doesn't mean a rush of fire or rending of earth won't consume them, but until you become more disciplined, you would be wise to avoid the Currents."

"You said the Seekers could disrupt a summoning," Darr said. "Why were you able to summon fire against them when we first entered the forest?"

Nidic Waq's face was hidden when he answered. "I did not summon fire. I summoned the Light to aid me, balancing the Seekers' essence of death with life."

"But how's that possible?" Darr asked.

"It's possible for anyone who's able to travel the Currents," Nidic Waq replied. "It's possible even for you, one who can walk in both worlds."

The power of life and death. Cold sickness swept through Darr at the thought.

"The Light is rarely given up willingly from the spirits," Nidic Waq continued, "which is the only way it can be effective. You could steal the Light from the Currents, like the Devoid, but you risk damaging both your body and soul."

"I don't want that kind of power," Darr said, his voice swelled with distress. "The summonings I performed in Stern and outside Oasis were rooted in power I can understand. But the power of life and death..."

"It will become necessary for you to understand, if you ever hope to survive the Soul Seekers and complete your quest." Nidic Waq's features were stern. "You'll undoubtedly face the Seekers again. Without the proper defenses, you'll be shattered both in body and spirit."

Darr forced his fear aside. "Go on," he said, prepared to listen.

"In order to summon the Light, you must remember there's nothing physical about the Currents," Nidic Waq said. "Your strength is determined by the strength of your spirit, by your courage and your wisdom of what you know to be true."

"How am I supposed to prevent my fear from overtaking me in front of the Soul Seekers?" Darr asked. "You're talking about erasing my instincts, about forgetting the rules of the physical world, rules I have known all my life."

Nidic Waq shook his head. "I haven't told you to forget anything. Instead, open your mind and realize there is another world overlapping this one, a world that reflects your own Light. In the physical world, your strength is determined by others. In the Currents, you're strength comes from yourself."

Nidic Waq rose from the log they were seated on and looked down at him. "This is the knowledge you must accept in order to improve your skills. Only through examination of your own spirit will you be able to master the power required to see you through to the end." The prophet leaned down. "You have the heart to accomplish this. You wouldn't have been selected otherwise."

The prophet turned and marched back to the camp, leaving a void in the space before Darr. Had he just been reprimanded, or did Nidic Waq merely stir his inner fire? Either way, Darr was certain he could do as he'd been told.

On his next voyage into the Currents, he wouldn't be so easily swayed by his perceptions. He would master his fear with the true strength of his Light.

Chapter Twenty-Five

"Though the Ancients had long departed the world, some remnants of their power remained. A few among the races could listen to the Currents in the same way the Ancients once had. Caeranol found he could still reach into the physical world. These few individuals became known as Spirit Summoners."

~From A Current History of Ictar, as told by Nidic Waq

For two more days and nights, the small company made their way through the Triker Forest as a steady rain soaked them through. Darr wasn't used to such miserable conditions, and the weather reflected his mood.

On the morning of their third day, the rain turned to drizzle before fading away, but the company remained in poor spirits. No one had slept well in several days. Everyone needed a change of clothes or a fire to dry out the clothes they had. Darr's heart dropped when Lacdur advised they wouldn't make it to the Crossroads before nightfall. Likely they wouldn't reach the village until late morning the next day.

The company trudged on. Mist curled around the trees, making shadows and light appear from nothing. The Triker took on an eerie feel, but Lacdur and Feywen took them through without hesitation.

Nightfall brought them to a cave like the one from their first night though much deeper, made so by the rocky terrain in the area. Screened away by the heavy trees, this refuge would allow them a fire for the first time in days. Their fire would have to be kept small, but for one night, they'd get some hot food, dry clothes, and a measure of comfort. Conra went to work preparing a meal, and within an hour, the Elf had concocted a stew they consumed almost before he took it off the fire.

Lacdur bellowed out, "If Elves could do business as well as you cook, we'd all be in better spirits."

The words were strange to Darr, and his face must have showed it because Feywen sat down next to him after supper and explained.

"Lacdur doesn't mean to be cruel by what he says," Feywen said. "It's an ingrained belief among the Dwarves that the Elves are responsible for our struggle. A long time has passed since the Aeon Wars, but much of the old bitterness remains. My people have exerted much effort into rebuilding our nation, and our efforts would be less of a struggle if trade routes stayed open. The Men of Kurflin won't let us pass into Cortaz, and the Elves are self-sufficient on their own without the need for trade."

"But the Cortazians, and even some of the Kurflinese, are helping you fight the Soul Seekers," Darr replied. "That has to mean something, despite the inability to trade."

Feywen nodded in agreement. "It means much more than I can explain. These small steps couldn't have been taken without my father. He knew the other kings of Ictar well enough to establish some small trade with them. He went so far as to open up civil talks with the Ogres, which inspired Elf King, Lendor Terwin, to do the same. However, with my father's death, I fear the Dwarf Elder Council will do nothing to aid his previous efforts."

Darr fell silent, but Feywen continued. "My hope is things will change after this war. I believe this war will help instigate reliance between the races. If all goes as planned, the three races of Man, Elf, and Dwarf will all be fighting for a common cause, and when the dust clears the battlefield, we'll see we accomplished it by working together."

"That's a very noble idea," Darr replied. Before he could think better of it, he asked, "Feywen, why are you here?"

"Do you mean, here in the Triker, or here, avoiding any responsibilities I might have in Jacova?" Awkward, Darr shifted, unable to think of a correct response, but Feywen laughed. "I'm here because I believe my father would have wanted me here. If there's anything I learned from the events at the Tower Castle, it's that my father believed whole-heartedly what Caeranol told him. Whereas Lendor Terwin and Ariel Forn expressed disbelief, my father was filled with hope after the encounter. He believed our destiny was in the Chosen of the Light. Yes, my father would've wanted me right here, guiding and aiding you and your sister in any way possible."

Feywen smiled, and rose from his seat. "I'll leave you with that thought. Lacdur and I have some scouting to do."

Darr smiled. Feywen Dery might by a man of mysterious ways, but he was bound by his beliefs. Without him, Darr had no idea how they would've gotten this far.

* * * *

Screams echoed through the Currents. After shaking off his initial shock, he put his ear to the spirit realm. The voices were disjointed and distant, close one second and moving away the next. The spirits themselves were in a state of commotion, their voices long and eerie. It took Darr several moments to focus his mind enough to move.

The Summoner sat up. The walls of the cave glowed red from the embers of the dying fire. Erec and Jinn slept beside him, and the Dwarves hadn't returned from their watch. Nidic Waq and Conra were nowhere to be seen. Darr got up and stepped over his siblings, walking lightly towards the entrance of the cave. Outside, Conra stood motionless, his face turned out into the blackness of the forest.

Darr walked to the old Elf's side. "What's going on?" he whispered.

"I can't be sure, Boy," Conra answered. "I heard screaming. The sound startled me and I woke up, and right away I could smell smoke."

After a few deep breaths, Darr shook his head. Conra

glanced sideways and grinned. "You wouldn't be able to smell it. Whatever's burning is a long way off." The Elf turned back, looking out into the night. "I might not be young anymore, but my Elven senses are as strong as ever."

Conra eased back inside the shadows of the cave, and his gnarled hand came up and brought Darr back with him. The Summoner kept his mouth shut, placing his trust in Conra. Two shadows materialized out of the darkness, they were on top of them so quick Darr couldn't react. His stomach jolted up into his throat, and though Lacdur and Feywen came into view, it took a moment for Darr to relax.

"'Aos—what're you two doin' here?" Lacdur grumbled, his large frame taking up every possible inch between them.

"Calm down," Conra said, "we just came out here to investigate."

"Investigate what?" Feywen asked.

"I heard screaming," Darr replied, "but it came from the Currents."

Conra nodded and added, "I heard something too, but not like the boy did. I *heard* them, and I could smell smoke."

"Elf blood," Lacdur muttered but Feywen silenced him.

"We haven't heard anything since we left," Feywen said. "In fact, there hasn't been a single sign of the Soul Seekers. You really heard screaming?"

Darr hesitated and said nothing.

"I need to know what you heard."

Darr couldn't think how to proceed. Feywen and Lacdur might not know anything about the Currents. Potentially, he'd be exposing a secret known only to a select few. But if Feywen had proven anything, he was a man who could be trusted.

Darr took a deep breath. "As a Spirit Summoner, my mind is connected to the Currents. The realm connects every living creature on Ictar, and because of this, I can feel and hear..."

"Bah!" Lacdur grunted, his voice rising into the night.

Feywen remained reserved, his face sincere. "I have heard of this phenomenon, Darr. It is rarely documented, but the oldest of the Dwarf histories record accounts of Summoners who can feel and hear the presence of other living creatures across the Currents. So, what is it? What did you hear?"

Darr shook his head. "My memories are fragmented, like a dream, but I felt pain and fear. I heard the screams of people far away. And I heard the spirits. They were crying out, I think."

Feywen fixed his gaze on Darr as if measuring his credibility. "Lacdur and I will take one more pass through the area. Perhaps there is something we missed." Lacdur grumbled muttered something, but he didn't argue before he disappeared into the trees.

Feywen paid him no attention and followed after, but after a few paces, he stopped and turned his head. "Where is Nidic Waq?" he asked. "If anyone knows what's happening, it would be him."

Darr shook his head. "I don't know. He was gone when I woke."

"He was missing when I woke as well," Conra added.

Feywen nodded, a dismissive gesture, before stalking off into the woods after Lacdur. His lean frame melted into the shadows. For a time, he stood alongside Conra, staring off into the Triker Forest after them.

"So," Conra said with a sigh, "you can read the Currents, huh? That's how you took care of the crab, isn't it?"

Darr grinned. "I suppose it was something like that."

For a long time, the Elf didn't say anything. "You know, Boy, one of these days I'm gonna have to know more about this magic you work." Conra looked at him for a moment longer before turning with a sigh and disappearing back inside the cave.

Darr considered going after him and telling him everything. Conra had been patient from the beginning, and still he knew next to nothing about his summoning abilities.

With a quick glance back out into the trees, Darr decided to save it for another time. Where had Nidic Waq gone? He couldn't worry about it.

Tired again, Darr left his thoughts outside the cave, and retreated to the comfort of his blankets.

* * * *

The warm smell of pan bread filled Darr's nose. He stirred within his blankets. With the realization that morning had arrived, he threw off his bedding and leapt to the side of the fire. Erec, Conra, and Jinn were awake and eating breakfast. Nidic Waq continued to be absent.

Erec looked up at him and said, "Feywen and Lacdur left early this morning. They said they're still scouting."

Darr sat down and let the warmth of the fire sink in, troubled, but also relieved that the Dwarves had not found anything last night. Conra offered him a slice of bread and a piece of cheese. He accepted them and devoured both within minutes.

He was in the middle of gathering his things when Feywen and Lacdur appeared through the sun-washed cave entrance.

Feywen bent down to Darr and said, "We searched for nearly three hours last night. I'm sorry, but we found nothing."

With a quick nod and a smile, Darr thanked him for his efforts and returned to packing his things. Did I dream it all? It wasn't possible, unless Conra had dreamt the same thing. He finished packing and hurried outside the cave to gather with the others.

"We're a few hours from the Crossroads," Lacdur announced when Darr appeared. "We'll be there by noon if we push it. I've got contacts there who will resupply us and give us horses from the remainder of our journey. If we're lucky, we might ever get to sleep in some real beds."

Abrupt as always, Lacdur turned and led the way. He kept a path parallel with the rocky terrain leading south. The day was pleasant and warm, filled with fresh smells of pine and the soft chirping of birds. An hour past midmorning, Lacdur took them sharply away from the mountains, leading them east.

A few minutes into their new course, Conra called a halt from his position at the rear of the procession. The five members of the little company huddled around the Elf. He stood looking up as if testing the air.

"What is it, Conra?" Jinn asked.

The Elf shook his head, his gaze still directed upwards. "I can't tell exactly. I smell smoke again." He lowered his eyes. "I smell death."

"From where?" Feywen asked, his voice calm but firm.

Conra pointed in the direction they were heading. "It's definitely coming from up ahead."

"I don't smell anything," Erec stated.

Lacdur laughed and said, "That's cause you don't have the magic-tainted senses of an Elf."

"That's enough, Lacdur," Feywen retorted without a trace of patience. "Put whatever prejudices you have aside and use your instincts, for spirits' sake."

The Dwarf warrior lapsed into silence, his face a mask of humiliation. Conra shook his head and said, "I can't be certain, but I'd guess from up ahead."

Feywen's face remained unreadable, but his fear rippled out into the Currents. "We must hurry," the once-prince said.

The line reformed and this time Feywen led the way, forging through the trees with single-minded purpose. Darr hurried alongside Jinn, and together they struggled to keep up. Darr gave his sister an encouraging smile, but it didn't dispel the look of worry on her face. The smell of smoke began to waft through the trees. Something terrible waited for them, and Darr knew with certainty the screams in the Currents last night weren't a dream.

Feywen fell into a dead sprint, his legs flying effortlessly over fallen branches and underbrush. The others struggled to keep up, but only Erec had the stamina to keep his pace. Feywen had thrown caution to the wind, and it occurred to Darr they could be heading into a trap. Hopefully, Lacdur still watched for the presence of Soul Seekers.

Sunlight flared before them, pure and warm. The trees broke apart and a field of long grass appeared. Smoke billowed before them, thick plumes centered on a dark smattering of deadwood across the field. No, not deadwood. Houses and buildings, structures reduced to blackened timber and rubble. Feywen raced ahead, and this time, even Erec fell behind.

The others slowed but they didn't stop running. The fields leading into the Crossroads became bumpy and rough, the grasses burnt through in spots. Darr tripped and fell into a heap, but Lacdur lifted him up.

At Darr's feet, a Dwarf child stared lifelessly up at him.

The body, along with many others, lay strewn throughout the fields. Some were bloodied and torn. Others were motionless heaps. They all stared into the morning sunlight, their eyes drained of color. Darr dropped to his knees, retching and coughing with the images burned into his eyes.

"I know it's hard," the Dwarf warrior soothed while hefting him back up. "We have to get moving. We have to see if any one made it."

Darr nodded, but the images of those Dwarves, broken and lifeless, were stuck in his mind. Lacdur dragged him for several paces before his legs could keep up with the mechanical motion of running. The others were far ahead now. Darr didn't really care. He wanted to run in the other direction.

Darr Reintol.

The voice came from the Currents. It belonged to Nidic Waq.

Walk the path you must, but do not let your fear get the

better of you.

The voice, imagined or real, made him remember. His fear weakened him. Darr shut out the images of the dead, focusing instead on his sister and brother, Feywen and Conra.

The first of the smoldering buildings appeared. Smoke billowed past, making it difficult to see, but the others of their company were gathered in a circle around a dark shape. Darr and Lacdur moved closer. Feywen knelt before someone with Conra at his side, their hands working over the body. Jinn stood alongside Erec, looking down at the dark shape on the ground.

Darr's breath caught in his throat.

It was Nidic Waq.

Chapter Twenty-Six

"The centuries passed and the fighting continued. The races evolved and learned from their wars, and sometimes, short periods of growth would erupt across Ictar. Alliances formed and often resulted in betrayal, but progress inched forward, aiming for a day when the races might find peace among one another. The memory of the Ancients, and the thing that drove them from the world, became like thin smoke, insubstantial and caught only in small pieces."

~From A Current History of Ictar, as told by Nidic Waq

The spot on the ground Darr had been studying disinterestedly for the past hour hadn't changed. Dusk had arrived, the sky turned crimson with the setting of the sun. The trees standing around him were dark sentinels, witnesses to the hideous deeds done to the Dwarves they once watched over. Tranquility fell over everything. The smallest chirp of an insect didn't intrude on the dead city.

"How are you holding up?"

Erec stood over him. Darr leaned forward, burying his head in the crook of his arms. "Not too well, Erec," he replied, his tone distant.

The breeze carried pieces of ash and the smell of smoke on its back. The burning in Darr's stomach told him he might retch again. In a swooping motion, Erec swung around and eased himself against the crumbling wall Darr sat against.

"It's been a hard day," Erec said, his voice sincere. "I thought you did well out there. You kept it together."

Darr shrugged. "No, I didn't. I ignored it. I wouldn't have gotten through it otherwise."

"Well, whatever. You showed courage when it counted. Not many could've done what we did today."

With Feywen and Lacdur, Darr and his brother had

helped inter several dozen bodies. They found a cold cellar that survived the fire, and for most of the day, they wrapped and carried bodies into the makeshift crypt. Unfortunately, there was no way they could bury all the dead, nor tend to them all. Someone else would have to finish.

"Lacdur said several hundred people lived at the Crossroads up until last night," Erec said, as if in a trance. "Over half of that number died. The Seekers didn't care who they killed. They gave no quarter except to those who had managed to escape, and from the looks of it, not many had managed to do so."

Erec looked over at Darr. "Do you think he helped them?" Darr didn't have to ask who he referred to. "You don't think he was working with the Soul Seekers, do you?"

When they found Nidic Waq, he was bloodied and unconscious. Burns ran down the length of one arm, and a series of deep slashes penetrated the flesh of his ribs. Conra had him carried to a building that'd been partially destroyed in the fire. With Jinn's help, the old Elf went to work treating the prophet's injuries.

"No, I don't think he was helping them," Darr whispered. "I would've known."

The two were silent for a moment while Darr studied the same spot at his feet. "You didn't know about Caeranol's prophecy to the Kings of Ictar," Erec said. "He hid that from you, little brother. Why not this?"

"Because the spirits wouldn't have let me near him!" Darr shouted, his face burning with frustration. "They confirmed everything he's said since Tyfor. I would've been able to tell if he was lying."

Darr's voice trailed off, lost in the heat of his words. He relaxed his body and focused, letting deep breaths settle into his stomach. The fact remained the spirits had said nothing to him about Nidic Waq except to confirm what he told him. Every word the prophet had ever issued, Darr heard echoed through the Currents. The spirits had never told him anything directly about the man. If he were in league with the Soul Seekers, wouldn't the spirits tell him? Wouldn't Racall?

"I think he was here trying to help," Darr said.

Erec let out a short sigh. "Well, we'll find out soon enough. Conra says he should wake soon. Speaking of which, the old Elf found some food in that burned out shell we're calling a shelter. I don't know what he found exactly, but..."

"I'm not hungry."

Erec's stare burrowed deep, but Darr didn't look up. "Suit yourself," Erec said in an oddly gentle tone. "We'll be inside when you're ready. Lacdur and Feywen scouted the area. They say the Seekers are gone for now. You should get some rest."

Darr nodded and thanked his brother for checking on him. Erec's footfalls faded into the dusk. Inside, where his emotions ran deepest, images of the dead townspeople were etched into his mind, and he couldn't escape their feel. The depthless gaze of dead eyes spoke of the horror that would soon run rampant through Ictar.

From Lacdur's examination of the scene, the first of the fires began around midnight, exactly when Darr heard the screams in the Currents. The Summoner couldn't ignore the fact he hadn't recognized the danger. He should've known something, but instead, he'd pushed the spirits away, and with it, any hope the Crossroads would be spared.

−The fault does not lie with you−

−The fault lies with the others−

−Your choices were good ones−

Whispers voices drawn from the Currents. Darr trembled and breathed deep. With the straying of his thoughts, his mind had strayed into the Currents. The spirits, detecting his pain, had come to him to dispel the negative emotions he forced into their realm. Darr slowed his breathing, yet their voices persisted.

−What has been done cannot be undone−

—What has been done can be prevented in other places—

"Go away!" Darr yelled, leaping to his feet. "Leave me alone! You should've stopped this!"

His screams rose into the coming night sky and the small smattering of stars as his raw emotions bubbled to the surface. "I could've helped the Crossroads. I could've saved them."

"Darr?"

Jinn's voice was small but recognizable. His sister stood motionless along the end of the wall, her body and face sketched by the light of the stars. She gave him a look of concern, but also love.

Everything drained away from the Summoner and he crumpled to his knees. Jinn ran to him in an instant, the strength in her arms evident while she cradled him close. "What's wrong with you?" she whispered.

Tears rolled down the Summoner's face and he tucked his head into her shoulder. "This is all my fault, Jinn. I heard them last night...I heard them in the Currents, and I could've stopped this, I should've stopped this, but I ignored it..."

Jinn held him, running her fingers along the back of his head like she might a child. "Don't hold onto this guilt, Darr," she whispered. "The Soul Seekers did this, not you."

She held him for a long time. When he finished, Darr lifted his head away and wiped at his eyes, ashamed at his outburst.

"I'm sorry," he said. "All I wanted to do was take responsibility. I thought if I could do that, I could stop this from ever happening again."

"But don't you see, Darr," she urged, leaning close. "You're helping stop the Soul Seekers. You're preventing this from happening again."

Darr let the strength of her words seep through him. Jinn was right, and so were the spirits. Despite the odds stacking against him, he promised himself he'd see the end of the Soul Seekers and their master.

* * * *

Nidic Waq woke an hour before dawn. Though his burns had been wrapped and the lacerations to his ribs sewn up, he walked unassisted into the side room of the blasted house where the others waited, a testimony to his incredible endurance.

Nidic Waq braced himself against the wall and stretched his hand out to his companions. "We don't have much time."

Feywen bolted to his feet without a word and supported the prophet's large frame. Darr and his companions all rose to their feet, and both awe and skepticism radiated through the Currents. Feywen led Nidic Waq to a scattering of blankets next to the woodstove and sat him down. Conra passed a bowl of soup to him, but Nidic Waq waved it aside.

"We don't have time for this," the prophet scolded. "The assault has begun much sooner than I anticipated. Navda is in danger. The Seekers move east, while we stay here."

It sickened Darr to think another town faced a massacre such as this. "They must be warned," he said. "We must go there."

"Not yet," Erec said, his voice cold and demanding. He rose to his feet. "No one's going anywhere until the prophet tells us why he's here."

"Erec, sit down," Jinn demanded, her round face pinched with anger.

"No. Not until we find out why he left without telling us and why he's at the center of this butchery. I won't take another step until he gives us a reason why we should trust him."

No one objected. The fire burning in the woodstove made hardly a sound, as if it too was unwilling to disrupt the tension. Did everyone believe as Erec?

"You're right to question me, Erec," the prophet admitted. "Your questions, all of your questions, are warranted."

Nidic Waq adjusted his body and leaned into the glow from the woodstove, his skin pale amid the wash of red from his beard and hair.

"My decision to leave you in the Triker was selfish," the prophet began. "I would only be able to protect myself, and that alone proved difficult. When I first detected the Seekers, they'd recently emerged from their mists. They were advancing on the Crossroads. I was still too far away to stop anything from happening, but I had to try. To bring you with me would've put all of our lives in danger. The number of Seekers which had assembled to destroy the Crossroads was larger than anything we've seen before."

Nidic Waq's face turned hard. "Nothing could've been done to stop it. The town had no preparation and hardly any defense. The Seekers washed through the town like a tidal wave. When I arrived, the Crossroad's had been burning for some time, a result of the townspeople who'd hoped to flush out the Seekers with fire. I helped those few who remained by sending them into the forests. I did everything possible to hold off the Seekers long enough for their escape. In the end, only daylight saved me. The Seekers retreated to their mists, and I collapsed where you found me."

Darr knew he told the truth. Despite whatever character defects Nidic Waq possessed, the spirits recounted his story as he told it. He'd done everything possible, and that hadn't been enough.

"'Aos—all those people and no one escaped," Lacdur said, shaking his head in disbelief.

Nidic Waq raised his head and replied, "Some escaped, but how many actually made it to the safety of Jacova, I do not know. Regardless, it's more important now to focus on those we can still save in Jacova and Navda. As I said before, the Soul Seekers are massing along the peninsula leading east. They're in such great numbers their presence is unmistakable."

"What is your plan?" Feywen asked.

"There are horses in a field south of here that the Seekers missed. I can see them in the Currents," Nidic Waq said. "You must secure them and head at once for Navda. The Summoners there must be warned, and they must be prepared either to flee or fight. I will go to Jacova."

"You're too weak, Prophet. I should know. I stitched you up," Conra countered.

"I'll be fine." Nidic Waq stood upright. He looked down at Darr and said, "I'm sorry, Summoner, but your quest must be deterred for the time being. The time spent warning Navda will inevitably slow the Seekers and ultimately give you more time to restore the remaining Sephirs."

The Summoner understood the importance of what they were required to do. He wouldn't ignore his instincts this time. Navda would be saved.

Lacdur and Feywen went out to find the horses while Darr and his siblings packed their things. A lot of the gear they'd brought would be left behind to necessitate a speedy journey. Conra helped, but in the end, each of the four would carry only a rolled blanket with some foodstuffs tucked inside.

Erec and Conra left to find weapons, leaving Nidic Waq alone with Darr and Jinn.

"I realize this must be very difficult for the both of you," Nidic Waq said, his voice soft. "You've both been patient despite everything that's happened. I sense your unease with where things are heading. Darr, your quest for self-discovery has turned into a destiny you cannot break from. Jinn, what once seemed to you an unconditional following after your brother, has since turned to a condition of your very soul, a following you cannot abandon. I ask you only to look after one another. Your mutual survival is what truly matters."

The prophet lifted his head as though he searched for something, but he whipped his cowl over his head, his face vanishing into darkness. "Keep yourselves safe," was all he said.

Nidic Waq swung around, a whipping of tattered cloth, and he stalked away into the darkness, his body melting away, leaving a void in the wake of his departure. When Nidic Waq traveled with him, Darr couldn't tolerate his deceptions. With him gone, Darr longed for his support. The Summoner saw the same confliction of emotions layered on Jinn's face.

"It's as if he has no place in this world," Jinn said, "yet we all rely on him to save us."

Darr nodded. His thoughts were the same.

Chapter Twenty-Seven

"The Devoid, long imprisoned and forgotten, was still alive, surviving on the only Light remaining within its body. Symdus's Light, so small and corrupt, could not escape the Devoid. It took many centuries before the Devoid gained enough strength to begin pressing against the bars of its prison, but when it did, Caeranol took notice."

~From A Current History of Ictar, as told by Nidic Waq

Erec and Conra returned shortly after Nidic Waq's departure. Their search for weapons turned up one short sword so Conra could arm himself. He wouldn't abandon his crossbow, but it didn't work against the Seekers. They settled down amongst their meager supplies and waited for Feywen and Lacdur to return. The fiery glow of dawn broke through the trees before the horses arrived.

"Sorry it took so long," Feywen said, leading three horses by a set of crude reins.

Lacdur appeared behind him with the remaining three. "We mutilated my pack to make bridles for these beasts." The Dwarf warrior slapped his rolled up blanket into Erec's arms. "Ha! You're strong enough to carry two blankets, aren't you, Tyfran? Or did I misjudge you?"

Erec laughed. "Are you sure you need a horse, Lacdur, because you've been riding me since we got here."

The Dwarf warrior laughed heartily. Despite the gravity of their work yesterday, cleaning up the Crossroads had finally brought Lacdur and Erec to a mutual understanding. Whenever Erec pushed Lacdur, the Dwarf would push back, and vice versa. As a warrior, Lacdur had a wealth of knowledge to teach Erec, and Erec knew it.

"I'm not used to riding without a saddle," Jinn said as she patted down the flanks of her horse.

"You won't have to worry about it," Feywen told her. "The horses are trained by Dwarves, and we're the best in Ictar. They'll follow my commands. All you have to do is hold tight."

By Feywen's estimate, it would take two days to reach Navda at a moderate pace, but he hoped to reach the city in half that time. Sleep and rest of any kind would be allowed only when the horses were required to stop. Though it would be a tough ride, Darr was excited. Since first learning about his summoning abilities, he'd always wanted to visit Navda, the City of Summoners.

Once everyone was situated, the once-prince gave a low whistle and took his mount into a steady gallop. Darr's horse responded by dashing after. Through the early morning hours, they rode steadily along the main road leading from the Crossroads. Sometimes they let the horses relax at a quick jog, and sometimes they walked, but for the most part, Feywen kept them galloping fast. Upon reaching the eastern edge of the Triker Forest, they were met with a torrential wash of rain.

Feywen led them to an outcropping of cedar to wait out the weather, cursing under his breath the entire time. Feywen's misery ran deep since leaving the Crossroads, and Darr recognized it without having to think too much on it. While he'd only imagined his responsibility for what happened at the Crossroads, it must be ten times worse for Feywen Dery.

When the rain had subsided to a slow drizzle, Feywen didn't hesitate to forge ahead. They rode across the boulder-strewn plains, and after a while, Darr's mind slipped into the Currents. He did so without knowing at first, but when he realized when he was doing, he forged ahead out of curiosity. Racall had told him the Lights of other living creatures carried their memories and feelings. Perhaps he could find a way to help his friends by listening to the Currents.

The emotions of his companions flooded Darr, making

him feel things like frustration, anger, and sadness. In his own heart, he felt tired. Images came next, a disjointed flashing of pictures portraying things he hadn't seen or done.

Darr redirected his mind and focused on the emotions rather than the connecting memories, keeping his own thoughts locked away so as not to invade the privacy of his friends. But things weren't so simple. Memory and emotion were closely connected, if not indistinguishable, and Darr couldn't read one without reading the other, so he forged ahead.

Feywen felt rage at what the Seekers had done, but that came as no surprise. His anger burned over the things done to the people of the Crossroads and his own father. His emotions and memories indicated the two events were inseparable in his mind. At the same time, Feywen struggled for restraint, but he couldn't command it.

Lacdur, on the other hand, could hardly be read at all. He kept everything hidden away, and only a glimmer of his memories revealed themselves. His body and mind were focused on his surroundings. Conra acted in much the same way, but Conra kept himself closed off from his emotions and memories. Both the Elf and the Dwarf lived very much in the moment.

Darr shifted his attention to Erec, finding a storm of frustration and sadness. Erec had mostly blocked off his memories of the Crossroads, though fragments of the atrocities infiltrated his Light. As a result, he couldn't distinguish his past memories from the troubled present, a difficult variance for anyone.

Last, Darr focused on Jinn. Though her insecurity and fear both loomed within her Light, they were overridden by her resolve. She pressed onward, adamant to follow through even though her fears told her to run in the other direction. She possessed great strength. She'd have to be. Along with three others, she would have to stand up to and defeat the most reckless evil Ictar had ever seen. The spirits wouldn't have chosen someone of any less character.

Darr relaxed his body, pulling his mind away from the Currents. The experience, though rudimentary in nature, had taught him much about how to control his ability. While rewarding, it was also an invasion. People kept their feelings to themselves for a reason, and it wasn't up to him to decide what they should share.

The day moved on, and the rain came and went in fits. Sometimes it would pour for several minutes at a time, only to stop long enough for the party to forge ahead and be caught in another downpour. Progress slowed, but Feywen didn't relent. He forced the horses into a wild gallop, keeping them moving when they could, and stopping them when the rain required it.

When they stopped for an hour to water the horses and rest, Feywen stalked around their shelter beneath the drooping limbs of a willow. Because Darr so recently felt what Feywen did, he approached the once-prince in an attempt to help. Feywen stopped pacing, his face kind but cautious. The emotions roiling within him invaded the Summoner's mind, but Darr shut away his connection.

"What is it?" Feywen asked, though not in an unkind tone.

Darr flipped his hair from his eyes while searching for something to say. "I wish I understood more about the Soul Seekers." As soon as he said it, Darr regretted opening his mouth. Feywen didn't need a remainder of the thing fueling his anger.

Feywen looked thoughtfully at Darr, perhaps to decipher the true nature of his intrusion. The once-prince settled himself at the base of the tree and welcomed Darr to sit as well. The others in their company were huddled on the other side of the trunk, tucked away from their conversation.

"Despite the time I've spent searching out the Soul Seekers, I understand very little about them," Feywen said. "They are single-minded in their need to hunt, but I've never seen them attack a group larger in number than ten or twelve. An attack on an entire town is unheard of. They don't notice movement or sound, but several times Lacdur and I got too close, and within moments they'd found us,despite all our efforts to stay hidden."

"What about the mist Nidic Waq talked about?" Darr asked, his mind racing for a way to keep Feywen talking.

"I'm not sure exactly how it works," Feywen answered, his brow furrowed. "It's not normal mist. It's thick and stagnant, and it moves unnaturally, like steam billowing from a kettle. You would recognize it if you saw it. Lacdur and I tracked it once, followed it while it moved through the Borderlands. Inside it, the Seekers don't appear to physically manifest themselves, but we didn't risk getting close enough to test the theory. We think the mist protects them from the daylight, but they retain their ability to move while in it."

"I suppose that makes sense considering what they're trying to do," Darr said. "It's just one more advantage..."

"What brought you over here, Darr?"

Darr steadied himself. "I wanted to know something more about the Seekers. I wanted to know how to defend myself."

"That isn't what brought you over here," Feywen said. Darr hesitated. Feywen glared at him.

The Summoner thought it over, then decided. "My connection to the Currents allows me to sense emotions and memories within other people. Ever since the Crossroads, it has been easier to read everyone because of the intensity of their emotions."

Feywen didn't break eye contact. "So, you know what I feel?"

"I felt your pain," Darr answered, "and the memories attached."

Feywen's gaze was fierce. "Some people might consider your ability an attack on their privacy. Worse yet, an attack on their very souls." The words set Darr on edge. He'd made a mistake.

Feywen smiled, disarming Darr. "Fortunately for you, Summoner, I'm not one of those people. I am a little shocked you saw something so private, but I understand something about your abilities. Nidic Waq has the very same."

"But, I don't use it the same way he does."

"No, you do not. He uses it to gain an advantage, to keep others in check and his plans in line. Don't misunderstand me. I have great respect for Nidic Waq and the things he is trying to accomplish, but I don't agree with his methods."

Darr nodded. He hesitated again before saying more. "I thought I might be able to help you. You've done so much for us."

Feywen waved the air in a dismissive gesture. "There's nothing anyone can do for me, Darr. You're a good friend for trying though. I think the reason people keep certain memories and emotions to themselves is because they try to make sense of them before sharing them. Sometimes we feel and experience things so pure and real, we want everyone to know. Sometimes we see things that make no sense, and our emotions reflect our inability to decipher what's happened."

Darr kept his gaze riveted on Feywen. "I'm sorry, Feywen. I didn't mean to pry."

"Your apology is unnecessary. Your heart was in the right place, and I can respect that." The Summoner smiled and got to his feet.

"Darr," Feywen called out. "The next time you want to know what I'm feeling or thinking, please ask me."

The air between them felt stressed. Regretful for what he'd done, Darr knew what it meant now to wield the power of the Currents. He'd never be normal again. Darr had always relied on his ability to arbitrate and put others at ease. Now, he'd forever be fighting the urge to dive into the Light of another and seek out their suffering in an attempt to make it better.

Feywen stood and looked out across the plains of the

peninsula. The rain lessened, and by the brightening of the sky, it appeared the clouds would clear soon.

"Go prepare the others," Feywen told him. "We're still a few hours away, but this will be our last rest."

Chapter Twenty-Eight

"Realizing a more permanent solution would be required to free Ictar from the Devoid, Caeranol established a covenant with the races of Ictar. He did so through a group of scholars called the Divine. Through them, his covenant and his teachings would be passed down through the generations until the time came they would be needed."

~From A Current History of Ictar, as told by Nidic Waq

With muddy ground beneath their hooves, the horses couldn't run, but they still made good progress. Everyone kept to themselves, but the mood lightened somehow. Darr couldn't describe the feeling, but everyone's determination was renewed as they traveled closer to Navda. Another tragedy like the Crossroads wouldn't happen again, he told himself, and that oath strengthened him. His friends probably felt the same.

As the sun crept into the horizon behind them, shadow tendrils stretched out towards Navda. The ground became more solid and Feywen pushed the horses into a steady gallop. By the time dusk had arrived, they were well into the hill country leading to the city situated on a steep rise overlooking the Arktary Sea. From there, Navda could ward off attacks from anywhere except from the west. A single stone wall stretched the length of the rise, low bulwarks no more than eight feet in height, their surface bathed in the red glare of the sunset. Darr's awe of the city he'd always dreamed of seeing was unsettling considering the current situation.

Feywen brought them to a halt a few hundred feet from the city gate.

"Stay put," he said. With Lacdur at his side, the Dwarves rode to the walls. They were gone only a few minutes when

Lacdur turned and rode back for them.

"Come along," the Dwarf warrior grumbled. "I don't think our prince is in the mood to wait."

Lacdur turned back towards the wall. Darr and the others followed, their own mounts matching Lacdur's pace. Within moments, it became obvious what had made Lacdur and Feywen so upset. The ironbound gates stood open to the night. One guard stood on duty, a Dwarf still in adolescence, looking somewhat terrified as Feywen Dery looked down on him with eyes of blue fire.

"Why are there no other guards on duty?" Feywen demanded, his voice calm but forceful.

The guard shook his head. "Aratan Bolgros ordered the change almost three months ago. He said it was unnecessary to have more than two soldiers on duty at any position. No one wanted to argue with him."

"Let me argue with him then." Feywen looked around. "How many soldiers are active?"

"I'm...I'm not sure...maybe two hundred. The rest have been dismissed."

Darr's heart dropped at the guard's statement. The city had no idea the danger it was in.

Feywen's brow furrowed. "You know who I am, do you not?"

The young guard nodded his head like it was about to disconnect from his shoulders. "You're Lord Dery, but the proclamation from Jacova says the monarchy no longer exists."

"That's correct, you aren't obligated to follow my orders, but hear me out," Feywen said, his command stern. "An enemy force is approaching. I need you to inform your commanding officer, and rally all active soldiers. Get them to this wall immediately, light the torches, and for spirits' sake, close the gate."

The guard acquiesced immediately, his lean frame darting to pull the gates in while Feywen and his companions entered. "We ride to the Aratans," Feywen told the guard. "Remember what I told you, soldier. I want to see two hundred men at this wall by the time I return."

With a high-pitched whistle, Feywen signaled the horses and bolted out along the road leading into Navda. Gardens surrounded them on either side of the cobblestone road, a buffer separating the city from its wall. Flowers and trees glistened in the twilight by the light of lamps. People walked along little trails winding through the mass of greenery, turning their heads at the sound of the racing horses, oblivious to the danger they were in. Darr wanted to scream at them, to warn them, but he held his tongue.

When the city's buildings came into view, Feywen kept the horses running. The city sat quiet and brightly lit, with nothing to indicate the citizenry suspected an impeding attack. As they raced past the buildings, a few people appeared to investigate, crouched down low against window sills and from around corners.

Feywen led them through the center of town to a large mansion set on the cliff overlooking the sea. He rode his horse up to the wrought-iron gate and leapt clear. He drew the sword from his belt, kicked open the gate, and rushed towards the mansion without waiting for his companions. Darr, followed by Erec and Lacdur, were the first to reach the gate. Jinn and Conra had fallen behind, but they weren't more than a few paces away.

"Better go after him." Lacdur said with a rough laugh. "There's sure to be something good when he finds the Aratans."

Like a man possessed, Feywen's anger radiated from his body. Darr had no trouble identifying where his anger came from. Navda stood on the brink of annihilation, and yet, the everyday defenses of the city were missing.

With incredible strength, fueled by the intensity of his emotions, Feywen lowered his shoulder and charged the front door. The jamb split wide where it was latched and the door swung inward, hard. Feywen stumbled inside the mansion and righted himself. His sword pointed straight ahead. Three men stood before him, all of various ages and sizes, but dressed in the same long, crimson robes. Feywen had his sword drawn on the largest of the three men.

"You're dead, Bolgros," the once-prince said in a calm voice. "You are all dead."

The Aratans stared at him in apparent shock.

* * * *

After their initial shock wore off, the three Aratans of Navda were thrown into different states of confusion.

Aratan Bolgros, the tallest and thickest of the three men, was a Cortazian. Despite his pale and waxy features, he commanded frightening arrogance. The big man yelled for guards, his face contorted in rage at the indignation he'd received.

Aratan Vanheila, an Elf and the youngest of the three, quietly turned away from the scene and sat down. He appeared as though he didn't know how to respond.

Aratan Fereta stood looking small and fragile, a Dwarf of considerable age, his hair wispy white like cobwebs. Unlike the other two Aratans, Fereta remained motionless, his face reflecting nothing.

When Fereta finally spoke, his voice sounded brittle and hard, but his words came unexpected. "It's good to see you again, young prince." The Aratan gave a slight bow, showing his respect. "While the monarchy of your family has been dissolved, you should know I trusted deeply in your father. You may not have kingship, but in my eyes, you should still be treated as one."

"What are you saying, Fereta?" Bolgros raged. "He's nothing now except a citizen of the Dwarf nation, and citizens have no power here."

Feywen Dery remained quiet to Bolgros' debasing

comments. "Please calm yourself, Aratan Bolgros," Fereta soothed. Bolgros turned in a huff, the look on his face a mask of loathing. "Give the prince a moment to explain himself,"

"Thank you for your consideration," Feywen said with a slight bow. "I apologize for the abruptness of my entry..."

"Abruptness?" Bolgros yelled, his pale features turned crimson. "You smashed in our door and who knows what other destruction you've brought!"

"Let him speak," Aratan Vanheila said, his voice a whisper, but commanding.

Feywen continued. "I acted as I have in order to prove a point. You've no defenses in place. Your gates were standing open, and your soldiers have been dismissed. Navda has always been a place of peace, but you've taken a risk in lowering your guard."

"Are we to expect an attack?" Fereta asked.

"Yes," Feywen replied at once. "Soul Seekers are massing on the peninsula. Navda and its citizens are next in their sights."

The anger drained from Bolgros' face, and he asked, "If we're next, who was first?"

Feywen met the big Aratan's gaze before answering. "Two nights ago, the Seekers attacked the Crossroads without warning. At least half the population perished. The prophet, Nidic Waq, was there to witness the attack. He confirmed that it was the Soul Seekers."

"Caeranol save us," Fereta whispered.

Aratan Vanheila rose to his feet, his Elven features strong as he took a few steps forward. "We must evacuate immediately," he said. "We'll organize a withdrawal across the peninsula."

"I can't recommend that," Feywen said. "The Seekers would find you during your retreat. They don't care about the city. The people are the only thing that matter to them. What about ships? The Dwarf Naval Fleet stationed here could easily move your people."

Bolgros raised his face, showing his arrogance and defiance in one mean stroke. "The Dwarf Navy has been dismissed on my orders."

"'Aos, you madman," Lacdur rasped in horror. "What would make you do such a thing?"

Bolgros' demeanor didn't change. "I was given control of Navda's defenses when the monarchy was dissolved. We didn't need the navy here. The operation was too expensive to keep up in a time when there is no war."

"Is that why you dismissed your soldiers?" Feywen asked, taking a step forward, his body rigid. "Do you know what you've done, Bolgros? You've sentenced this city to death."

"I have sentenced nothing," Bolgros retorted with a roll of his eyes. "How was I to know the Seekers would come here? The Dwarf Elder Council told me almost nothing about the Soul Seekers when I was given command. They told me only to keep my eyes open."

"And so instead, you have kept them shut." Feywen turned away in disgust.

Darr's stomach knotted up while the Aratans and Feywen continued to argue. The city would be swallowed whole before it could react to the oncoming threat. He glanced sideways at Aratan Vanheila. The Elf had been staring at him since he'd arrived.

"Aratan Fereta," Feywen implored. "Are you still in control here? Are you still the highest among the Aratans?" The wizened Dwarf nodded. "Then I ask you to remove Aratan Bolgros as captain of defense. Appoint me instead."

Fereta took a minute to consider, but he shook his head. "I can't do that, Lord Dery. This city would panic if it knew it headed for battle. The people here are not warriors. We must investigate other methods."

"We don't have time to find another way," Feywen insisted. "Our options are to fight or flee, and fleeing is no longer an option."

Fereta shook his head, and Bolgros began chastising

Feywen for attempting to take away control of the city's defenses from him. Lacdur and Erec shouted as well. Even Conra spoke up in an attempt to plead the case. Helpless, Darr watched the argument. Somehow, they must find a way to convince the Aratans of the danger they were in. He met Vanheila's gaze once more, the Elf's gaze riveted on his own. What was it about Vanheila that no one else saw?

Darr nudged his mind into the Currents, keeping his gaze steady with Vanheila's. He felt the Aratan's Light within the spirit realm, faint and obscure, like the shadow of a body pressed up against stained glass. Vanheila was listening to the Currents. Darr smiled. He knew how to break the stalemate between the Aratans and Feywen Dery.

He checked the Currents for any distruptions before he plunged himself in...

...the wisteria light surrounded him, familiar and welcomed. When had that happened? When had the Currents begun feeling so comfortable? The fuzzy balls of white, that were the spirits, danced around him, their whispered words urging him on in approval of what he was about to do.

The Lights of his companions glowed around him, their bodies a mass of white sparkle. Their Light didn't glow the same way the Aratans' did. Vanheila, Bolgros, and Fereta— their Lights responded to his own, dancing in the wisteria glow as if they were ready to come alive at any moment.

And so they will.

The Aratans were practiced in the known arts of summoning, their minds always connected to the Currents. Although one practice remained a mystery to them, for they had no notion of how to enter the spirit realm. Darr would show them the way. He reached out to them, no longer practicing the physical motion. His Light connected with theirs, and gently, he brought them into the Currents.

The shock and confusion of the three men roared like something tangible, wild with fear. The spirits flitted around them in swarms, feeding off the intensity of their Light, but Darr willed them away.

"Where are we?" Bolgros demanded, his Light brimming with terror.

"You are in the Currents," Darr answered.

"You," Vanheila said. "You're a Summoner. How have you brought us here?"

"I can explain when we're done, but for now I only need you to trust me, and trust Feywen Dery. You know I can't tell lies here."

The Aratans were resistant, but they could do nothing about it. As Racall had shown him the Currents, bending him into understanding, Darr would have to do the same for them.

"You must see something," Darr said.

He let his memories surge to the surface, painting a picture so vivid the Aratans experienced the moment with him. The lights of the Currents softened, replaced with a scattering of colors that exploded into a rendering so real it hurt.

The *Aratans* ran alongside Darr as he ran through the trees of the Triker. They felt his guilt and fear. The trees fell away, the late morning sky opened up, and smoke stretched in billowing plumes to the sky. Dead Dwarves, men, women, and children lay scattered all around, their bodies torn, their eyes white as snow. Darr let the Aratans taste his sickness, he let them experience that moment of terror with his own thoughts and feelings. They smelt the smoke and the carnage. They tasted the bile in his mouth. They lived the memory like it had happened to them.

Once they understood, Darr retreived the memory and with it, he released his hold on the Aratans. Without another word, the men slipped back into their physical bodies and left the Currents behind...

Feywen and the others were still yelling when the Aratans froze. Their faces went blank with confusion, and their voices stuck in their throats. Vanheila still had his gaze fixed on Darr. Fereta and Bolgros turned to look at him as well.

"What have you shown us, Summoner?" Fereta asked, his words distant.

Feywen and the others turned to Darr, but he didn't move. He answered confidently. "I showed you what happened at the Crossroads, so you would know. The Seekers come now to do the same to you."

The silence in the room grew depthless. Darr and the three Aratans looked at one another across the room. Aratan Vanheila took a step forward and knelt down in front of Feywen Dery. Aratan Bolgros hesitated for a moment, then knelt with his head bowed.

Aratan Fereta walked towards Feywen and placed a gnarled hand on his shoulder. "We pledge our support to you, Lord Dery," the old Dwarf said in a near whisper. "You may not be king, but we'll trust in you to do whatever is necessary."

Despite his old age, Fereta lowered himself to his knees and bowed his head. In the ensuing silence, Feywen Dery stood in place, confusion evident on his face as he nodded.

Chapter Twenty-Nine

"One day, the Chosen of the Light would put an end to the Devoid. Four individuals selected by the spirits and imbued with a fraction of Caeranol's Light. A talisman held by each would name them: one a Bearer, one a Guardian, one a Warrior, and one a Healer. Together, and only together, could the four rid the world of the Devoid."

~From A Current History of Ictar, as told by Nidic Waq

Jinn Reintol lifted her eyelids with the slow, lazy motion that comes with a good night's rest. She took a moment to get her bearings, letting her dreams fade away while reality seeped into her body. Hazy sunlight came into the room from a wide window, its panes covered in lacy, white curtains reminding her of a dress her mother once wore. Paintings hung on the walls depicting the faces of serious men, their features cast in iron rather than oil.

This room, this mansion, wasn't familiar. It was the home of the Aratans, and Jinn spent a long time examining the various sights, taking in and becoming acquainted with the strangeness of her surroundings. She might've done so last night, but the prospect of sleep had been too appealing. When she'd reached her room, she followed her first impulse and slid under the sheets.

Cozy in her bed and satisfied with what she saw, Jinn let her mind wander to those little pieces of reality nagging at her. She'd guessed where Feywen and Lacdur had gone with the Aratans after she left last night. Planning a defense would've come first, and the two Dwarves were seasoned veterans in the war against the Soul Seekers.

Something had come between them, stopped the dangerous confrontation between them, changed the attitude of the Aratans that discouraged their argument immediately.

253

Darr had something to do with it, and Jinn was sure he'd done something in the Currents.

Content with her small conclusions, Jinn threw back the sheets and leapt from bed anxious to start the day. She washed in a basin and dressed in a fresh set of clothes, provided by her hosts.

She fastened a belt across her waist.A knock came at the door. A visitor wasn't unexpected, but it might be later in the day than she thought. Perhaps she should be out doing something. She pulled on her boots and walked to the door. Conra entered before she could pull back the latch, his gray head appearing through the opening.

"Oh, I'm sorry." The Elf hastily pulled his head back, but Jinn stopped him.

"It's okay, Conra," she said with a laugh. "I was coming out anyway."

"I'm sorry. I thought maybe you'd left," he said.

Jinn smiled at his sheepish appearance. Because Conra kept to himself, she hadn't talked much with him on their journey, but she liked him. He treated her like an equal, always kind and straightforward with her, listening with open ears to anything she had to say.

"I woke up a while ago," she told him. "Where are the others?"

Conra raised his head and let loose a slow sigh. "Well, it would appear we're as useful today as we were last night. Lacdur left early this morning to track the Seekers and find out how far away they are. Feywen and Erec went out to the wall, and Darr and the Aratans are off helping the people in town. I would've gone, but I wanted to stay here in case you needed company."

Jinn wasn't bothered that her brothers had left her behind, but she felt uncomfortable being taken care of. Since learning of her role among the Chosen of the Light, Jinn perceived herself as being in the way. She had become a commodity in need of protecting.

Silence passed in the wake of Conra's words, and Jinn hastened to find something to say. "Maybe we can go find them."

Conra smiled, forcing a crinkling of his lined face. They walked down the hallway of the Aratan mansion, and after descending a small staircase, they stood outside the large anteroom they'd been in the night before. A serving man appeared and approached them.

"Good morning," the man said. "Aratan Fereta has asked to meet with you. He'll be along shortly if you'd care to wait."

Jinn and Conra bowed their heads, and the serving man showed them over to a small stuffed couch.

"Would you like anything? Breakfast, perhaps?" he asked.

Jinn and Conra shook their heads in unison. The serving nodded and dismissed himself.

Conra leaned back casually and said, "Darr did something to those Aratans last night."

Jinn didn't know how to answer. Conra knew almost everything concerning their journey, but he knew next to nothing about Darr's summoning abilities. Jinn understood Darr's reason for keeping it secret, but at the same time, Conra had proved to be a trusted and willing ally.

"I think he did something too," she replied, keeping her tone uninterested.

The Elf sighed. "Hmm, I wonder how he could've made them change their minds so easily."

"The Aratans said he showed them something. He probably did it through the Currents."

Engulfed with curiosity now, Conra set his hands on his knees and leaned forward, his fierce eyes riveted on her. "Tell me something about the magic he works."

Jinn hesitated. It wasn't her place to tell Conra anything. "Darr's different from other Spirit Summoners. He doesn't only listen to the spirits, he can talk to them. He can put himself in the Currents and ask them to do things for him."

"So, the spirits are the source of his magic," Conra said. "I never would've imagined they possessed that kind of power."

Jinn shook her head. "I don't think it's only the spirits. It's the Archons, also."

The look Conra gave her suggested fascination beyond what she could see written on his face. "The Archons," he whispered. "Everything I've ever known says the Archons are confined to the Sephirs."

"They are to some extent," Jinn answered. "It seems the Sephirs are linked to the Currents, as is everything living. The way Darr explains it, if something has life, it's connected to the Currents."

"Amazing. I'd never thought such a thing was possible. So, we're all connected?"

"It would seem so."

"What a revelation that would be for the rest of Ictar," Conra laughed. "If everyone could see into the Currents like Darr does, could you imagine the impact it would have? Everyone would see themselves as equals."

Jinn shook her head again. "I don't think it'd necessarily work that way. Just because you see someone as an equal doesn't mean a thing. Look at the power struggles going on now, in a time when the races view themselves equally."

"I suppose you're right," Conra agreed.

A door opened across from them, and a small, hunched form wrapped in robes of crimson stepped into view. Aratan Fereta's friendly face smiled. The old Dwarf amused Jinn with his white beard obscuring his wrinkled face. Despite, his appearance, he had her respect.

Fereta gave a short bow and said, "Thank you both for waiting. I apologize for the sluggishness of my ageing body. Your brothers are tending to matters concerning our defense. I thought I'd offer to show you the city while they do so."

Conra looked as though he wanted to get out of the mansion, so Jinn nodded to Fereta. "We would like that," she said.

A broad smile stretched across the Aratan's face. "Come

then." He shuffled towards the anteroom, and Jinn and Conra followed after.

Out in the morning air Fereta said, "I must say, Jinn Reintol, your brother is quite a fascinating boy."

Jinn gave a disarming smile, unsure of what to say. Conra, always blunt and to the point, forged ahead without her.

"What do you mean?" the Elf asked.

"I'm not sure I know my exact reasons," Fereta said with a shake of his head. "I've been a Spirit Summoner my entire life. I've instructed many, but I've never met a Summoner that I can feel like he were a spirit himself. He has a presence in the Currents, as if he's there all the time."

"Is that what happened last night?" Conra asked.

Fereta cackled and shook his head. "I'm not sure what happened last night. I'll confess, I feel as if time disappeared last night. Somehow Darr showed us the error of our ways. I don't know how he accomplished this, but it felt like he took us inside the Currents."

Darr mentioned Racall had done a similar thing to him once. If Darr possessed power similar to Racall, what were his limitations? How powerful had her brother become since leaving Tyfor?

At the end of the walkway, the city of Navda opened before them. The sky shone blue overhead, except for a smattering of white clouds dotting the western horizon. The clean streets were bordered by carefully maintained yards, and people hurried in a pleasant manner from one place to another. If Jinn didn't know any better, it was just a normal day.

"Long before the end of the Aeon Wars, a group of Spirit Summoners and their families settled here," Fereta told them as they walked. "This peninsula was far removed from the rest of Ictar, and it had no resources that were particularly valuable. It was a perfect spot for a people who already felt removed from the rest of society."

"Why did they feel removed?" Jinn asked.

Fereta sighed as if he'd been asked a difficult question. "During the Aeon Wars, Spirit Summoners met with discrimination, and in severe cases, torture and death because of the abilities they sometimes displayed. A group of Summoners found their way here, and together, they learned how to control their abilities. Over the years, the colony attracted scholars and historians, people who strived to learn and expand their minds. After the wars, the city was born into the Dwarf territories. We adhere to the laws of the Dwarf Elder Council, but mostly we're governed from within, by elected Aratans."

The old Dwarf gave Jinn a wink. She liked Aratan Fereta. While she'd never known her grandfather, she imagined he would've been something like Fereta, full of stories and little secrets.

As they approached the city center, the amount of people and activity increased. A singular race didn't make up the population of the community. Elves, Dwarves, and Cortazians all worked side by side gathering and organizing weapons and supplies.

Fereta's attention turned to a garden shed off the road with workers gathered around it. "Most of the work being done in town is focused on opening up the tunnels running beneath the city," Fereta explained, gesturing to the workers. "In Navda's early history, tunnels leading to the Arktary Ocean were dug in case the city fell under attack. They haven't been used in over a century."

Debris hauled from the shed passed from worker to worker and then tossed in a pile behind them. The shed appeared to be a hiding spot for the tunnels Fereta spoke of.

"Is that really going to work?" Conra asked. "I thought Feywen said running wasn't an option."

Aratan Fereta didn't look back. "Any options we have must be explored. We have so few left to us."

They left behind the ruckus of the city and entered into

the vast garden area fronting the wall. "Cerian Gardens," Fereta said with no small amount of pride. "Prospective teachers and students wanting to practice here are required to bring seeds or bulbs from a plant native to their home. The result is a collection of flowers, trees, and shrubs from every corner of Ictar. These gardens are a symbol of our perseverance to learn regardless of race, creed, or age."

The feeling of harmony in the garden was omnipresent. Colors diffused and radiated through the various beds, and trees both familiar and foreign grew together in small thickets. The gardens were a promise of the peace that might one day spread through Ictar. Beyond the protective shelter of the gardens where the low wall rose up, the sounds of men shouting and the sharp clang of metal broke the soothing morning air.

Fereta's face changed, becoming less jovial. "Nearly five hundred soldiers have gathered," he whispered. "Most are trained soldiers who've come from Jacova over the years and did not return home after their dismissal. Roughly a thousand able-bodied men from many different age groups have joined them, though these men are mostly untrained. They are teachers, students, and farmers, but they can wield a sword. Right now, that's all we need."

Fereta led them beyond the gardens to a wide clearing fronting the walls. Men were busy training both within and outside the wall. Fereta took them to a small stairway near the city's gate and led them up to the top of the wall. Feywen Dery worked nearby with a small group of men along one of the battlements. Aratan Fereta signaled to the once-prince and Feywen came over to them, his face tired.

"Good morning, Jinn. Conra. It's good to see you," he greeted.

"Has your man returned yet?" Fereta asked.

"Yes. Lacdur returned less than an hour ago. You can already see what he found." Feywen gestured out towards the plains, pointing to a spot west and north on the horizon. Jinn saw nothing at first, but what she'd mistaken as a low bank of storm clouds became apparent as something else. On the horizon where Feywen had pointed, a heavy gray blanket, swelled and heaved, its eerie bulk sliding forward. Her heart skipped a beat.

"The Seeker mists," Feywen said. "They'll be here by nightfall."

Jinn's stomach spun in circles, threatening to fold her over. She resisted the urge to move and focused on keeping her balance.

Fereta tried to smile and failed. "I'll have to dismiss myself now. Feel free to walk the gardens. Your brother, Erec, trains with the men below, but Darr should be in town. If you find him, I'm sure he'll find something you can do." The Aratan bowed once more, and with a polite nod to Feywen, they climbed down from the wall.

Jinn stood alongside Conra for a time, looking out at the men on the fields below them. She looked over the ranks of soldiers, trying to pick out Erec. With all the activity going on, she couldn't tell one soldier from another. Some fought each other with sticks to hone their skills. Others stood in rows and fired volleys of arrows at distant targets on the field.

Training, Jinn thought desperately. Training and the Seekers will be here tonight.

"Do you think they stand a chance?" Jinn asked.

Conra said nothing. Like her, he probably didn't want to say the answer out loud.

Unable to watch any longer, Jinn and Conra stepped down from the wall and walked back through the gardens. In silence, they made their way back to the city where people ran about in complete ignorance of what came for them. It frightened Jinn the city could be so unprepared, so unheeding of the danger.

In the early afternoon, they found Darr. Her brother worked outside a small school that had been converted to a shelter. He talked with several others while they sorted a variety of supplies, but as soon as he saw them, he stopped his work and ran over.

"Have you seen the city?" he asked, his face beaming with excitement.

Jinn nodded. "Yes, Aratan Fereta showed us around. What've you been doing?"

Darr gestured towards the school. "Soldiers wounded during the battle will be brought here. We've been working all morning to prepare it." He looked like he would burst at the seams with excitement.

"So, I take it you like it here?" Conra asked.

"I do, very much," Darr replied. "Everyone here knows about Summoners. For the first time in my life I don't feel like an outcast."

Stung by her brother's words, Jinn refused to show it. "You were never an outcast in Tyfor," she said. "We always took care to make sure you would never feel that way."

"It's different here, Jinn," he said. "Most of the people I've met know what it's like to be a Summoner. They've struggled with the voices of the spirits and how to shut them out. No one in Tyfor ever knew that feeling..."

"I did," Jinn interrupted. "I knew because you always talked with me about what it meant."

"I'm sorry," Darr said, his brow furrowed. "Of course you understood me. You've always helped me, Jinn, but I don't have any explaining to do here. Here I can learn things about myself that I couldn't learn back at home."

Still hurt, Jinn forced a smile. There was no point in arguing the matter. Her pain came from the thought Darr might one day come to Navda to live, and with Erec going away also, she would be left behind.

"Enough of this," Conra said. "We still have a long journey ahead of us, Boy. We'll see if you still feel this way about Navda once this quest is over." The Elf shrugged and his face cast in iron. "Have you heard about the Seekers?"

The excitement drained out of Darr's face. "Let's walk," he said, taking them to a side path along the school which led back to the gardens.

"I didn't want anyone to overhear," Darr said. "In reality, only a select few in the town know that it's the Soul Seekers coming to attack. Everyone else has been told it's Ogres."

Jinn shook her head in disbelief. "You're joking. You mean to tell us nobody knows it's the Seekers?"

"Only the people in town, those who can't fight," Darr answered. "I'm sure the soldiers know. That's what the Aratans said they would do. Many rumors have been floating around, and the people in Navda believe the Soul Seekers are remnant pieces of magic from the Aeon Wars. They don't believe they can be stopped. Telling them the truth would lead to mass hysteria."

"That's just the opinion of the Aratans, isn't it?" Conra asked. "They don't know for a fact it'll really come to that."

"I suppose not," Darr replied, shaking his head. "But they've been in this city a lot longer than we have. They don't think the Seekers will even breach the wall."

Conra gave a look of confusion, a mirror of Jinn's feelings. "How can that be possible?" she asked. "We saw the soldiers training out there. Half of them don't even know what they're doing."

Darr leaned towards his sister and Conra. "I talked to Erec a few hours ago and he spent the morning spilling casks of oil over the fields outside the wall. He said it starts about a hundred yards out, and once it's lit, the whole field will go up in flames. That's Feywen's plan, to burn the Seekers up."

"What happens if the Seekers break free?" Conra asked. "What if they gain the wall before the fields can be fired? You can't be telling me that's his entire plan?"

"No," Darr said. "No, that's only what Erec heard. Feywen's been studying the Seekers for months, and he has enough military experience to know not to rely on one plan." The Summoner looked unsure of himself. "I would hope he has another plan."

Jinn shook her head. They'd put faith in Feywen Dery to lead them through the Triker, and he'd done so successfully. Why start doubting him now?

Darr didn't look so sure. "I wish there was something I could do to help in this fight. Both Feywen and Lacdur have banned me from setting foot on the battlefield, and if the Seekers break through the wall, I'm supposed to retreat through the tunnels with you two."

"Well, isn't there something you can do with your magic?" Conra suggested, his grizzled brow lifting in anticipation.

"No, there's going to be too many Seekers. Nidic Waq said it wouldn't be wise in any case, and this time there will be a lot more than the three we fought in the Triker."

"Yeah, but this city is filled with Summoners," Conra said followed by a snort. "You'd think the lot of you could come up with something."

"Maybe, but none of these Summoners know how to control the magic. They don't even know how to reach the Currents..." Darr's voice trailed off and his brown eyes grew distant.

Several moments passed and Darr didn't move. Finally, Conra broke the silence. "What's the matter with you, Boy?"

The Summoner flinched, and his eyes shot to Jinn, burning with fascination. "We have to go see Feywen," Darr said. Without another word, he took off running in the direction of the wall.

Jinn watched after him and attempted to make sense of his actions. Conra looked to be doing the same. They wouldn't be able to figure it out by standing around.

She gave Conra a shrug and dashed towards the gardens after her brother.

Chapter Thirty

"For many generations, the Divine spread the teachings of Caeranol throughout Ictar, and the covenant remained safe. The Aeon Wars, like everything else, changed even the ranks of the Divine. Many Divine turned from the roots of their founding and sought ways to twist their knowledge into power. The Divine sided with the monarchies rising up across the land, and together, they ended the Aeon Wars."

~From A Current History of Ictar, as told by Nidic Waq

At sunset, Darr walked to Navda's wall with Jinn and Erec at his side. He walked in silence, content with his siblings' company. Around them, the city stood rigid in anticipation of what was coming. Some believed Ogre raiders approached, while others knew it was the Seekers coming for them. None of them would be prepared. The soldiers were too unprepared to hold the walls all night, and the citizens taking refuge within their homes didn't possess the bravery to take the place of their defenders. Feywen hoped for the best, but he wasn't optimistic the walls would hold.

Of course, Darr had a plan in case they didn't.

"Look," Erec said at his shoulder. His brother pointed beyond the city wall. "Do you see?"

Where the sun set in the west, a great gray cloud rose up against the glare of the sun. The Seeker mists. Having appeared a few hours ago, the mists were rising and growing to enfold the hills below the city, a great massing wall prepared to swallow it whole. The sight was unsettling, and Darr hoped the townspeople didn't see it.

At the edge of the gardens, the level of activity increased from a buzzing of people to a swarm. Feywen and Lacdur led the more experienced soldiers, their position established outside the wall and on the low battlements. Reserve soldiers stood ready and at attention, prepared to march inside the city wall when required. Erec would stand with the reserves, his warrior instinct unquenchable. Darr and Jinn both tried to talk him out of going, but their brother wouldn't hear it. Although untested, Erec had trained as a soldier. He would fight and no argument could change his mind.

Erec stopped once they approached the front lines. He turned to his siblings and said, "This is where I leave you."

Conflicted, Darr watched his brother, studying him. He didn't want his brother to fight, but at the same time, he didn't wish to take away Erec's warrior heart. His brother would fight as a brave and fierce warrior, the same way Darr would fight with his Summoners.

"Keep yourself safe," Jinn whispered.

She moved forward and embraced him. Erec hugged her back and smiled, the first genuinely happy emotion he'd displayed in weeks. Jinn released her grasp and took a step back. Erec extended his hand out to Darr. The Summoner took his arm and pulled Erec close.

"I don't want you to do this," Darr said.

Erec shook his head. "Enough of this. We've been over it already. I'm fighting because it's the only thing I'm good at, and because I don't think anyone else can do the job of protecting you two better than I can."

Darr nodded his head, not in understanding, but because he didn't know what else to do. "I wish there was another way. You could protect us from back here, in the city."

"If I fight up towards the front, you might not need any protecting in the city. Perhaps I can take down every one of the Seekers that comes over that wall." Erec smiled and his face lit up. "You just worry about yourself and Jinn. Be ready to work your plan if the Seekers get too close. And if that fails, you run."

Feywen and Lacdur would do everything in their power to hold the wall, but if the Soul Seekers broke into the gardens, the people within the city would be ordered to evacuate through the tunnels. If the soldiers couldn't stop them in the gardens, Darr would initiate his plan as a final defense. If that failed, fate would decide what happened next.

Erec fastened the buckles of the thick leather plate he wore and checked the short sword at his side. He acted nervous, but Darr believed it came more from his inexperience, rather than fear. Erec wasn't the least bit afraid, and that single fact was more upsetting than any other. His brother should be terrified.

"Well, this is it." Erec let loose a quick breath. "You two look after each other. I don't want to have to come running if you get separated." He gave a perfunctory nod, rigid and tight like Darr would expect from a soldier, and turned to find his place.

Darr and Jinn stood for a time at the edge of Cerian Gardens, watching the daylight leak away over the heads of the troops. Within a few minutes, the unit commanders gave their signals, and in single columns of four across, they moved to the wall. Darr tried to pick out Erec among them, but he failed. He wished his brother safe.

"Should we head back?" Jinn asked in a soft voice, her eyes still focused on the looming mists.

Darr nodded. "The Aratan Fereta and Vanheila will be waiting for me," he said. "They want me to explain to the other Summoners what to do."

Jinn looked up at him, her concern evident in her face. "Are you sure you'll be able to do this? After what happened with the scattercrab, don't you think this is risky?'

She was right, but Darr shook his head. "We have to try something, and this seems like the best plan. If I'm careful and check the Currents beforehand, I don't see what could go wrong."

Jinn didn't look convinced, but she said nothing more. Darr watched her, trying to figure out her doubts, but he didn't want to pry. Instead, he turned and walked back to the city with his sister at his side.

* * * *

At the edges of Cerian Gardens, Darr stood with Aratan Vanheila and watched the city walls. Behind them, Aratan Fereta and his Summoners stood motionless and silent. Though distant, Darr could hear Feywen Dery's voice in the night, his words booming. He wanted to see what happened outside those walls.

Carefully, Darr put his ears to the Currents, reaching out across the ether to Feywen. Brief flashes of memory and emotion were all he could detect. He felt Feywen's camaraderie with Lacdur. Fear and excitement came in waves, rising and falling. Above all else, the looming blackness of the Seeker mists bore down on Feywen's Light, and Darr shuttered in response.

"They're very close now," Vanheila whispered at his shoulder.

Darr pulled himself away from the Currents and nodded in agreement. Although younger than the other Aratans and most of the other Summoners in Navda, Vanheila possessed a strong connection to the Currents. The Elf could almost pull himself into the spirit realm, though something held him back. Perhaps his fear, or perhaps other forces were at work preventing him from doing so, but his skill was impressive.

Cold settled into Darr's stomach as the mists rose and fell outside the walls, heaving and shrinking, inhaling and exhaling. Since nightfall, the cold had grown stronger. It was only a matter of time before the Seeker's emerged.

"Such fear," Vanheila whispered at Darr's side. He didn't have to ask for clarification.

Even though Aratan Vanheila was unable to reach into the Currents by himself, he was adept at reading them. The fear he spoke of was the same fear Darr sensed, endless waves radiating outward from the soldiers gathered before them. The threat of the Soul Seekers, whether you believed in them or not, was very real.

"They will be strong," Darr said softly, firmly. "They will be strong, because they have to be."

Erec was among the soldiers, and he was an outsider to the people of Navda. If even half of the soldiers gathered were as strong as Erec, the Seekers would have a hard time getting to the city.

Vanheila stiffened his frame. "They're here," he said so soft Darr could barely detect the words.

The cold was now so intense, so numbing and silent, there was no doubt the Seekers had broken through the mists. Cries echoed from atop the walls and from without, but the Seekers themselves made no noise, like a light breeze rushing the city.

A hail of arrows, blazing orange, flew up into the night. They arched across the sky and then fell, exploding into an angry glare above the heights of the wall.

Darr's heart solidifed against his fear. He could show no weakness in the Currents. If he were to succeed, he must be strong, not only for himself, but for the Summoners he would lead into battle. Their summoning would save them all. But at what cost?

Whether they lived or died this night, Ictar would be forever changed.

* * * *

An orange glare rose against the black of the Seeker mists. The cold breath of fear blowing against Darr lessened. As the fires died away, the shouts of the men outside the walls came infrequently, but not frantic. Smoke rose into the night, blacker than the Seeker mists, reflecting back the red light of the embers below. Victory, it seemed, was close.

Darr's hope fell away when the cold returned, vengeful and piercing. Somehow, the Soul Seekers had found a way past the dying fires. Cries of pain rose into the blackness. More fiery arrows rained down from atop the city walls, but the cries increased in frequency. They became frenzied.

Darr let his mind slip ever into the Currents. All he could detect were flashes of memory and emotion, so potent and clear one moment and gone the next. The fear was overwhelming. Had Darr not prepared himself, the emotions of the soldiers fighting before him would've swept him away.

Darr took a moment and refocused his efforts. He closed away his emotions this time and listened to the Currents without getting too close. He let the voices of the spirits come to him, their words giving him small images of the battle unfolding around him.

Men he didn't know flashed before his eyes, some covered in ash, others in blood. Many lay dead. Darr turned his attention to the wall, hoping to find good news there. He let the spirits take him there.

The spirits whispered words gave life to the thoughts in Darr's mind. He saw a flash of Aratan Bolgros with his sword lifted high. He thought he heard Lacdur's booming voice. The flash of a silver sword might've been Feywen. The Seekers were on the wall, but again, the images were too fragmented and chaotic to be of use. Nothing he'd seen told him if they were losing this battle or not.

"What are you doing?" Aratan Vanheila asked. The Elf looked worried.

Darr shook his head. "I'm trying to see what's happening out there."

"How?" Vanheila asked, arching his already slanted brow.

"I don't want to risk going into the Currents, not yet anyways," Darr replied. He returned his gaze to the battle. "I want to be prepared, so I'm listening in on the Currents and trying to find something of use."

Aratan Vanheila leaned closer. "And have you found anything?"

Darr said nothing. While listening to the Currents, a single Light shone through. The Light may have been lost or captured, but for the briefest moment, Darr touched it, connected with it, and its memories exploded in his mind.

He looked down from the walls of Navda as if he were actually there. His heart stopped pumping. His bones turned to ice.

A wave of darkness spilled soundlessly across the fields below, glittering with the silver claws of Soul Seekers. No sound emanated from the mass, not the beat of a drum or the thud of booted feet, or the clang of armor. Terror, pure and silent, washed over him.

The Seekers scaled the walls with silver claws digging deep into the stone. They shredded the solid oak of the gate below. They slaughtered and they killed so many in that brief moment, Darr lost count.

A wash of black spilled across his eyes, followed by the glitter of claws. The Light snuffed away, and with it, the final memories it bore vanished as well.

Darr swallowed but his throat felt too dry. "I saw the Seekers," he rasped. "I don't think there's anything we can do but wait."

Aratan Vanheila didn't respond with words, he only nodded his head. On the city walls, the glitter of the Soul Seekers' claws danced in furious motion.

* * * *

The way the soldier ran towards him instinctively told Darr what the message was he brought. The man's fear and panic rang across the Currents. The time had come. Darr didn't wait to hear the message. He raised his arm, a signal to the other Summoners.

In a soundless rush, he sank into the Currents...

...*The spirit realm was as chaotic as he expected. The spirits flew around in a flurry of discontent, their fragile forms raking through the wisteria light like mad bees. The soldiers who fought the Seekers were a mass of sparkling white roiling with rage and desperation. The Soul Seekers were there, a scattering of white also, but the feelings they projected were numb. Darr guarded his Light, protecting himself in the strength of his convictions and his courage. He wouldn't be turned away.*

He did as Nidic Waq and Racall had taught him, checking the lines of power between the Sephirs. He wouldn't allow himself to repeat past mistakes. He took his time and examined the balance between the Four Elements, checking for frays that might cause him trouble. Satisfied that all was as good as it could be, he set to work.

Darr reached out and touched the Summoners who were gathered around him, their own Lights reaching to him from the physical world. He envisioned a net, a gathering of each of their Lights. Swiftly, he pulled them into the Currents. Confusion ran rampant through them, but Darr turned his thoughts to attention and focus. Already, he could sense a few had been left behind, their minds incapable of breaching the gap between the spirit realm and the physical, but he couldn't go back for them.

—Be strong—

Darr spoke to them with his thoughts, forcing his Summoners to listen.

—Ignore what you see around you—Focus only on me—

Darr waited while their concentration refocused. The net he wrapped around them wouldn't let them stray, but he didn't think it would make them follow either. They would have to do it on their own.

—Follow me—Don't turn away—

Darr's thoughts settled on the Sephir of Fire, the pulsing red light in the distance of the Currents. He willed his own Light towards the Sephir with slow and precise thoughts, giving time for his fellow Summoners to do the same. The mass intrusion of so many Summoners caused unease with the spirits, but Darr ignored them. He had to press forward.

Once he had the attention of his peers, Darr sent his Light soaring to the Fire Sephir. Some of the Summoners lost contact and drifted back into the physical world. Those who could follow, latched onto him intently.

The glare of the Fire Sephir exploded before them, its Light shinning brilliant crimson.

–Archon of Fire–

In response to his thoughts, a sensation of discontent radiated out of the Sephir.

–Archon of Fire, I implore you to listen–

Anger erupted through the Currents as the Archon of Fire emerged. Darr solidified his resolve, ignoring the spirit creature's emotions.

–Why have you come here– The Archon asked.

–I come seeking help– Darr answered. –Please lend to me, and those with me, your power and wisdom–

–They do not belong here–They are not prepared–

Darr galvanized himself against his fear, making his commitment as hard as iron –I've done all I can for them– We need your help–

The Archon scoffed at him, a strange repetition of Darr's thoughts. –You need more than my help–You are lost in this endeavor–What you ask is impossible–

Rage burned inside the Archon. It wasn't happy with what he was trying to do.

–Why won't you help me– Darr pleaded.

–To spread my power among so many is impossible–

–Then lend it to me alone–

–You are not prepared for the power you ask for–It will destroy you–It will destroy us all–

In frustration, Darr projected his emotions and memories into the Archon, letting his desperation and motives drive his thoughts forward, but the Archon didn't listen. If anything, she resisted and retreated back down within the Light of the Sephir.

What do I do? Darr thought. What more can I ask?

A cold seeped into Darr from somewhere in the Currents, followed by a cry so piercing its memories cut through him. He saw a village like Tyfor, and a family resembling his own. He felt frustration and rage, but also sadness and longing to return to a home, a house...and an old man...

A Light drained away, and a life excruciatingly important to him was lost to the Devoid.

Erec's memories?

Those had been Erec's memories!

Power born of rage and sadness welled up within the Summoner. His soul hardened and congealed until nothing could reach him. What once had been fear and distress turned numb. Darr's thoughts focused tight, before exploding into the Sephir before him.

–Give me what I want, Archon–

The response came without restriction. The crimson Light of the Sephir burst into Darr's own Light, filling it until he felt nothing, not even his own thoughts.

From the Archon of Fire, only a hint of its sadness came to Darr before he shut it out completely.

–You are not prepared, but your Light is stronger than we thought–

The magic of the Fire Sephir filled Darr's Light with the white hot heat of its element. The Summoners gathered around him faltered, sensing the rage boiling within Darr, but he held them fast, refusing to let them go. The red light of the Sephir filtered from Darr and into them. Some resisted, but Darr broke through their defenses. He didn't care. They were conduits for the magic, nothing more. He would wield the Element of Fire, and he would do so through them.

The magic filled him, radiated through him. He knew what he would bring to the Soul Seekers, how they would be destroyed. He would make them suffer like he had suffered...

...The physical world closed around Darr once more, but his awareness, as seen through the lens of the Currents, enfolded the entire city of Navda and its people. Darr and his Summoners burst into flames, torches against the darkness. They felt heat, but they didn't burn. They wielded the magic now, and it would only hurt its intended target.

With arms outstretched wide, Darr released the magic.

In a blast of heat and light, the line of Summoners exploded into a wall of flame. Firehounds erupted into the night sky. The beasts screamed in high-pitched wails. They ran along the currents of air, buttressed by the breeze, searching out the Soul Seekers. As if from a distant place, Darr's eyes burned with the same intensity as the hounds. His thoughts propelled them forward. Their fiery paws and the gaping white heat of their maws tore through the air and landed in the thick of the Seeker masses.

The firehounds attacked relentlessly, tearing through the Soul Seekers, their fire racing like spilled oil. There were a few dozen of the elementals, each one born from the Light of the gathered Summoners, but driven by Darr's commands. Without mercy, he hunted the Seekers in droves, consuming every black form that crossed his path. He snarled and spit. He breathed the fire of the hounds as he snapped and clawed his way through hundreds of the black robes.

The attack ended in minutes. Fires remained where a few Seekers still burned, but the firehounds were gone, sent back to the Currents. The magic rushed back into Darr, an agonizing flood of fire and heat.

He thought briefly of Erec, of the brother he'd lost and would never see again, before collapsing into the black quagmire of his mind.

Chapter Thirty-One

"In return for their help in ending the wars, the kings of Ictar entrusted the Divine with the Sephirs. A decree passed down, forbidding the use of the Sephir's magic, and the Divine became the enforcers. Only a few of the original scholars remained within the Divine, and with those few, Caeranol's covenant remained safe and well hidden."

~From A Current History of Ictar, as told by Nidic Waq

In his dreams, Darr fell into the blackness.

He drifted without knowing where he was. The place he came from only brought pain, rife with sorrow and filled with people who were lost and would never be found. Darr sunk deeper into the darkness. His thoughts dulled and his emotions scattered. He remembered nothing, and he found solace in the dark.

A light appeared in the void, and despite his desire to resist, Darr drifted towards it, intrigued and repulsed at the same time.

The light flared blood red. Flames danced all around, enfolding him in their heat and intensity. Dark shapes moved in the distance, but Darr's own hands controlled the fire. He sent it spinning into the darkness, wielding the fire like a giant sword, cutting through anything that threatened.

The black shapes turned and ran, their indistinct features torn, but Darr went after them ruthlessly, sending the fire out, obliterating anything trying to escape. In moments, they were gone, reduced to ash and blown away, consumed in the red glare of the fire. A final black shape rose up, and Darr sent the fire hurling into it without hesitation. The dark creature shuddered and turned as fire ate away its body.

Its face belonged to Erec.

Enraged, Darr screamed out a cry so loud he heard nothing else. The red of the fire burned into him and the darkness closed around once more.

He awoke in a familiar place. The gardens surrounded by thorns. The tower covered in ivy rising hundreds of feet into the air as if to pierce the heavens. Darr watched through dead eyes, his soul ruptured, his consciousness faltering. The familiar scene unfolded, of the black-haired man arguing with the man in regal white.

The argument concluded the same way it always did. The black-haired man retreated, and Darr turned to watch him go.

"I know you, Boy."

The black-haired man stood before him, his face pale, his eyes burning red. Darr backed away, but the man reached out, fastening his hand around Darr's neck, his grasp tightening.

"I...Know...You...Boy!"

This time when Darr cried out, his howl echoed through his ears until it became a blazing whirlwind, and it consumed him in its fury.

* * * *

Darr's dreams had ended, but his nightmare lived on.

At dawn, he found himself alongside Jinn, standing on a secluded cliff behind the Aratans' mansion overlooking the Arktary Ocean. Feywen, Lacdur, and Conra were there, but they where indistinguishable shapes. Pine trees, tall and dark, prevented anyone in the direction of Navda from seeing them, a sharp contrast to the omnipresent sunrise before them. Darr pulled his cloak tight to ward against the chill in the air.

Erec was dead.

Lacdur told him the story of how it happened, even

though Darr already knew his brother had fallen.

"You're brother fought well, Darr," Lacdur had told him. "He saved my life, and the lives of a hundred more. He saw the Seekers trying to cut us off, and he led the counterattack that drove them away."

Darr listened with dead ears while the Dwarf recounted the story, hearing the words, but already knowing the outcome.

"I tried to reach him," Lacdur told him. "Though he'd driven off the Seekers, they overwhelmed him. I just couldn't get to him in time. I wish I could've helped him, but it happened so quickly. If those hounds had come just a moment sooner..."

Those words, though they were spoken over twelve hours earlier, still rung in Darr's ears as if Lacdur had just said them. A few moments earlier, and Erec would have been alive. Darr nearly collapsed after hearing that, and Lacdur retracted his statement in haste. The words he spoke were out and they couldn't be taken back. Darr might've saved Navda, but he'd done little to save his own brother.

Now, the gravesite lay before him, a small pile of stones marked with Erec's sword. Darr's anger gave way to the deepest sorrow he'd ever known. He collapsed to his knees, a crumpled figure crouched over the stones of the grave, tears streaming in warm rivulets down his cheeks. While Jinn held tightly to him, Darr's grief consumed him from the inside out, threatening his life. He'd lost a part of himself, a part he'd unknowingly kept as part of himself. He could never get it back.

It didn't matter he and his brother were so different, or they had fought throughout their lives. There could be no reconciliation and no more bonding. Erec was gone, and the damage done was irreversible. Worse, he had only himself to blame.

He let Jinn hold him for a while longer, the warmth of her body seeping into him. His pain melted away, warmed by his sister's love and his own anger. His connection to the Currents strengthened in the wake of his recovery, and Jinn's emotions manifested within him. Her memories of Erec and the depth of her grief became equal to his. Together, they sat on the ground before his grave, speaking in hushed voices to one another of their brother. They shared remembrances and silent oaths they would all meet again. The thoughts felt futile. The Light belonging to his brother had gone to the Devoid, and it would take its destruction to free it.

When they were finished, Jinn rose and looked back towards the pines. Feywen and Lacdur were gone. Conra lingered, his presence small and unobtrusive.

"Are you coming?" Jinn asked him, her eyes red from tears.

Darr shook his head. "I'm going to stay here for a while. I want to be alone." She gave him a sympathetic look and smiled gently.

As Jinn turned away, Conra came close, raising his gnarled hand to Darr's shoulder. "I'm sorry, Boy. I wish I could've done something..."

"It's all right, Conra. Thank you."

Hesitant, the old Elf smiled and turned back to Jinn. They walked away and disappeared into the trees. Gratitude welled up within Darr. He had two great friends in Conra and Jinn. He didn't know what he'd do without either of them.

For a time, Darr stood before Erec's grave, remembering all the times they had fought, and all the disagreements driving them apart. There were other memories, small fragments which weren't recognizable at first, but they gained power the longer he dwelled on them. Erec had always been a brother to him, looking out for him when no one else would. Knowing he wouldn't be there to look after him left a tremendous hole.

This journey is exactly why this happened, Darr thought. If I'd stayed home, none of this would've happened.

He knew he was wrong. If he'd stayed home, the Seekers would've come for him sooner of later. Still, he'd abandoned his father and lost his brother. Jinn's fate had tied her up in something so dangerous Darr couldn't imagine how to save her from it. His own body and mind had been thrown asunder to the point where he couldn't recognize himself anymore.

"It's a horrible thing."

Darr didn't turn. Conra stood behind him. Though unwanted, Conra's presence comforted him. The waves of the Arktary and the rise of the sun were equally silent in the world beyond Erec's grave.

"I lost a brother once," the Elf said, hushed and ragged. "Belmon. He was Erec's age when it happened."

Brief images flashed in Darr's mind, a fragment of memories belonging to Conra which were brought to the surface along with the emotions which fueled them. They were quick and vague, and painful for the old Elf to remember.

"I'm sorry," Darr said, unable to think of anything else.

Conra stared out at the Arktary, his face reflecting a kind of anguish not easy to detect, but the Currents helped Darr to see it.

"Not much I can say about it," the old Elf grumbled. "It happened a long time ago, but even now, I can't really let it go."

"How did you deal with it?" Darr asked in a whisper.

Conra laughed without warmth. "I ran. I left behind my family and my friends. I decided to do what Belmon and I had always talked about, and I traveled." The Elf's gaze turned on him. "But I wasn't traveling. That was my excuse. I ran from what'd happened. I felt responsible because regardless of how it happened, he was my brother, and I should've protected him. Because Belmon died, it must've been my fault, and so I ran away from Qued, from the Elves, from everything I ever knew to try to escape my guilt."

As the Elf spoke, the full weight of Darr's emotions crashed down. Conra had somehow removed a wall blocking his true feelings. Funny it should be the same memory that had caused the Elf to be so distant. Conra had been petrified by what had happened to his brother, and he'd spent his entire life trying to recover.

For the first time, Darr understood what drove the Elf. By coming along, by leaving his little haven, Conra had finally come to terms with his brother's death.

"Don't make the same mistake I made," Conra said, his eyes watery as he turned away.

"I think I can try," Darr said at last, but too late for Conra to hear.

The Summoner returned his gaze back to the sea, and as he did so, doubt settled in. Darr couldn't avoid Conra's mistakes for one important reason. Conra believed he'd caused his brother's death, but he discovered his belief to be wrong. Realizing he was innocent allowed him to face it and then forgive himself.

Darr could find no such forgiveness with Erec's death. The fault belonged to him alone.

Interlude

"The Aeon Wars, centuries long, had caused much imbalance between the Sephirs, allowing the Devoid to create a small fracture in its prison. Though the Aeon Wars ended, and the balance between the Sephirs strengthened, the Devoid began its assault. First, it tainted the Currents with its deceptions, masking its intentions. It summoned Ovids, the counterparts to the Archons, that began draining the Light from the Sephirs. As time crawled on, the Devoid weakened the Sephirs enough to summon his Soul Seekers. It would be only a matter of time before it gathered enough Light to break free completely.

Caeranol searched for the Chosen of the Light, but he couldn't find them in the badly distorted Currents. Even the spirits couldn't remember who they were.

Time grew short, the Devoid grew stronger, and still, the Chosen did not appear."

~From A Current History of Ictar, as told by Nidic Waq

From the high wall of Jacova, Nidic Waq looked out over the Triker forest from the Dwarf city's high bluff. Night had fallen, but the leading trees and boulders stood defined by shades of light and dark. Watch fires lit at the edge of the trees did little to penetrate into the Triker. The vastness of the forest astonished him, even for someone who'd seen things no one on Ictar had seen. He was insignificant before their mass, a small participant in a game played amongst more powerful beings.

Spirits and Ovids. Archons. The nothingness of the Devoid. A secret war persisted between them, and the people of Ictar would be caught in the middle. Of course, one didn't always get to choose a side. Sometimes you fought only to stay alive.

Nidic Waq breathed in the cold air until it hurt his lungs, and he released it in a soundless rush. Both within the Currents and without, so much relied on chance. Neither world claimed any stability, and there would be much to upset both in the days to come.

It had started with the Soul Seekers attack on the Crossroads. The slaughter of the people there meant the Devoid was through waiting. Its Seekers would begin scouring the land, feeding the dark creature in order to aid its escape. Nidic Waq had reached Jacova as quickly as possible, and fortunately, plans for the city's defense had already been put into motion.

The Cortazian Army had arrived the day before, and their king, Ariel Forn, had established a perimeter to protect the Dwarf city at once. It'd been nearly two hundred years since the races had met in such large numbers, and never before had it been done in cooperation. The Ictarian people faced a tough battle ahead, and Nidic Waq believed they stood a chance of surviving, but only if they stayed united.

Of course, the war between Ictar and the Seekers meant nothing in comparison to what was happening in the Currents. The magic flowing between the Sephirs and out into Ictar was spinning out of control. The balance between the elements had been tipped, and the Archons were working hard to repair the damage. A small possibility remained that both chaos and the Devoid would be set free, and then all of Ictar would die.

All because of Darr Reintol.

Nidic Waq doubted the Summoner knew what he'd done. Consumed by his anger, Darr was blinded to the truth. After the loss of his brother, Darr sought to exact his revenge against the minions of the Devoid. What Darr didn't understand was his summoning in Navda was never actually a summoning at all. In his anger, he'd torn the magic of the Fire Sephir from its Archon, like pulling a block from an unstable foundation. Now the entire structure threatened to fall. One more block and everything would crumble. The Devoid would be searching for a way to make that happen.

A smile crept up the sides of his face. He didn't smile out of secret satisfaction or madness. He smiled because he knew Darr wouldn't give in easily to his base emotions. Darr held more strength inside himself than anyone suspected. The boy was resilient, contemplative, and intuitive. He'd been chosen for that very reason.

In the aftermath of the Current's violation, some hope remained. Darr's stolen magic had erased the Soul Seekers from Ictar for the time being. It would be a while before the Devoid could muster the strength for another summoning.

Nidic Waq lifted his head to the cloudy skies above, and the dim firelight of the city reflected bloody red. He wished he could speak with the spirits, to get a glimpse of the future, a taste of what lay ahead. The Currents were in an uproar, disrupting any sort of communication.

The prophet sighed. He centered himself and let his thoughts cool. He must stay alert and aware of everything happening around him. He must focus his efforts, helping Caeranol search for the remaining Chosen of the Light. If the spirit realm cleared, he must reach Darr Reintol and help him. These were the only ways to gain an advantage over their enemy.

Nidic Waq straightened his frame. Satisfied with his conclusions, he walked down from the high wall, leaving the night's shadows to dance between the watch fires.

Darr's story will continue, along with the fate of the Ictarian Army, in Book Two of The Chosen of the Light: Soul Seekers.

Author Bio

Over the last twenty years, Jon Carlin Shea has been putting his love for fantasy stories down on paper. With interests in writing, woodworking, parenting, comic books, movies, and RPG video games, he always has something new to inspire him.

We lives in Western Washington with his wife and son.

You can learn more about him at www.joncarlinshea.com.

www.ingramcontent.com/pod-product-compliance
Lightning Source LLC
Chambersburg PA
CBHW021949170626
46808CB00001B/84